RAMSEYER'S GHOST

Manu Herbstein

RAMSEYER'S GHOST

Also by Manu Herbstein

Ama, a Story of the Atlantic Slave Trade

Brave Music of a Distant Drum

The Boy who Spat in Sargrenti's Eye

Akosua and Osman

President Michelle or Ten Days that Shook the World

CHAPTER 1

Shit! Am I crazy? Or something? I'm in Africa! Fucking Africa. Sitting on a beach with my back against the rough trunk of what must be a coconut palm. My jeans are soaked with salt water. God only knows the condition of the kit in my backpack. It's dark, so dark that all I can see is the dial of my wristcom. 3.14 a.m. 3.15 now. At least that's working. 3.15 a. m. Greenwich Mean Time. What'll that be in Washington? 4 hours back. 11.15 p.m. I'd better give Millicent a call before she turns in. Probably fast asleep in front of the TV.

I told the fucking bosun, "Beach your boat so that I can step out onto dry land."

He says, "And bust my outboard? That's not part of the deal. And who know what African darkies, excuse the expression, will be waiting for us there? This is as far as we go, Buddie. It's low tide and only waist deep. Now git or I'll take you right back to the tanker."

My back is itchy. I stand up and rub it against the tree. There are lights on the surface of the sea, twinkling, like stars reflected in a smooth pond. But there are no stars, the sky is overcast. And the surface of the sea is no way pond-smooth. There's no rational explanation. Unless it's a species of marine fireflies or maybe some kind of African witchcraft.

Witchcraft? Crash, get a grip. Best to strip off and hang my pants up to dry. But hang them on what? I'll just have to lay them out on the sand and wait for the sun. I feel in my bag for my towel. Wet! Everything's soaked. Fucking fucking bosun.

I sit down and call up Millicent. Fergus answers. Fergus? What the hell is he doing up at this time of night? I hear a male voice in the background. It says, "Fergus, who is it?"

"Fergus," I say. "It's Dad. I'm calling you from Africa. But how come you're up so late?"

Fergus says, "Hi, Dad," and then, "Uncle Bud, it's Dad."

"Fergus, give that to me," says Bud.

"But I want to speak to my Dad," I hear Fergus say.

Then it's Bud on the line.

"Crash, where are you?" he asks.

"Bud, I'm in Africa. Just landed. Now let me speak to Millicent, please."

"Millicent's having a bath," he says.

"And what the hell are you doing in my house at this time of night. What's going on?"

He starts to reply but I interrupt him.

"Let me speak to Fergus," I tell him.

Then the instrument goes dead.

I find the hip flask in one of the bag's side pockets. I'm a teetotaler and the brandy's intended for use in an emergency, but what the hell. If ever I needed a drink, it's now.

We're in a restaurant. I recognize one of the side booths at the Stars and Stripes in the Old African Quarter of Washington, D.C. My farewell dinner. Millicent, dressed up to kill and drunk, Bud, in his uniform with his new Silver Oak Leaf. The band strikes up. Bud gets to his feet and extends a hand to Millicent. She staggers after him, leaving me with Selma. Selma the mouse.

"Well, Selma?" I say.

"Well, Crash?" she says.

On the dance floor Bud and Millicent are in a clinch. They're hardly moving, just swaying to the music. Bud's hands are on her buttocks, holding her tight. Selma turns to follow my gaze.

"Well, Selma," I ask her, "What's it like to be married to a Lieutenant Colonel?"

When I open my eyes they are standing there, staring at me. The sun is behind them. I raise my hand to wipe the sleep from my eyes and the dream from my mind. They take a step back. Two boys, one perhaps six years old, Fergus's age, the other a little older; both stark naked. I'm naked myself, from the waist down, with a morning hard-on. I stretch for my pants and cover myself.

I curse myself for falling asleep. And then this. It was for Ham's looking on Noah's drunken nakedness that the Lord God punished us blacks.

"Buzz off," I tell them and raise my fist.

They look back over their shoulders as they run. Once they see that I'm not chasing them, they stop and turn. I raise a fist again and they make off. I allow myself a smile and for a moment imagine Fergus and Marilyn playing naked and carefree on that beach. Technology has spoiled the childhood of our kids.

I go down to the water and wash my face. The tide has risen.

Turning, I see the coconut palms for the first time, a whole ragged plantation of them, extending into the distance east and west as far as I can see, without a single distinguishing landmark. I must bury some stuff but how will I find my way back to collect it? I enter the code on the wristcom and record my position. Then I cut some notches in a coconut trunk.

I need to take my morning shit. There is no one in sight but modesty leads me to look for a private location. Wandering back inland through the palms, I catch sight of a shack and decide to investigate. As I have been taught, I call out "Agôô" to give notice of my presence. There is no reply. I take a closer look. The corrugated metal roof seems intact. So are the wooden jalousie shutters. But the door hangs askew, its top hinge rusted away. Cautiously I poke my head through the opening. I pull back so quickly I hit my crown against the door frame. Instinctively, my trained Marine mind takes over. I do a quick reccy: north, south, east, west, no one in sight. Then I do some slow stretches. Only when my heart stops pumping do I think of taking another look.

In the course of my career, I've killed a man or two. To my regret, some women and children, too. Sometimes that's unavoidable. And I've seen more than a few corpses, not a pretty sight. Nor, for that matter, a dainty smell. But this is different. I've never seen anything like this before.

Slowly, carefully, I stick my head through the opening. Morning light filters through the jalousies. The single room is sparsely furnished, a table, a chair, some sort of shelving against the far wall. On the chair sits a human skeleton, the bones held together by jeans and a faded patterned shirt. The chest and shoulders lie on the table, the skull enclosed by the arms. There is a book. Man perishes; his books survive him, it strikes me.

I strain my eyes to read the title. "Four years in Ashantee," it says.

I shiver, hoping that that is not some sort of bad omen.

On the floor, partly covered by a plain cloth, lies another skeleton, smaller, a woman perhaps, lying on its side in a fetal position.

I mutter a prayer and withdraw.

Outside, I stand for a while and reflect. Is this crude mausoleum of any relevance to my mission, my missions, I wonder? There is none that I can see. I record a brief note of the incident. Doing that reminds me that Bud will be waiting to hear from me. At this moment he'll still be snoring in his warm bed in D.C. His bed or my bed?

Or maybe Selma, needing some sleep herself, has tried to close his mouth and he has woken and decided the time is right for a screw. As for Bud, any time is right for a screw, at least, that is, if you can believe even half the stories he tells. The wristcom works perfectly. I hear his phone ring. It rings ten times. Then he picks it up.

"Who the fuck is calling me at this unearthly hour?" he growls.

Typical of Bud. What if it had been some senior officer?

"Hi, Bud," I greet him, in the sweetest of voices, as if I were chatting up some dumb broad. "This is Crash. Remember me? I'm in Africa. I just thought you'd like to know. Sorry to disturb your beauty sleep. Will you forgive me, old fellow? And by the way, how's Selma? Do give her my fondest greetings, will you?"

He doesn't say a word, just slams the phone down.

"Well, fuck you, Bud," I say aloud, as if he could hear me.

Then, like a cat, I dig a small hole in the sand and shit in it. Thank God for the training they give you in the Corps. Next stop, the sea. To wash my hands. Cleanliness, the Good Book teaches us, is next to Godliness. Especially in the tropics.

I haven't walked twenty paces when something hits the ground behind me. I swing myself round the nearest palm. Hey, do I feel a fool? It's just a coconut. I relax. I look up into the fronds of the palm the thing has fallen from. Two eyes look back at me. Another small boy.

"*Oburoni, maakye,*" white man, good morning, he greets me. "*Wobenom kubé, anaa?*" Would you like to drink some coconut milk?

Silently, I curse. He has been spying on me. He has seen me using the wristcom and has heard every word I've said. I wonder whether he understands English.

"Good morning," I reply. "Do you speak English?"

"Please, teacher, yes. I am hearing English small. Please, what is your name?"

Damn, damn, damn, I curse. I haven't been in this country a day, I have yet to meet an adult native, and I'm already being made to look like a fool. I smile up at the lad. He grips his cutlass between his teeth and shins down the trunk of the palm, no rope, no ladder, just the alternating grip of legs and arms.

"What were you doing up in that tree?" I demand.

"Please, I cut *kubé*," he replies.

Evidently he doesn't know the English word for coconut. That doesn't stop him using his cutlass to slice off the top, exposing the contents of the fruit.

"Drink!" he commands.

I do as he orders. The milk is cool and refreshing. When I have drained it, I am about to drop the nut. Vegetable matter, biodegradable, you understand. The boy takes it from me and with a single expert stroke splits it into two. He returns one half to me, together with the slice he has taken off the top, to use as a spoon.

"Eat," he commands.

I scoop up the soft white flesh. Delicious. And filling. Before I know it, I've had a great breakfast.

"Please, teacher, what is your name?" he asks.

"You know my name. You called me *Oburoni*, white man," I complain. "I'm not a white man. I'm darker than you. Why did you call me that?"

The poor lad is confused. My flood of angry English is more than he can handle and I take pity on him.

"Back home," I tell him, "they call me Crash. But here in Africa my name is Ekem. Or Yaw, because I was born on a Thursday."

"*Ye fre wo sen?*" I ask him in Twi.

That surprises him, my speaking to him in Twi. I gather that his name is Kwabena, but beyond that his answer comes in such a torrent of words that I'm unable to keep up. So instead of making an attempt to answer, I ask him two questions which I have prepared in advance.

"*Wo firi he?*" where are you from, I ask; and, in case he doesn't understand, "*Wo kurom wo he?*"

CHAPTER 2

AN OLD MAN sat on the ground. He was mending the fishing net that was stretched between his legs. He looked up as I approached. Kwabena had run off to join other small boys swimming in the sea, so I was alone.

"Kofi," the old man called once and then again, more urgently.

I rehearsed my options. Should I greet him with the morning greeting, *maakye*, or the greeting for one who is at work, *adwuma ôô*? And when he answered, how should I continue? Learning a language taught in a classroom by a non-native linguist is one thing; using it in practice is quite another.

I needn't have worried, for Kofi appeared at the door of a hut, wearing a pair of khaki shorts and pulling a faded red tee-shirt over his head. I thought I saw the glint of gold on a finger as he passed from shade to sun and wondered at the incongruity of it.

"Me papa?" I heard him ask.

The old man indicated my presence by an inclination of his head. Kofi smiled, almost as if he had been expecting me.

"Kwesi Buroni, akwaaba," he said by way of welcome.

For the second time in an hour I was being addressed as a white man. I decided to deal with the issue once and for all.

"Yenfre me Kwesi Buroni," I told him: that is not my name.

"Me paa wo kyew," Kofi apologized and was asking for my name when his father interrupted him, reminding him, I suppose, of his manners.

"Kwabena," Kofi called.

When Kwabena did not appear, Kofi went himself to fetch a stool and invited me to sit.

"Would you prefer to speak English?" he asked.

Somewhat relieved, I nodded. I made a mental note that I would have to work on my Fanti.

"My name is Ekem Ferguson," I told him. "Back home they call me Crash. But here, since I was born on a Thursday, I guess you'll call me Yaw."

The old man looked up from his work and mumbled something to Kofi again.

Kofi brought an old beer bottle and a glass. The bottle looked as if it had water in it. I was thirsty after my walk, but I feared diarrhea.

"You don't have a Coke by any chance?" I asked.

Kofi suppressed a laugh. I ended up taking some stuff from a calabash which he said was called palm wine, assuring me that it was a product of nature and guaranteed not to harm the constitution of a visitor. He lied. That palm wine was real sweet and by the time I had had half a dozen bowls, I was ready to go back to sleep. That's something they didn't warn me about at the Special School.

When I woke up it was past noon. Kofi explained that the Chief and Elders were in session and wanted to see me. He and his father led me to what Kofi called "the Palace," a single storied mud building with a long veranda. A fence of palm fronds enclosed a sandy area in front of it. The Chief, or "King" as Kofi sometimes referred to him, sat on a real chair at the center of the veranda. Several old men, bare to the waist, sat on benches on either side of him. Facing this row, another bench had been set in the shade of a tree.

As we entered this space, Kofi called out, *"Agôô"* and those present answered, *"Amêê."* I recognized the exchange and that pleased me.

Kofi led me to the bench, where I sat between him and his father. I looked around. In one corner of the yard, a woman was sitting on a low stool stirring a pot over an open fire. She raised her head, saw me gazing at her and at once looked down and returned to her work. There were several children, young girls and infants, playing quietly or just idly watching the proceedings.

The man at the chief's right hand held a wooden staff with a carved animal of some sort, painted gold, at its head. He stood up. One of his colleagues handed him a green bottle, not round but square. From this he dribbled clear liquid onto the ground. Then he began to speak.

"He is pouring libation," Kofi whispered to me, "Praying for the goodwill and support of our ancestors."

"I know," I replied.

When he finished, Kofi stood up and, signaling to me to follow, headed for the elder on the right. He and I and Kofi's father then shook hands with each of the elders in turn.

When it was my turn to shake hands with the Chief, he murmured, *"Akwaaba,"* which I recalled means "Welcome." Without hesitating I replied, *"Yaa agya,"* and saw from his smile and the nod of approval of the staff-holder that I had got it right.

We returned to our seats. It was only later, with increasing experience of such matters, that I realized that at this stage it might have been proper for me to have presented the Chief with a gift. I had no gift to offer, so we moved on.

The man with the staff asked Kofi, as the representative of our party, for our *"amanee,"* the purpose of our visit.

Kofi spoke in Fanti but for my benefit translated everything said on both sides.

"This our visitor," he told them, "arrived at our town of Mpoanokrom this morning, walking along the beach. He told us his name and we gave him some palm wine to wet his throat after his journey. He was tired, so we gave him a place to sleep; and while he was sleeping, my father, Opanyin Kwabena Kom, reported his arrival to Nana. Nana asked that the stranger introduce himself and that is how we come to be here. He hears a little of our language but he may prefer to use his own, so if Nana permits, he will speak in English and

I will translate what he says."

"Now, my brother," he said to me quietly, "you must tell them your story. Tell them who you are and what your mission is."

That word he used, "mission," startled me. Did he know more than he was letting on? I dismissed the thought. Kofi was just a simple fisherman who had been fortunate to go to school and learn a little English.

"*Nananom*," I addressed them in some semblance of their own language, "*Eye me anigye se me hyia wonyinaa ha enne.*" That means, my grandfathers, or my seniors, it gives me great pleasure to meet you all here today. That was one of the speeches I had learned by heart in the States. It produced a round of applause and a string of private conversations amongst the Elders, in which I heard, again, the words Kwesi Buroni and Oburoni repeated.

I went on to request their indulgence as my friend Kofi had done, for me to speak in a language more familiar to me. I told them that I was a true son of their soil, that my natural parents were Fantis (which wasn't quite true) and that my grandparents, on both sides, were also Fantis though they had lived for many years in Kumase, the Asante capital.

"In the year 2008," I told them, "my father was studying in the United States. His studies were sponsored by his father who had grown rich working for the old United Nations, before returning home to retire. 2008 was the year in which I was born. It was also the year of the collapse of a great American company, in which my grandfather had invested all his savings abroad. He was reduced to poverty."

I paused for Kofi's translation. There were sympathetic noises.

"My parents had no money and had to go home, or should I say, to come home. They thought that my father would soon be able to return and resume his studies. So they left me, at the age of six months, in the care of friends in America, friends who came from Cape Coast. Those friends were called Ferguson. When my parents did not return, they adopted me and gave me their name. And that is how I come to be called

Ekem Ferguson. However, because of the circumstances which led to my being placed in their care, they gave me the nickname Crash and that is what people call me."

Then I told them that I was born on Thursday and that they could call me Yaw. They liked that.

I was ready to resume my seat but Kofi, who had been cutting in to translate every few sentences, whispered, "Your mission. Tell them your mission."

That word again. I looked at him closely but saw no guile in his eyes.

"Pa and Ma Ferguson died recently," I told them.

There were murmurs of condolence.

"Before they died I told them that I planned to come here and look for my natural parents. They gave me their blessing and we pored over maps together. They recommended that I start my journey on this stretch of the coast. Ma Ferguson drew a large arrow on a map, pointing to this very village. In Fantiland, she said, I would find civilized and helpful people with a long history of friendship towards the Western nations. Indeed, she told me, Pa Ferguson's illustrious forebear, after whom they said I was named, was a distinguished and faithful servant of the British Empire."

I was taking a chance on that one. I had no idea how they felt about the British Empire, whatever that was. I hardly knew what it was myself. But to my surprise they broke into applause. I thought that that was a good time to sit down.

They went into huddle. I guess Africans love a story and that they found mine intriguing. The man with the staff collated their questions. One of the Elders wanted to know more about the Fergusons. I knew little about their family in Cape Coast but I dredged my memory for a few anecdotes and that seemed to satisfy them.

Then the Chief himself wanted to hear the details of my journey, how I had traveled from America, or Aburokyiri, the country of the white man, as he called it. Fortunately I had foreseen this question and prepared my answer well.

"I am sure I don't have to tell you that there are no longer any air services to your country; and of course the old ports of Tema and Takoradi are silted up so that ships cannot dock there. The only way to get here was to hitch a lift on a passing American oil tanker. They sent me ashore in a motor boat."

Again they consulted amongst themselves. At last the staff holder expressed the consensus. He said that their King, Nana whatever his name was (I forget), welcomed me as a long-lost son of Fantiland and was honored that fate had made his town Mpoanokrom my first port of call. Mpoanokrom, Kofi added, means the town at the mouth of the ocean.

"You will see," the spokesman told me, "that we are poor, that apart from the sea we have few resources. Nevertheless Nana instructs me to tell you that we are resolved to do whatever lies in our power to help you to achieve your mission."

How, he wanted to know from me, could they help?

I did my best to hide my elation. What a story I had to tell that cocky bastard Bud! I had these naïve but friendly natives eating out of the palm of my hand. I expressed my thanks with some effusion. Then I told them that I thought I should start my search for my parents in Kumase, their last location known to me.

The small boys were a trial. They followed me everywhere. I had to find a private place where I could communicate with Bud unheard and unobserved.

I found a solution almost by accident. The next morning Kofi shooed everyone away, small boys included, so that I could use the public toilet in privacy. Once was enough. The stench! And the wooden floor was so rickety that there seemed to be a distinct danger of falling into the deep pit. I pinched my nose and shook my head.

Kofi laughed. He had had nightmares about the pit latrine as a child. Now, like most of the townsfolk, he did his thing on the beach and relied on the Atlantic Ocean to wash away the waste.

"Sea Never Dry," he told me with a laugh.

That didn't seem to inhibit them from allowing their kids to swim in that very same Atlantic Ocean. I suppose they reckoned on a safe dilution factor. Or maybe they just didn't reckon at all.

Anyways, I didn't see myself squatting on the beach in company. The next morning I headed off into the coconut groves, small boys tagging along behind me.

I turned on them.

"Firi ha!" I told them, meaning, get lost.

One of the bolder souls asked me, *"Wo ko he?"* where are you going?

"Me ko baabi," I replied, meaning literally, I am going somewhere.

They nodded sagely and turned back. It seems that that phrase is used as a euphemism for "I am going to shit." And it is extremely bad manners, even for small boys, to treat another's defecation as a piece of theatre to be observed. In fact, I noticed that these people don't even greet each other before they've had their morning shit. If you say good morning to one of them when he is on the way to the beach, he'll just ignore you.

So I found myself a quiet place amongst the coconut palms, dug myself a little hole in the sand, pulled down my pants and squatted over the hole. And while I was doing my business, I rang Bud. Trouble was, of course, that while it was dawn in West Africa, Bud, in Washington, was still fast asleep. Or if he wasn't fast asleep, he was doing his thing with Selma. I sorted that one out by remotely setting his machine to record mode. That way, I reckoned, I could send in my report without having to endure Bud's short temper and malign sense of humor.

Bud, Lieutenant Colonel Bud Power, to give him his full designation, 42 years old and quite young to reach that rank, responded by calling me back, me, Crash, also 42 and still a Captain. You'd think he'd have more sense, putting me at risk. I bet he hasn't even taken the trouble to read the rules. Millicent thinks Bud's right on the ball and, as for me, I'm... well never mind. How wrong can you be?

So Bud called me back.

I was sitting with Kofi in the shade of a beached canoe,

drinking palm wine.

"What was that?" Kofi asked when he heard the wristcom beep.

I pressed a button.

"I must have set the alarm on my watch by mistake," I told him. "Sorry."

That night I slipped away quietly from my hut and walked down the beach. I caught Bud in his office, just back from the usual expense account lunch.

"What the hell do you mean by beeping me like you did today?" I demanded. "That could have meant the end of my mission and maybe…"

Bud never takes criticism lightly. Before I could complete my sentence he swung to the attack.

"Crash, it seems to us all here that you are having a fine holiday at Uncle Sam's expense. When are you going to get off your ass and start heading for Kumase?"

"Bud, I'm in Africa," I said, "Things take time here. I'm waiting for the Chief to give me a guide and the go-ahead to get moving."

"Crash," he told me, "you forget that I've spent some time in Africa myself. Now you remember, Captain, that the Corps has entrusted you with an urgent life or death mission. There is no way that some no-good native chief can be permitted to interfere with your duty."

"Bud," I replied. "You been in Africa? You mean you once visited St. Thomas and helicoptered in to one of our offshore oil rigs. That ain't Africa. Where I am is the real Africa and here nothing happens overnight. Now just trust me, will you?"

Well, I know not to take Bud too serious, but that conversation upset me some. I admit that I was a shade melodramatic. Kofi and Co. were unlikely to know the difference between my wristcom and a regular tick tock watch. But why chance it?

"Don't call me," I told him, "I'll call you."

And then I rang off.

I stood for a while, listening to the surf and looking out over the dark sea. There again were those dancing fireflies. But this time I understood what they were: the flickering lamps of the night fishermen.

I called Millicent at work but she said she was in a meeting and couldn't speak.

Next morning I took my usual place in the shade of the old canoe and sent Kwabena to bring me a calabash of palm wine. Soon the canoes began to return. I went to help pull in Kofi's net.

"Kofi," I told him as he walked up the beach, leaving his meager catch in the hands of the womenfolk, "we need to talk."

"Bra Crash," he replied, "I beg you. Later. I tire small."

And he tilted his head and rested his cheek on his hands.

"I go-come," he said.

It was noon by the time he joined me. There wasn't much left in my calabash. Kofi sent for another.

I had prepared what I was going to say to him. I would be diplomatic, thank him for his hospitality, but tell him that I couldn't expect to depend on that indefinitely. Well the palm wine undermined my good intentions and I ended up demanding to know when the King would appoint the guide he had promised me and when it would be possible for me to leave for Kumase.

Kofi, as I recall, was the diplomatic one. He apologized for the delay. He knew, he said, that Americans were always in a hurry. However, going to Kumase was not a simple matter. For one thing, it was impossible, or at best, inadvisable, without a visa.

"A visa?" I demanded. "There is not one single sovereign, independent state in the whole of West Africa and you speak of a visa? Who has the authority to issue me with a visa?"

"Bra Crash," Kofi asked me, "If I were to arrive in your New York in my canoe and tell the first passer-by that I had come to look for my lost parents in Washington, D.C., what would he say, or do?"

The thought made me laugh: Kofi, unshaven for the past week, barefooted, wearing an old tee-shirt with the words,

'KISS ME IN THE DARK, BABY" in faded luminous letters across his chest and his ragged khaki shorts, approaching a New York cop.

"First thing, they'd put you face forward, hands up, against the nearest wall and search you for a gun, or drugs or whatever. Then they'd ask you for proof of identity. Hey, Bra Kofi, you'd be in deep trouble."

He gave me a look, curious-like.

"Body-search, eh? Proof of identity? Seems like we've been rather casual. But the Asante might not be. Be prepared, Bra Crash."

Not for the first time it occurred to me that there might be more to Bra Kofi than appeared on the surface.

We had the same conversation, with minor variations, every day. Bud's impatience increased exponentially. Some of it must have worn off onto me.

"This visa business," I asked Kofi. "How does it work? Are there forms? How do you communicate with Kumase? E-mail?" and then as an afterthought, "You know what e-mail is, of course?"

He said nothing but the look he gave me spoke of contempt. I tried again. He spoke to me as if I were an ignorant child.

"E stands for equine," he said, and then, "You know what equine means, of course?"

It was two weeks before the equine mail arrived, two horses with riders, leading three more with saddle-bags.

Kofi announced, "Bra Crash, I have good news for you. I have been appointed as your guide. And we leave at dawn tomorrow. So I suggest you get yourself a good night's sleep."

I think he added, "And no nocturnal strolls along the beach, mind?" but when I thought about it the next morning I couldn't be sure. Perhaps, I thought, I had been dreaming. Had Kofi been spying on me? I gave him the benefit of the doubt.

I took my leave of the King and his courtiers who wished me good luck and a safe journey, warning me to beware of the activities of brigands and ruffians, but assuring me that Kofi would look after me.

16

CHAPTER 3

THERE WERE JUST three of us. When there was enough space Kofi and I rode abreast. Kofi's son Kwabena followed. This was his first trip to Kumase and he was clearly excited.

"When we reach Kumase, Uncle Crash," he said, "I'll go with you to America."

"Great idea," I said but Kofi just turned and gave him what I took to be a silent warning.

"I'm surprised," I said, "I read somewhere that the tsetse fly has made it impossible to use horses in this part of the world."

"Out of date," Kofi replied.

"How come?" I asked.

"Vaccination," he said.

"And where do you get the vaccines?"

He tapped his saddle bag.

"Bra Crash," he said, "you ask too many questions. Take my advice, when we reach Kumase, ask about your parents, nothing more. The Asante don't like outsiders prying into their affairs."

I took his advice and for a while I kept my questions to myself.

We had a journey of a hundred and twenty miles ahead of us.

"We must conserve the horses' energy," Kofi said, as we moved along the beach. "We'll set off at dawn and walk them for a few hours before it gets too hot. And then another hour or two in the late afternoon. If all goes well we should be in Kumase in a week."

An hour after our departure an enormous white building loomed up ahead, situated right on the coast.

"What's that?" I asked, surprised to see a manifestation of advanced civilization in such an undeveloped area and wondering, if it were ours, why I had never heard of it.

"Elmina Castle," Kofi replied.

"Elmina Castle, huh?" I asked, "And who lives there?"

"Ghosts," he replied.

"Ghosts? Whose ghosts?"

"Bra Crash," Kofi asked, "do you mean to tell me that you've never heard of Elmina Castle? Of the slave trade? There are millions of blacks in your country, not so, people of African descent? How do you think they got there? In canoes?"

"Are you telling me that they were sent from that place? By whom?"

"My brother, it's a long story. But I'll do my best to tell you."

And tell me he did. Four centuries of unthinking cruelty and suffering.

Kofi's history lesson brought to the surface a memory which I suppose I must have repressed.

"When I was a kid," I told him, "Pa Ferguson used to say to me, 'Crash, my boy, there's one thing you must never forget: you're an African. That's something to be proud of. Stand tall and say you're proud to be an African.'

"And Ma Ferguson would nod her head.

"Then one day at school I was hanging out with a crowd of black kids (most all the kids in our school were black) and I had occasion to say, 'I'm an African and proud of it.'

"There was this other boy, a big strong feller. He wasn't too good at studies but he was tough and he ruled our gang. His name was Bud Power and he was the school bully.

"And he says to me, 'You may be an African but that ain't nothin' to be proud of. If you're an African, you're one of those who sold us African-Americans into slavery.'

"I didn't have the slightest idea what he was talking about, but remembering Pa Ferguson's counsel, I stood up for myself. I got a good beating as a result. Not just one good beating, but two. When Pa Ferguson saw the mess I was in he used a strap on me. Only time he ever did that.

"From that time on I was proud to be an American. I never told Pa Ferguson. He would still give me the same old pep-talk and I would nod and agree. But I never again told anybody that I was proud to be an African."

The road from Elmina to the next town, Cape Coast, was something to see: men, women and children in their hundreds, all carrying head loads, a bag of cement, a 5-gallon drum of kerosene, a bundle of the discarded clothes of the West, which the locals call *Oburoni wawu*, meaning the white man has died.

Four men pushed a small steel trolley, heavily loaded with sacks of cement. As we came abreast of it, one of the wheels fell off and it tipped. Some of the sacks fell to the ground. We dismounted to help.

"Barter trade," Kofi explained, "from a passing tanker. The Elmina canoes have ferried the goods ashore. These people are traders, hoping to get a better price at the big market in Cape Coast."

"Barter," I asked, "barter for what?"

"Plantain, corn, palm oil, coconut oil, yams. Many of the seamen on the tankers are our people and they don't fancy a diet of canned food. But mainly wee, what you call marijuana. Your people on St. Thomas and on the oil platforms can't get enough of the stuff."

Some time in the early hours of the next morning, I awoke, stiff from the ride and wet with sweat in the humidity of our unventilated hut. Kofi had apologized: this was the best accommodation could find at Yamoransa Junction.

My story of Bud the bully had returned to me in a bad dream and I found it difficult to get back to sleep. It was cooler outside. I lay back and gazed at a sky full of stars. A flotsam and jetsam of repressed thoughts floated to the surface of my mind. Millicent repeated the drunken speech she had made at the Stars and Stripes and I wondered whether our marriage could survive. The sexual passion of our youth had evaporated. Her energies were absorbed by a corner-cutting drive for money. I couldn't share her compulsion to compete with Bud and Selma. I would rather devote my spare time to Fergus and Marilyn than help her with her business. A captain's pay just wasn't enough to satisfy her material needs. Success in this mission would guarantee promotion, Bud had assured her.

"You'd better succeed, or else…" she had warned me.

"Or else what?" I had asked.

My musings turned to Pa and Ma Owusu-Ansah. Why had they abandoned me, never taken the trouble to call or send me a present at Christmas? They were complete strangers to me. The only photograph I had seen of them was more than forty years old. Would I recognize them? Not likely: I would have to rely on the name and my story. And if I were to find them what would I say? I had no idea.

Then there was Pa Ferguson's long forgotten admonition. Was I indeed an African as he wished me to believe? What did that mean, anyway? Did I have more in common with Kofi and his crew, apart from a similar complexion, than I had with Millicent and Bud and Selma, who certainly didn't consider themselves Africans?

Questions, questions, but no answers. I returned to the hut and fell at last into an uncomfortable, troubled sleep.

We set off the next morning without breakfast. Africans, I have already learned, take their first meal in mid-morning. We stop at the next village and I break my fast with some grilled plantain, purchased from a woman sitting by the roadside. I say purchased but I see no exchange of cash.

"Kofi," I ask, "How did you pay?"

"My credit is good," he replies and says something to the woman. She smiles.

"What did she say?" I ask.

"She says you should bring something for her on your way back from Kumase."

"Like what?"

"A pair of gold earrings would do fine, she says."

We laugh and then I say, "Kofi, seriously now, how I am going to pay you for all this?"

"All what?"

"Accommodation, food, transport, your services as a guide and teacher. All that."

"Gold dollars," he says, raises his head and looking me in the eye must observe my discomfort.

I get a grip. He surely can't be aware of the coins sewn into my jeans. I return his look.

"Sure," I reply. "No problem."

He says, "Seriously now, Crash. In this part of the world we pride ourselves on our hospitality, especially to strangers. So there will be no charge."

After a minute of silence he continues, "Except, perhaps, if and when one day you leave our shores, you might consider dashing me that fine wristwatch of yours. As a parting gift."

My wristcom. My super-miniaturized link with the outside world. Not likely.

"Well thanks," I say. "No problem."

And so it goes. Our road once served automobiles but I guess that it is years since the last one passed this way.

Every few miles there is a small village of crude houses with crumbling mud walls and roofs of rough thatch or, sometimes, rusty corrugated iron.

"Why do they put rocks on the roofs?" I ask Kwabena.

He seems intrigued at my ignorance.

"Big wind like roofing sheets too much," he explains.

Kwabena looks after the horses when we stop, unsaddles them, rubs them down, inspects their hooves and finds them water and a place to graze. He's a bright lad and eager to practice his limited English on me but Kofi makes it clear to him, speaking in rapid Fanti whose meaning I can only guess from the context, that he should not get too friendly. When we stop in the midday heat, Kwabena is left alone with me while Kofi goes off to report our presence to the village chief. I try to shake him off to let me call Millicent or report to Bud, but he won't let me out of his sight.

The road rises and falls past forest and farm. The upper reaches are in a surprisingly good state of preservation but the tarmac in the valleys is so heavily potholed that we sometimes have to dismount and lead the horses.

Kwabena points out the crops, corn, cassava, plantains, oil palm and, in the valleys, swamp rice, the ragged edges merging into the bush, no fences, nothing in straight lines.

In the predawn light a man marches to his farm, cutlass in hand, followed by his wife, child on her back, a hoe in the empty basket on her head, two children gamboling behind her. They turn off onto a bush path and then, seeing us, stop to call greetings and wave us on our way.

As we start looking for a place to take our midday break, another family emerges from a bush path. I look down into the woman's basket and see plantain, cocoyam, sweet potato, oranges and bunches of cocoyam leaves, the local spinach. As we make a temporary camp at the edge of their village, they catch up with us and greet us as old friends. Kofi engages them in conversation and they take him to greet their chief.

On the outskirts of a larger village we camp at a derelict gas station, complete with the skeletons of what once were pumps and the steel frame which once supported a canopy. A rusting sign reads "Shell." Nothing worth scavenging remains intact.

There is hardly any twilight in the tropics. It will be dark before we reach the next village and we run the risk of the horses stepping into a pothole. Kofi decides that we should camp out. We lie on our backs on the road, using the saddles as pillows. The sky is clear and full of stars. Only the intermittent hooting of an owl breaks the silence.

Kofi asks me for my impressions of the country.

"It's a disaster," I tell him.

"A disaster," he muses. "Natural or man-made? What would you say?"

"You'd know better than I," I reply. "I wasn't here to see it happen. A bit of both, perhaps?"

"One thing strikes me, though," I continue. "I haven't seen a single beggar. You might think America is rich, but our downtown streets are infested with panhandlers. Every day the cops round them up and deport them to the Abandoned Territories, but they just filter back."

"Our towns were like that when I was a child," Kofi says. "Even Elmina, in the days when the tourists were still coming. In Accra they used to gather at the traffic lights. Now we hardly use cash and even if we did, we'd have little to spare for alms; in any case there's no motor traffic and the lights don't work."

"So what's happened to the beggars?" I ask. "From what I've seen, there must be many in need."

"I think those who can, have fallen back on our old social security system."

"You have a social security system?" I ask.

"Our extended families," Kofi replies. "In our villages. Some of our old customs and obligations have survived. You'll see that when we get to Asante. But Crash, my brother, we have a long day ahead of us. Let's try to get some sleep."

"Pray that it doesn't rain tonight," he says, "and wrap yourself up against ants and mosquitoes."

I fall asleep considering an enigma: Kofi. For the simple fisherman he professes to be, he has a pretty good mind. But then, why not?

There is only one large river between Yamoransa Junction and Kumase, the Pra. In times past, the road crossed it on a steel truss bridge. That bridge is broken and its mangled remains lie rusting in the river bed, obstructing the flow.

"The wrath of the ancestors," Kofi says as the wrecked structure comes into view.

"What do you mean?" I ask.

"Nana Osei Tutu was the founder of the Asante Kingdom and Empire. That was in the year 1700. Fourteen years later, he was being carried across this river in the course of a military campaign, when his enemies shot and killed him. That was on a Thursday, which in Twi is called Yawda, on account of which the great oath of the Asante is "Meka Yawda," I swear by Thursday, an oath which is not lightly taken.

"For nearly two centuries afterwards, no Asantehene crossed the Pra and when one did, in 1896, it was not by choice, but as the captive of British invaders. In Asante eyes that was an abomination, an insult to the memory of Osei Tutu.

"And so too, perhaps, was the construction of this bridge. And so too, perhaps, that is why the ancestors, in their own good time, have destroyed it."

"Are you serious?" I ask.

He returns my question.

"What do you think?"

There was a crude ferry, a floating platform fashioned from old oil drums, pulled across by a steel cable turned around a manually operated winch, a slow business but safer than swimming the horses across. Kofi sent me and my horse first.

Once across I had the first chance in days to make contact with Bud.

"Crash, where the fuck have you been?"

Bud was shouting so loud I reckon I could have heard him without the wristcom and its satellite.

"Calm down, fellow," I told him. "I'm already in Asante."

"What the fuck are you doing in Asante? You're supposed to be in Kumase, remember? You're already three weeks behind schedule. Listen to me. The shit is flying here. I've been instructed to write you off, to set up an alternative strategy. This stuff is political dynamite, do you hear? We need news of our guys in Kumase and we need it quick. Now get off your ass and get up there. Quick. Anyway what are you doing in Asante? That's not on the route to Kumase. You on vacation or something?"

"Bud, will you give me a chance to put in my report?" I asked him and then he calmed down a bit, small, as they say in this country.

I gave him a brief lesson in geography and told him that the roads were a disaster, that there were no vehicles in working order and even if there had been, there was no gas to run them on. I explained that we traveling to Kumase on horseback

"On horseback?" he exploded. "Those guys might be dead by the time you get there."

"Bud, we're almost there. I've just crossed the last river into Asante. We should be in Kumase in two or three days. I'll be in touch as soon as I can."

Kwabena was leading his horse off the ferry, so I cut the connection.

We were now in Asante proper. Up on the bank, beyond the reach of floods, I guess, there stood a wooden shack with a crudely painted sign translated to me as "Asante. Immigration and Customs." Two men sat on a bench, facing one another, balancing a ten by ten checker board on their knees and taking turns to bang down the pieces. Kofi waited and watched. In due course they finished their game and while the loser swept up the pieces, the victor looked up and said, "Yes?"

Kofi introduced himself, "Kofi Kom."

The man nodded. It seemed that we were expected.

There ensued a long to and fro conversation of which I understood nothing except Kofi's tone and body language. He nodded towards me. The immigration officer or whatever he was, gave me the once over, then shook his head.

"Bra Crash, there's a problem," he told me.

"What now?" I asked.

"They're not ready to receive you in Kumase."

"Oh, shit," I said recalling what I had told Bud.

"Take care with your language, Bra Crash," he said, "Some of the Asante still understand English and they dislike the careless use of obscenities."

I was humbled.

"So, what now? Back to Mpoanokrom?" I asked, struggling with my pronunciation.

"We must find the Chief," Kofi interrupted my reverie.

"What, again?" I groaned.

"Yes, again."

I could hear the impatience in his voice. Kofi was getting pissed off with me. Perhaps we needed a break from each other. Like me and Millicent. A long break.

Absence makes the heart grow fonder, I had told her. She had turned her head away.

What I hadn't told her was how long I expected to be away. Truth is, I hadn't any idea of how long this mission was going to take. I still hadn't. "Four years in Ashantee?" I hoped not.

We'd arrived at a town called Bekwai late in the afternoon.

"We might be here for some time," said Kofi, "I need to find some decent accommodation for you."

I boiled. He let me rant and rave for a while and then quietly, gritting his teeth, explained. Our entry visas, such as they were, had only so much validity. We had to send ahead to Kumase, to make sure they knew we were coming and would let us in.

They have a proverb in this country: *abotare ye* it says; and its meaning is that patience is a virtue. That is not putting it strongly enough. The truth is that it is impossible to survive here without an infinite store of patience.

"*To wo bo ase*, Crash," Kofi told me, with a forgiving smile now, "Keep your cool, my brother."

That night we had reasonable accommodation in the rest-house of the Cocoa Marketing Company, or so the faded sign read. But I still had to bath out of a bucket.

Cocoa, it seems, was once Ghana's main export. A century ago, Kofi told me, Ghana led the world in cocoa exports, both as regards quantity and quality. Cocoa is what chocolate used to be made of before our chemists found ways to synthesize it.

I said I supposed it was cheaper to make it that way than getting peasants to grow the stuff in far away tropical countries.

Kofi said, "The invention of synthetic cocoa ruined Ghana's

economy. Almost overnight."

We had a look inside the main cocoa shed. The cocoa beans used to be supplied in sacks. When the demand ran down, there were still unsold stocks, sacks piled twenty or thirty high. The sacks were made of jute, a vegetable material, and in the course of time the jute had rotted.

"That ain't worth a hill of beans," I said.

Kofi let that pass. I considered telling him about Bogart in Casablanca but thought better of it.

We shared a room. Kofi and I had comfortable four-poster beds complete with mosquito nets. Kwabena slept on a mat on the floor. I waited until I was sure that Kofi was asleep. Then I stepped outside and called Bud to tell him the bad news. He was his usual bullying self, threatening to call off my mission and send a force to Kumase without my guidance. He said that he might lead it himself.

"You take the high road and I'll take the low road and I'll reach Kumase before you," I whispered. With a name like Ferguson, I'm almost a Scot.

I rang off without waiting for his response. The man is really insufferable.

When I returned to my bed, Kofi turned over.

"Who were you talking to," he asked.

"Talking to? In this place? Did you hear me talking? You must be imagining it. I just went to piss."

"Oh yeah?" he said and turned over and went back to sleep.

A boy delivered a message to Kofi the next morning.

"We're to head for a village called Abono and wait for a call," Kofi said.

I had visions of the villages we'd slept in the past few nights and flinched. I was badly in need of a long hot shower, a shave and a laundry of some sort. I was traveling light and both sets of clothes were beginning to stink.

Millicent. I should only present myself to Millicent in this condition, I thought, and that would be the end.

Abono, as it turned out, was paradise.

CHAPTER 4

THE HORSES HAD been sent to their stable and there was a taxi rank. Well, sort of. The taxis were three-wheeled cycles, with a saddle for the driver and a shaded seat behind for passengers. There was a choice: some of them were motorized, powered by a DC battery. And there was a bank of solar panels with batteries being charged. Wow! In darkest Africa!

While Kofi bargained, I went over to inspect the charger. The battery-master switched to English when I greeted him.

"Made in here," he answered my question, "At Suame Magazine, Kumase."

I have to say that they showed it: not much design and crudely made. Yet they seemed to work.

"Crash, let's go," Kofi called. "Meet Osei. He'll take us to Kuntanase and we'll pick up another taxi there, or a bus, or walk."

I groaned.

"Why can't he take us all the way?" I asked.

Osei explained in English, "From Kuntanase to Abono is too steep. Taxi there get special motor, two or three batteries."

Once we were on our way Osei proceeded to cross-examine us. He would ask a question and then turn his head around to look at us.

The third time I said to him, "Mister Osei, you no fear accident? Look front, I beg you."

They all laughed at my attempt at pidgin.

Kwabena, who was wedged between us in a seat for two, mimicked me.

"Mister Osei, look front, I beg you."

Kofi reprimanded him at once in Fanti and he fell silent.

Osei continued to turn, as if he were deaf and had to read our lips. Kofi and I were both cagey with our replies. Osei seemed satisfied with Kofi's explanation that I was a tourist from America and that Kofi, now exposed as a Fanti, was my guide and companion. He clearly assumed that both of us were ignorant of Asante and offered to give us a history lesson at no extra charge.

"I am historian, you know."

"Sure," I replied.

He must have sensed my disbelief.

"E-be true-o. In the old days, before the troubles, I was tourist guide, professional, registered with the Ghana Tourist Board. They sent me to Kwame Nkrumah University to study history. They awarded me diploma. It says, 'This is to certify that Christian Yaw Osei attended a two-week course on Asante history for tourist guides.' I have it in a frame, with glass in front, hanging on my wall. But these days no tourists come."

Coming to a small river, we had to get down and walk across the makeshift wooden bridge, one at a time, Osei pushing his precious taxi.

"Where shall I start?" he asked.

"Start?"

"The history."

"At the beginning?" I suggested.

"OK," he agreed. "In the beginning Onyankopon created the heaven and the earth. That was at Adanse, about twenty miles from here, near Obuasi."

"Hold on," I said, "I thought that happened in the Garden of Eden. Was that in, what did you say, Adanse?"

"Garden of Eden is for white men," Osei replied. "Adam and Eve. God. Bible. Church. White man's history. You be white man?"

He turned round again to look at me.

"No," he said. "You be black man like me and Mr. Kofi Kom and his boy. For us, Onyankopon did his work at Adanse."

"OK, I get it," I said. "Please go on."

Kofi leaned across and grabbed my arm. Then he shook his head from side to side. I guessed he didn't want me to encourage the guy. But hell, this was better than watching trees and cassava farms. I ignored him. I had already set the wristcom to record his story.

"One thousand years ago, Onyankopon sent a beautiful lady, Ankyewa Nyame was her name, down from heaven on a golden chain. She arrived at a place called Asantemanso. We will reach the place soon, it is just past Asumegya, but in the bush. It is holy ground. We don't go there. Anyway at Asantemanso, there was a deep, deep hole in the ground.

"Using the powerful juju which Onyankopon had given her, Ankyewa Nyame drew our first ten ancestors out of that hole and also a leopard, a frog and a dog. The frog gave them water and the dog gave them fire."

"What about the leopard?" I asked.

"As for the Osebo, I don't know. Maybe he taught those ancestors how to hunt."

"Osebo brought a drum," Kwabena said. "It was Osebo who taught us to make music and dance."

Osei turned round and nodded. Kwabena grinned.

"Our ancestors," said Osei, "built a big city there with seventy-seven streets. Ankyewa Nyame showed them where to find wild yam and cocoyam and taught them how to make farm and cook. She showed them which fruits were for eating and which were poisonous; and which plants were good for medicine. When they needed meat she showed them where to find snails in the forest. She taught them how to make iron and how to use it to make hoes and cutlasses and spears. And she taught them how to use clay to build houses and to make pots for cooking and to keep water. We will pass Asantemanso soon, but no lives there now, only bush.

"Near Asantemanso is Anyinam. That is where Nana Osei Tutu, the first Asantehene, was born. That is history. That is what history tells us. Chapter one. Chapter two later."

Kofi had brought some bottles of palm wine from Bekwai. It was hot and humid. We drank the tepid stuff as if it were water. I dozed; Kofi too, I guess.

The road surface deteriorated. The rough ride woke me. I rubbed my eyes. We were making slow progress as we ascended a steep hill, I called out to Osei to stop. He turned to look at me.

"You want piss?" he asked. "Wait small. Make we reach the top of the hill first."

A little way past the crest he halted and quickly slipped a wooden chock under one of the wheels. A woman emerged from a bush path, a basket of foodstuffs on her head. She was followed by a small girl, also with a head-load, this time firewood. Bringing up the rear was a man carrying a machete. Osei and Kofi both greeted them and some conversation ensued in which I heard the name Asantemanso. They pointed vaguely back down the path. Heads nodded.

Here the going was tougher. Osei had to pedal on the short up-hill stretches and on the long ones we had to get out and walk, sometimes even push.

When the going became easier, he started to tell us about Lake Bosomtwe. It seems that it was discovered by a hunter who shot and wounded an antelope, of the species known to the natives as *otwe*. The hunter tracked the bleeding animal and it led him to the lake, which he named *Bosom-twe*, or the spirit of the antelope.

Now Osei switched roles from historian to conventional tourist guide.

"Lake Bosomtwe," he recited as if by heart, "is shaped like a circle, about five miles across and two hundred and fifty feet deep. Scientists believe that it was formed by the impact of a meteorite about a million years ago. All around the lake hills rise to a height of three hundred feet and more above the water level. The slopes are steep, making it difficult for the inhabitants of the twenty-four villages which surround the lake to make a living from agriculture. They do a little fishing but ancient taboos forbid the use of canoes, so each fisherman sits on a plank, his legs in the water, and paddles."

The language wasn't his. He must have learned that from some ancient tourist hand-out.

In the early afternoon we arrived at a town called Kuntanase and there Osei left us to recharge his taxi's batteries and look for passengers for his return journey.

And here I had another surprise: there was a bus, a twenty-seater bus, and it was loading passengers heading for our own destination, a village called Abono on the shore of the lake. There was a queue and it wasn't at all clear that there would be room for us. Kofi pulled out his visa with the King's stamp on it. I went off to chat up the driver who had his head under the hood.

"Hi," I said. "Great bus you have here. Where do you get gas for it?"

He stood up.

"Gas?" he asked.

"Fuel," I replied. "Petrol."

He laughed.

"Petrol? Petrol in Asante? This my bus uses *akpeteshie*, pure alcohol, made in here by our own distillery. And palm oil for lubrication."

I expressed my amazement.

"But alcohol cost plenty," the driver told me.

Kofi came up and greeted the driver.

"There's a conference center at Abono, where we're heading," he told me. "They have this special shuttle bus because the road is so steep. There are some actors going down but I managed to persuade two youngsters to give up their seats for us. They'll go down on the next trip."

Actors. One surprise after another. Were we going to see a performance during our enforced stay by the lake? Of what, I wondered.

I took my place in the line, behind two women. In the bus they split, one left, one right. I moved in beside the younger one before they had a chance to change their minds.

"*Ye fre me* Crash," I introduced myself, holding out my hand.

She ignored my friendly gesture and turned to look at me.

"*Wo firi he?*" she asked me.

I hesitated.

"From where you?" she asked the same question in pidgin.

"I'm an American," I replied, somewhat taken aback by her aggressive response.

"An American?" she asked in a fake American accent. "You're the first one I ever met."

Then she held out her hand and introduced herself as Yaa.

"They call me Yaa Amponsah. That's my stage name."

"You're an actress?" I asked.

"Somehow," she replied.

She couldn't have been more than twenty one or twenty two, quite pretty, with her hair in corn rows and a dimple on her cheek.

"Tell me more," I asked.

"Well," she replied, "in Asante every town has one drama group. We do one new play every year. Then we combine with twelve other groups and we put on a show in a different town every month. So the people in our town will see twelve different plays every year and we will perform our play in twelve different towns."

I was intrigued.

"What sort of plays do you do?" I asked.

"All sorts," she replied. "Mostly Asante, but some English. Some from books, some we write ourselves. Tragedy, comedy, all sorts. Last year we did a concert party, like they used to do in the old days."

"And what are you going to do at Bosomtwe?" I asked.

"Every year," she said, "we have a national competition. Each district sends a group. The judges give prizes to the best shows. They select the year's best actors and actresses and bring them together to put on a special show to perform for the Asantehene and to tour the whole country. That's us."

She indicated the others in the bus.

"Great," I said. "Congratulations. But you haven't told me what you're going to perform."

She took a small paperback book from her bag and showed it to me. The cover said, "AKAN SHAKESPEARE. William Shakespeare *nwoma*. Julius Caesar a B. Forson *akyere ase*." I opened it. Inside there was a bizarre but recognizable head and shoulders image of the bard, in color, wearing a kente cloth.

"Julius Caesar," I said. "I did it in my senior year at high school. I played Mark Antony. 'Friends, Romans, countrymen, lend me your ears. I come to bury Caesar, not to praise him. The evil that men do lives after them. The good is oft interred with their bones. So let it be with Caesar.' In English, of course. I don't think I could manage that in Asante."

That excited her. She called the producer and told him what I had said. They started to make plans to involve me in the production. But that was not in my schedule. What would Bud say if I asked him for leave to join a group of traveling players?

"What part are you going to play?" I asked Yaa.

It had to be either Portia or Calpurnia. Portia probably.

"Julius Caesar," she said.

We laughed at that, the producer and I.

"Men!" she said, spitting out the word. "Why do you laugh? You men have all the best parts. I'm going to tell Okomfo Anokye that. He chose the wrong play. Or the wrong author. He should send a message to this Shakespeare guy and tell him that he should write good parts for ladies too."

Just then we caught our first view of the lake below and the oohs and aahs brought that conversation to an end. Soon we arrived at the small village of Abono and took a turn to the Bosomtwe Paradise Conference Center. It had been a popular tourist hotel in the old days. They gave us a double room with all facilities and a small balcony looking straight out over the lake. The sun was going down as we moved in and the view was stunning. Surprisingly, lights began to come on in the villages around the lake.

"Solar power," Kofi explained. He had been there before. We would have lights until nine.

I took a shower. While Kofi was having his, I strolled down to the water's edge and called Bud.

"Bud," I said, "I have important news for you."

"Don't tell me," he replied. "You're in Kumase. At last."

"Not quite," I told him, determined to keep my cool, "Still twenty miles to go. I'm at a village on the shore of a lake called Bosomtwe."

"A holiday resort?" Bud asked.

"Bud, just listen to me for once, will you?" I insisted. "This could be important. How are you going to get a force in here? Someone told me today that Kumase Airport hasn't been used in years. The runway is full of potholes. Now this is a big lake, about five miles across, and deep. I'm told that the road to Kumase is in reasonable condition. I had a great idea. How about using seaplanes?"

There was a pause.

"Crash," Bud replied, "Now where would I lay my hands on one of those? In an aviation museum? My brother, the tropical sun must be frying your bloody brains. Now if you are twenty miles from Kumase, just pick yourself off your fucking ass, walk in there tomorrow and find dear Professor William bloody Franklin and his party."

"Listen," I said. "We have to wait here until we receive an invitation from the Asante King. That might arrive any time, today, tomorrow, next week."

"Next month, next fucking year," Bud said and switched off.

He was right. I was on holiday. But what choice did I have? I suppose I could have slipped away and walked into Kumase, but what then? Unwittingly, Yaa had taught me a simple lesson, a lesson I should have learned earlier. If I stood dead still, no one could tell me from any other Asante man; once I moved, once I opened my mouth to speak, even if I got the words right and the tones right, I gave myself away. By

Kofi's account and judging by his behavior, it seemed clear that the Asante were nervous about having strangers in their midst. I could see no alternative to playing the game by his rules.

An hour before dawn I would be woken by bird-song. Elsewhere I would have turned over and gone back to sleep; at Bosomtwe I would rise quietly so as not to disturb Kofi and go out onto the small balcony. Sometimes I'd hop over the balustrade and make my way down to the water's edge in the dark. Then I'd send a brief message to Bud's recorder, to let him know I was still at Bosomtwe and to check whether he had left me any messages about my seaplane plan. Once I called Millicent, even though it was two in the morning in Washington. She had taken a sleeping pill and managed to be at once angry at having been woken and incoherent. I asked her for news of the kids but she just put the receiver down.

Dawn was something to see. The appearance of the lake changed almost by the minute as the light crept over it. At that time of day there wasn't a breath of wind and the surface was like a mirror, broken only by the stumps of old trees, relics of a time when the water level had been lower. Then the first fisherman would appear on his board, legs immersed, quietly paddling across from the village to inspect his traps, raise his nets and fill his basket. By this time the birds would have stopped singing and gone off to their work, but now it was the fisherman who was singing quietly to himself. His voice would carry across the water as if he were sitting by my side. Then I would greet him with the work greeting, *"Owura, adwuma ôô,"* speaking, not shouting, and he would reply with the respect due to a stranger, *"Yaa, ohenebaa,"* son of royalty, I return your greeting.

I would compare the early morning bustle at home, the rush to the bathroom, getting the kids woken and bathed, dressed and fed, driving through the cold and fog and fumes, nervous about being late for work, listening to the bad news over the car radio. This fisherman, I guessed, would rise from his mat, go outside to piss and then stroll down to the lake to catch the family breakfast. Peace.

By this time a light breeze would have risen and the surface of the water would be rippled. Kofi would stumble out onto the balcony rubbing his eyes. Sometimes we would hobble over the smooth inshore stones, ease ourselves into the tepid water and swim out to the fisherman. Kofi, a fisherman himself, though in a different environment, would engage the man in conversation regarding the arcane mysteries of their shared craft. I would soon give up trying to understand and float on my back. Once I borrowed a plank from a fisherman and tried to ride it. I never did master that skill, toppling over again and again to the amusement of the owner.

By the time we had showered and changed and strolled down to the dining room for breakfast, it would already be warm enough to raise a sweat. After breakfast Kofi would walk over to the terminal to see if any message had arrived from Kumase. As I curbed my impatience, enjoying the break, his increased. He was clearly anxious to fulfil his obligations to me and get back to Mpoanokrom. But Kwabena had found friends amongst the village kids and seemed to be having a great time, most of it in the water.

I spent the mornings watching the Anokye Players, as I learned they were called, first auditioning and allocating parts and then beginning to rehearse. My recollection of the details of the play was a little hazy, so I borrowed a copy of the original and found a quiet place to read it. My memory refreshed, I went back to the rehearsals. Sometimes I could identify a landmark scene but by and large the language cut me out.

One day, when Kofi had gone off to Kumase, I had lunch with the producer, who was called Opoku.

"How did you come to decide to do Julius Caesar?" I asked him.

He laughed.

"It was Okomfo Anokye's request," he told me. "You know who Nana Anokye is? Nana Asantehene's Gyasehene. Like your Prime Minister."

He had clearly either confused our constitution with that of the Brits or maybe he though I was a Brit, a black Brit. I let it pass.

"But why Julius Caesar?" I persisted.

He gave the matter some thought before replying.

"You see, we have democracy in Asante now, grass roots democracy. In every town and village and even in the suburbs of Kumase, the people elect their own Chief and Elders. Once a month we have a big meeting of all the people and the Chief reports back to us. If we like his report we elect him for another month and tell him to get on with the job. If we don't like his work, we elect someone else. It was Okomfo Anokye who started this. In the old days, you had to be a royal to be selected as Chief and once you were selected, you had the job for life, unless you did something really bad."

Yaa Amponsah brought us our fufu and snail soup and a bowl to wash our fingers. I winked at her but she didn't respond.

"Now the power belongs to us, the common people. In my village we elected a woman as Chief. Now our Chief is a Muslim from the Zongo."

He beckoned to me to bring my ear closer.

"A descendant of slaves," he whispered, looking around to make sure that no one had heard him.

"We only managed to do this because there was no government in Accra, not even in Kumase. The new Asantehene told us he would be our teacher, not our ruler. He said he was as poor as us and that he couldn't help us in any way except with ideas. The first of these are peace and cooperation. Without those, nothing can be achieved. He advised us to be truthful and honest with one another; and that we should show hospitality and generosity to strangers, even those from the next village. He told us that we would succeed in building progress only if we observed those rules.

"Good advice," I said, thinking that I'd heard those words before in church.

"We had to make the best of what little we had. And I tell you, we have done it. Everything is different now from what it was before. Every year there is an improvement. We never understood before that we had the power; we thought we had to wait for someone else, the Regional Minister, or our Member of Parliament or the District Assembly, to help us with our problems. Now we wait for no one, we just go ahead and do what we can. Open your eyes, open your ears, open your hands (to give, not to receive) and, most important, open your minds. That is what Nana Asantehene and Nana Anokye taught us."

It sounded like some earthly paradise. I wondered whether the man was pulling my leg.

"Sounds great," I said. "But where does Julius Caesar come in?"

"Be patient," he told me. "I am coming to that. Now some of our people, those who used to be rich in the old days, the traders, the preachers, the transport operators and the like, those people have started to agitate. They say that what we have is not true democracy. They say we must have a constitution and parties and elections and a parliament, *Asantehyiamu* they call it in Kumase. Nana Anokye says that may come in time, but only when we, the common people, think we need it, when we think it will be useful to us. He says that first we must consolidate our power. Those are his words. Consolidate your power. He warns us that if we are not careful, that old class of lawyers and politicians will steal our power from us, that they will start to tax us, that we will have to bear the cost of paying them big salaries. They call themselves the Constitution Party; Nana calls them *Domo*."

"Julius Caesar. Julius Caesar," I reminded him, gently.

"*Yadu,*" he replied. "We have arrived. You have told me that you know the play, that you once acted the part of Mark Antony. So I am going to ask you, what is this play about?"

"Oh, it's some old story from Roman history," was all I could think of to reply.

I'm not exactly a literary scholar. I do read books, but for pleasure and relaxation. And, frankly, if I hadn't had to act in Julius Caesar at school I would never have read it.

"Ah, brother Crash," said Opoku, "if you are a producer, as I am, you have go deeper than that."

"OK, you tell me," I said.

"First of all it's about power, about the exercise of power, about its limitations, about the relationship between the ruler and the ruled. Also, it deals with superstition and the hold it has over us. Then it's about the use of violence as a means of solving disputes."

Yaa brought the finger bowl and cleared our table.

When she came back for the finger bowl and the towel, Opoku was saying, "And it raises issues of gender. That might not have been Shakespeare's intention, but today we have to ask, why Caesar and not Calpurnia; why Brutus and not Portia?"

He turned to Yaa, who had been chosen to play Portia.

"I lie? My young sister Portia-Yaa, I lie?"

"And why Opoku and not Yaa?" she asked.

She had him there. I warmed to her spirit. I'd been watching her rehearse and she was a talented performer. I really liked Yaa but she would have no truck with my tentative advances. I wasn't serious, mind, but I would have liked to have got closer to her, to have taken her for a walk along the lake shore and explored her mind. Just that. Nothing more. Can a man and a woman not be friends, just friends?

I've been faithful to Millicent through all the years we've been married, in the physical sense at least. Sure my eyes have wandered on occasion but I've resisted every temptation. I reckon that's been Ma and Pa Ferguson's good influence. Now Yaa was showing me how lonely I was.

"Bide your time, young woman," Opoku said. "It won't be long before you become a producer. But first you must develop your acting skills and get experience."

We rose. On holiday, I was going to have a siesta. Opoku and Yaa were going back to their rehearsals.

"Do you understand now?" Opoku asked me. "This is a political play. Nana Anokye wants to use it to help us open our minds. After each performance we'll invite the audience to discuss what they have seen. Was Caesar good for the Romans? And what about all the nations which he had defeated on his way to power? Why did Brutus and his co-conspirators want to kill him? Were they right? And, finally, and most important, how does this story, this 'old story from Roman history' as you call it, bear on our own experience and the political decisions we have to make?"

"Sir," I said, addressing him as my master and teacher, "Thank you. Now I understand. I hope one day I'll have the chance to meet your Okomfo Anokye."

That night I dreamed of Yaa. I still recall that dream with guilty pleasure but there's no need to record the details here. The escapades of our sleeping hours are beyond our control and we cannot be held responsible for them.

The next day was a Saturday. Kofi had gone to Kumase. At Kwabena's insistence he'd taken him along. So I was on my own, without a chaperon.

On my way to breakfast I stopped at the notice board to read a large new handwritten poster. The Ramseyer Memorial Church in Abono, it said, was celebrating the 180th anniversary of the arrival of the Rev. Fritz Ramseyer, of blessed memory, in Kumase, bringing with him the Holy Word of God. All were invited.

Opoku came up behind me.

"Are you a church-goer?" he asked.

"Yes, A.M.E Zion," I said.

"Ah, you'll find them in Kumase, when you get there. This lot are Presbyterians. We're all going. You'll be welcome to join us."

Later than morning I called home. On Saturday mornings Millicent leaves promptly at eight for her aerobics workout. I fix breakfast for Fergus and Marilyn and then, at nine sharp take them to the club, for a swim and for their tennis and horse riding lessons. I called at ten past eight Washington time.

Fergus answered, "Ferguson residence, Fergus Ferguson speaking. Good morning. Who am I speaking to and how may I help you?"

Smart kid, Fergus.

I said, "Good morning. I'd like to speak to Captain Ekem

Ferguson."

Of course he recognized my voice at once.

"Dad! Where are you? I've been longing to talk to you. Why haven't you called?"

I did my best to explain within the limits of security and we had a great chat; with Marilyn too. When would I be back, they both wanted to know. I couldn't tell them. Then Selma arrived to take them to the club.

The Sunday service was a special occasion. A pastor had come from Kumase to give the sermon. He was dressed in black with a white dog collar. The church was too small to accommodate all the visitors from neighboring villages, so they'd set out benches and chairs in the tree-lined public square, near the lake shore. The service was conducted in Asante, including the sermon. It went on and on and on. Understanding practically nothing, I dosed.

After the service the VIPs, the Pastor, the Chief of Abono, the local catechist and the headmaster of the school took their lunch at the Paradise. Opoku and I were invited to take our seats on either side of the visiting Pastor. Akwasi the waiter brought us fresh palm-wine and announced that *banku* and grilled *tilapia*, fresh from the lake that morning, would follow. Then he dropped his voice and whispered in the Pastor's ear. The Pastor nodded, raised his index finger and used it to describe a circle.

"Just APC, mind," he said.

"The Holy Book," he said to me in English, "does not forbid the use of alcohol, on the contrary. In moderation of course."

I nodded politely and said, "What, if I may ask, is APC?"

He laughed and called the others to order.

"Our American friend," I understood him to say, "asks the meaning of APC. Who can tell him?"

There was general laughter.

"A is for American," said the catechist.

"A can only stand for *akpeteshie*," countered the chief.

"No, no," said the headmaster, "African. African People's…"

"Comforter," suggested Opoku, "African People's Comforter."

There was general applause. The Pastor held up both hands, calling for silence.

"A stands for Aspirin, P stands for Phenacetin and C stands for Caffeine," he announced.

"What?" asked Opoku as the others murmured their disbelief.

"My father told me," said the Pastor. "It was a drug, a medicine, popular in his time. Good for headache, fever and hangover. They used to sell a hundred pills in a small bottle. The akpeteshie sellers used the empty bottles to measure one shot."

"Eh, Pastor," said the chief, whose age and status allowed him some levity, "You are a real *krachie*."

At which there was general applause, repeated soon after when the waiter appeared with a tray of glasses of clear liquid. These the men raised, saying "Cheers," and downed at a single swallow. When in Rome...I followed suit. Wow! Firewater. Opoku saw the tears in my eyes and laughed.

"Kill me quick!" he said.

"So you're going to Kumase," said the Pastor. "Be on your guard. It has become a wicked place, a den of iniquity."

Opoku stiffened but the Pastor didn't seem to notice. I made no secret of my interest.

"Wicked?" I encouraged him.

"The Devil himself has been reincarnated there, in the person of a man to whom the natives have given the name of a fetish priest of ancient times, Okomfo Anokye."

"Okomfo Anokye was a wise man," said the Chief. "It was he who showed Nana Osei Tutu how to make the Asante nation."

"With respect, Nana," said the Pastor, "that may well be true but, if so, it is only half the truth. In those days our forebears practiced slavery. Moreover, they killed innocent people and sacrificed them to their false gods. Even when Rev. Ramseyer of blessed memory came amongst us and revealed the word of the true God, they persisted in their wickedness. It was not until the British captured Prempeh I and sent him away that they were forced to stop. And even then that stubborn woman, Yaa Asantewaa, started a rebellion with the aim of restoring their evil customs."

"Sir, are you saying that the Okomfo Anokye of today wants to restore slavery and human sacrifice in Asante?" Opoku asked, barely containing his indignation.

"Not yet, at least not to the best of my knowledge," replied the Pastor, seemingly impervious to Opoku's outrage. "But he might try. I have it on good authority that he is trying to persuade the Asantehene that the source of all our troubles lies in our acceptance of what he calls foreign religions, especially Christianity. The next thing we'll hear is that he's planning to restore our old pagan fetishes. What did those fetishes do for our ancestors, I ask you? Did they spare them the suffering of the slave trade? Did they protect them from the colonial conquest? They did no such thing. Those are false gods; they are fictions, creations of the human mind. Christianity has revealed the only true God to us. So I say that a man who can take it upon himself to ban Christian worship throughout Asante is capable of anything. "

"Nana, I beg leave to ask you: do you share the Reverend Minister's assessment?" Opoku asked.

"The Church has its view," replied the Chief, "and the Stool has its own. Mr. Crash, since you are on your way to Kumase, you must pass by Abono on your return journey and tell us what you have seen there. We are village people. The ways of the big city are often a mystery to us."

"It is one hundred and eighty years since Rev. Ramseyer of blessed memory brought the true word of God to the us," said the Pastor. "These are terrible times. We sorely need a new Ramseyer to light the way for us."

"This Ramseyer," I asked. "Who was he?"

The Pastor seemed at last aware of the heat his remarks had generated. He wiped his brow with a handkerchief. Then he put his hand on Opoku's in a silent gesture of reconciliation.

That done, he accepted the challenge to shine the light of his erudition into the darkness of my ignorance.

"Reverend Fritz Ramseyer," he replied, "was a Swiss missionary of the Basel Mission as our Presbyterian Church was then known.

"In 1869, he was stationed at Anum, on the far bank of the Volta River, bringing the Word of God to the heathens there. The Asantehene at that time, Kofi Karikari, a bloodthirsty tyrant by all accounts, sent a large force of his brigands into the Ewe lands to capture slaves and rob the poor.

"They captured Reverend Ramseyer and his wife, Rosa, another Basel missionary and a French trader and brought them back to Kumase on a forced march. The whites suffered terrible hardships on the journey. Worst of all the Ramseyers' infant child died from hunger and disease. Yet God's purpose is revealed even in the severest test of the true believer's faith. Even in that den of iniquity the Lord guided Reverend Ramseyer to fertile ground in which to plant the seed of the Holy Spirit.

"It was not until 1874 that the British general, Sargrenti, occupied Kumase and freed the European prisoners. Reverend Ramseyer gave thanks to the Lord for their deliverance and even wrote a book about his time in Kumase. If you come to Kumase I can lend you a copy to read."

"I would like to do that," I replied politely.

"That is not the end of the story," continued the Pastor.

I groaned inwardly. Christian I may be, but Lives of the Saints does not feature in my personal list of literary favorites.

"In 1896 the British entered Kumase again, this time to stay. Reverend Ramseyer followed soon afterwards, determined to continue his civilizing mission. Yet the Devil was still at work. The Asante hated the Reverend and his works and refused to acknowledge the Gospel of Jesus Christ. Under the leadership of the woman Yaa Asantewaa, as I have told you, they rose up against the British and burned the Basel Mission House. Mr. and Mrs. Ramseyer were forced to take refuge in the British Fort.

"They had to stay there for nearly two months. When the British soldiers' food and ammunition ran out, the Governor decided to lead an attempt to escape. By this time the

Ramseyers were already old. Yet again God tested them. The good Reverend had to carry his ailing wife much of the way. One night she was almost burned alive when the hut in which she was sleeping caught fire.

"The Reverend would not admit defeat. After the British had again pacified Asante, he returned to Kumase to spread the word of the Lord to the pagans.

"That is the story of the Reverend Ramseyer, a saintly man if ever there was one, surely a man sent by God to open our eyes to the truth. Think of him as you enter Kumase."

"Thank you, Sir, for that short history lesson," said Opoku as the tilapia arrived.

"Mr. Crash," the Pastor said. "I understand that you are an American?"

"Yes sir," I answered.

"And what brings you to our country, if I may ask? We don't see many tourists these days."

I told him my story. Pa and Ma Ferguson had died recently and I had come to Africa to search for my natural parents who had left me in the care of the Fergusons when I was still an infant.

"What did you say your father's name was?" he asked.

I hadn't mentioned his name but I gave it now, "John Owusu-Ansah."

He raised his eyebrows, pushed out his broad lips and nodded.

"A distinguished Asante name and an historical one, too. If it hadn't been for a man of the same name, no doubt your forebear, the Ramseyers might well have died in captivity. But today the name is quite common. Do you have any clues that will help you find them?"

"Just a faded photograph taken over forty years ago," I had to tell him.

"If you like I'll make an announcement in my church," he said and gave me a grubby visiting card with his address. "Now it's time for us to take our leave."

I was elated, but controlling my excitement, I had one more question for him.

"Do you know of any Americans in Kumase?" I asked.

He shook his head slowly and then stopped suddenly and raised an index finger.

"About a year ago, there was a rumor in town. I generally pay little attention to this sort of gossip. These stories are usually spread by Anokye's people. No doubt they have their reasons."

My pulse quickened. Two possible leads in one day. And without any input from Kofi. The Pastor noticed that I was waiting for more. He smiled.

"As I recall, your government was reported to have sent a hundred spies into the country. Anokye's brave forces had captured them without any loss of life and had imprisoned them in the Fort. I heard no more. If there was any truth in the story my guess is that they are all dead. Executed. That would not be beyond the new anti-Christ. And now, my good American friend, Mr. Crash, I really must leave you. I see our transport is waiting for us."

CHAPTER 5

KOFI CAME BACK at last with the news that Kumase was ready for us and, what's more, that he had found us an apartment in the center of town. He had sent Kwabena to stay with friends of his.

The first bus to arrive in the morning brought a load of handicapped people, complete with wheelchairs, crutches and white sticks. They were coming for a working holiday, to a conference to discuss their needs and, as one voluble delegate told me, their potential contribution to society.

We took their bus up the hill and then a motor rickshaw to a terminus in Kumase, still called a lorry station, though there were no lorries in sight. Lorry, by the way, is British for a truck. Kumase was like a ghost town. It reminded me of places in our own Abandoned Territories. I remember wondering whether this was a portent of the future of all the world's cities when the last oil and gas have been sucked from the earth. We passed rusty sawmills, the crane gantries overgrown with creepers; and a railway yard and station which clearly hadn't seen passengers or freight for many years. On the other hand, every open space seemed to have been turned over to farming. Kofi said it was the same behind the high walls of the houses of those who had once been rich. The city of Kumase had become a huge village, its diminished population surviving on subsistence farming and petty artisan trades.

Our apartment was in a block called Cedar House, located in a quiet side street off Stewart Avenue, named after some long forgotten colonial master. It was on the second floor (what they call the first floor) over an old shop. The owner was an ancient bearded gentleman of Lebanese extraction who spent his days watching the world go by from a rocking chair which must have been at least as old as he was. Trade had come to an end years before, he told me later, and since, in his extreme old age he found it difficult to climb to his apartment upstairs he had had the shop converted into living quarters. His capital long since exhausted, he was happy to find a tenant. I mentioned my parents' name to him but his answer was incoherent and I soon gave up.

We had a bedroom each and there was a separate living/dining room and a bathroom and kitchen. My bedroom smelled of fresh paint and had a shiny new lock. Kofi gave me the key. One room on our floor was not available to us. Kofi said it was let to a writer who used it intermittently as his office. He might make use of our bathroom but wouldn't interfere with us otherwise.

There was a stair up to the flat roof where we found a table and chairs, a beach umbrella and some potted plants. There was also, lo and behold, a gnarled grape vine stretching up on a trellis from a small courtyard at ground level.

"The Lebanese use the leaves for cooking," Kofi said.

Now the high tech stuff. There was a solar water heater and a bank of photo-voltaic panels of somewhat archaic design that ran the lights and the ceiling fans. There was also a satellite dish. What, I wondered, could that be connected to? But, thinking that it was probably old junk, I held my counsel.

That first evening Kofi found us a keg of palm wine and we sat up on the roof, admiring a crimson sunset across a landscape of rusty corrugated iron roofs set in the greenery of the tropical trees which moderate the ugliness of the city. When Kofi isn't around, I thought, I'll come up here to talk to Washington.

While we were there we heard a noise down below. Kofi

went to investigate and found it was the writer, whom he promptly invited to join us.

"My name," he said, "is Saman," and he winked at Kofi. It seems they were having a private joke; and it was against me.

"Some of my friends call me Kofi Kanea," he continued. "Others call me Boafo. I think that's what you should call me. Boafo means helper, so if there's anything I can do for you, just let me know."

"Boafo," I mused. "I really should know that. My parents hail from Kumase; and my foster parents were Fantis. But my Asante is nothing to write home about."

I went on to tell him the purpose of my visit, that is to trace my natural parents. When I told him my father's name, Owusu-Ansah, he affected astonishment.

"That's a well-known family with a distinguished history," he said, "but they are many."

He hadn't heard of my parents but he promised to ask around.

I told him that Kofi had mentioned that he was a writer and asked him what sort of stuff he wrote. It turned out that the satellite dish was his. He worked through agents in New York and London, doing anything that came his way, mainly copy-editing.

"Cheap colonial labor," was his comment.

I wondered how he got paid in Kumase, but decided it would be impolite to ask.

After some more desultory chat he asked permission to leave us, which we granted. That is their custom.

"Crash," said Kofi. "I don't know how long you plan to spend in Kumase, but I need to get back to Mpoanokrom. I've been looking around for someone to take my place as your guide, so far without success. Now it strikes me, how about this chap, Boafo? He's a Kumase man and almost certainly knows his way around better than I do. And he can probably use the pocket money. What do you think?"

I told him I would be sorry to lose his services. That wasn't entirely true. At times I had suspected that Kofi was watching me as if he knew something about my hidden agenda. I knew I would be more relaxed in his absence. So I agreed to let him discuss the matter with Boafo.

"How long do you plan to stay here?" he asked.

I guessed he had been reserving that question until we were about to part.

Before I could reply he continued, "I take it that you do plan to go back to the States one day?"

"As long as it takes to solve the mystery of my disappearing parents," I replied.

I would always be welcome at Mpoanokrom, he assured me,.

He fixed things with Boafo the next day and left the following morning. So now I had a new guide.

"If you have any valuables," Boafo advised me, "hide them in your room and make sure you lock the door and take the key. We flatter ourselves that we have had a revolution, but that hasn't persuaded our professional pick-pockets to give their fingers a holiday."

"Revolution?" I asked.

"Oh, forget that I said that," he replied. "Not really a revolution. It's just that we've begun to learn to take charge of our own lives."

Boafo lived with his family on the University campus, five miles away on the Accra road. He used a bicycle to commute to his town office.

He had brought a kit-bag with him.

"I'll move in while you're here," he explained. "You'll need a guide if you decide to go out at night; and I don't want to be cycling home in the early hours."

Kumase had some rusting street light poles but none of the lights worked.

"I suggest that we spend our first day together touring the town, on foot," Boafo said. "You need to get your bearings. In case you lose me, you should know how to find your way back here."

He produced an old street map of the city, the torn pieces carefully taped together.

"I take it you can read a map?" he asked.

Inwardly, I laughed. What would the guy say if I told him I was a U.S. Marine?

"It's a skill," he apologized, "that eludes some of my best educated colleagues."

He spread the map and showed me the route he planned to take. Then we set off. We walked up Stewart Avenue, past the Ministries, bereft of bureaucrats, and the General Post Office, where no letters arrived and none were dispatched.

"That is Kumase Fort," Boafo told me, pointing out a curious red-brick building on the other side of the road.

"The one where Ramseyer was besieged?" I asked, pleased to display my knowledge.

He looked at me curiously. I must have persuaded him that I knew more than he gave me credit for. Charlatan, I accused myself, silently enjoying my small triumph.

"Correct," he replied.

The Law Courts were next. There, Boafo told me, black judges in white wigs, caricatures of their colonial predecessors, had received sealed envelopes before dispensing justice. We peered through a window. The fine dark furniture appeared to be intact but only the invisible ghosts of the jurists sat at their bench.

"These days it is the people who administer the law," Boafo told me.

"That is Okomfo Anokye," he told me next.

"Where?" I asked, expecting to see the man I had already heard so much about.

He pointed. Up ahead, on a traffic island, there was a statue on a pedestal. We waited for a gap in the flow of bicycles and crossed. The statue was of a small man dressed in a grass skirt, dancing. His face was painted white and he brandished a fly-whisk as if it were a weapon. Clearly it represented the original Okomfo Anokye, not the man of our times.

Our next stop was the Okomfo Anokye Hospital, named after the eponymous folk-hero.

"When the Central Government collapsed," Boafo told me, "so did our Medical Schools. Even in the good old days we were losing more than half of each year's new crop of doctors to emigration. Now not only were there no new doctors entering the system, but many of the mature doctors decided to invest their savings in a dangerous adventure, taking their families to the West. We had nothing left to export and foreign aid, the mother's milk of our politicians in the early years of this century, had dried up. So there were no rubber gloves and no syringes, which didn't really matter, because there were no drugs either. This hospital became an empty shell. Old diseases began to reappear. Even today, with our new health policies, our life expectancy is less than it was fifty years ago. By rights (I mean statistically) as an average Asante man I should be dead by now."

He laughed.

"But then our statistics are not exactly accurate these days, so maybe the Chief Statistician up there has forgotten about me. Or maybe I've kept him at bay with my cycling."

"You mentioned new health policies?" I asked.

"Okomfo Anokye again," he said. "not he of three hundred and fifty years ago, but he of today. Education, hygiene, good drinking water, regular exercise, sensible and simple diet, traditional herbal remedies, home care; and education again. Every one his own doctor, or her own doctor: the women are our betters when it comes to this. Medical education starts at six and continues right through the school years. And it doesn't stop there. But that's enough of a lecture for the time being. What about you? Are you well? Not been attacked by some dreadful tropical disease?"

Boafo was an interesting man; and a knowledgeable one, too. I learned a great deal from him in our short time together. But when I tried to get him to tell me something about himself, he would deflect my query. So he remained an enigma.

It was getting hot and by mid-morning my tee-shirt was already drenched with sweat. Boafo insisted that we should complete our circuit of the sights of the city. The old Cultural

54

Center, or what was left of it, Kumase Zoo, the only zoo I've ever seen that had no animals beyond the birds which populated its trees, the Central Market, thinly populated with goods and traders, Manhyia Palace, residence of the Asantehene, the Prempeh Assembly Hall, the Cathedral and then back across the disused railway line at the obsolete Kumase Station and up the hill to our apartment. It was three by the time we got back. I was too tired to eat or shower: I just flopped down on my bed, my bones and muscles aching, and fell at once into a deep sleep.

It was dark when I woke. I had a piss and then stumbled to the kitchen. There was a bottle of cold water in the frig and I drained it. Boafo must have heard the noise of the flush. His door opened and I caught a glimpse of a computer and what seemed to be a mass of electronic gear on a work table. He came out and quickly closed the door behind him.

"Fancy something to eat?" he asked. "There's quite a good chop bar just up the road. You might even get a can of beer there, if you're prepared to pay."

"Give me half an hour," I begged.

I lay down again, intending just to take a short rest and then get up and shower. When you take an afternoon siesta in Africa it really knocks you out. I dozed off and dreamed I was shoveling snow at home and throwing snowballs at the kids. I was woken by beeping from my wristcom. Shit! I had hidden it somewhere before going out with Boafo and now I couldn't remember where. By the time I found it the beeping had stopped. There was a message from Bud.

"Crash, where the hell are you? Millicent phoned and said if you don't get back soon she's going to divorce you. She's blaming me for your lengthy absence. You should teach your wife manners, man. I had to disconnect her. Call me back ASAP."

He said ASAP as if it were a word.

I put the cursed thing back in its hiding place. Fuck Millicent, I thought. I am out here serving my country on a dangerous mission and she threatens to divorce me. Women, I'll never understand them.

I knocked on Boafo's door when I was ready. We locked our rooms and walked up to the chop bar. It was called *Christmas in Egypt*. Boafo had to knock on the door to get us admittance.

"What's going on?" I asked him. "Is this place a speakeasy?" I had a splitting headache.

"Speakeasy?" he asked.

I guess it's an American word. I explained.

"No," he replied. "It's not possible for it to be illegal since we have no more than the shell of a central government and the old government's laws are in abeyance. No police, no judges, no laws. Not entirely accurate but you get the general idea. Nana Asantehene certainly wouldn't waste time on policing a place like this, even if he had a regular police force at his disposal. Maybe the proprietor thinks the speakeasy business enhances the ambiance. I'll ask him."

"Never mind," I said.

There was a bar right across the room at one end with a mural on the wall behind it. The subject of the painting was Paradise and it featured Adam and Eve, both naked except for their fig leaves, and both pink-skinned. Eve was offering the man a half-eaten apple.

There were two empty stools and we took them, casually greeting the other drinkers.

"What'll you have?" asked Boafo, as if the round was on him.

There weren't any drinks on show.

"What've you got?" I asked, looking around in case I'd missed the display.

"Whatever you want, sir" chipped in the proprietor, who happened to be behind the bar. "Scotch, imported beer, Kill-me-Quick. You name it, we have it."

"I'll have a dry martini," I replied.

"Your wish is my command, sir," he said.

The martini wasn't the greatest but it was drinkable. Boafo ordered an APC of *akpeteshie*. On ideological grounds, he claimed.

"What are you?" I asked him. "Some kind of communist?"

"Crash, my good friend, in this country we are all some kind of communist now. Except the DOMO, that is. The Constitutional Party, you know. The nut-cases. Let's drink to them."

And he raised his glass.

One of the other drinkers got off his stool and came and stood behind Boafo. Struggling to maintain his balance, he tapped Boafo on the shoulder. Boafo turned and looked at the drunk.

"Did I hear you insult the DOMO?" he asked, sticking out his chest and raising his head. His speech was slurred.

Boafo didn't answer. The proprietor had left the bar and was nowhere to be seen.

Boafo turned to me.

"Crash, as I was saying before I was rudely interrupted, the Constitutional…"

The drunk grabbed his shirt and pulled him off his stool.

Boafo slapped the man's face, all but knocking him off balance. He was smaller than the drunk but he was sober. I was bigger than either of them and I was a professional fighter. I forced my way between them, gently pushing both backwards.

"That's enough," I said.

The drunk was feeling his cheek.

"You American?" he asked.

He had evidently had second thoughts about picking a fight.

"Sure thing," I said.

I led him back to his stool.

"How come you're not in the Fort?" he asked.

"In the Fort?" I replied.

"All the Americans are in the Fort," he said.

"There are Americans in the Fort?" I asked.

At this point, Boafo took me by the arm. He was holding both our drinks in his free hand.

"Come on Crash," he said, "Let's go and get something to eat."

He led me to a table in the courtyard. A waiter brought a printed menu.

"Sorry about that," he said. "And thanks. If you hadn't

intervened I would have knocked him down, I was so angry. And god knows what that would have led to. What will you have?"

I read the menu but I wasn't seeing the words. Americans in the Fort! The Pastor's rumor was true. At last I would have something positive to report to Bud. And after just a couple of days in Kumase! I was tempted to ask Boafo what he made of that, but the rules were against it. In D.C. I had committed my instructions to memory. Rule 7: say nothing to a native that might lead him to suspect your true mission.

Boafo placed his order. I said I'd have the same.

I was sober enough when we left to observe that the drunk had left before us.

Boafo woke me for a late breakfast.

"Sorry, no bread, no coffee," he said. "These days we eat what we grow, what we can grow ourselves. Wheat doesn't grow in our climate. So no bread. We used to grow coffee, but only our elite drank the stuff, so we don't grow much any more."

I didn't ask him why they don't grow it for export. The answer was obvious: there was no easy way to get the beans to the foreign buyer.

So we had to make do with freshly squeezed orange juice, bananas, pawpaw, pineapple and avocado pear. Boafo had grilled some ripe plantain and a few rashers of bacon and boiled us an egg each.

"All from my own farm," he boasted. "Do you want to go and have a look?"

"Boafo, I'd love to," I said. "I'm really impressed. But I need to stay focused. My first priority is to look for my parents. Where would you suggest I start?"

Actually my first priority was to get rid of Boafo so that I could make a private call to Bud. And my second priority was to get rid of Boafo so that I could make a call at the Fort. Again I considered asking him about the Americans but again I decided against. I liked the guy but I didn't trust him. First, his politics. Second, all that electronic gear of his.

"Hold on," he said and went to his room.

I heard him unlock the door. He always locked the door behind him. I wondered whether he thought I was a thief. He came back with two Ghana telephone directories.

"I had a look in the University library," he said. "That was one of the few institutions that escaped without damage during the troubles. Unfortunately where explosives and arson failed, humidity and insects are succeeding. Anyway, this fat one is the 1994 directory. The thinner one came out later, I think, but the cover is damaged and I can't find the date. Have a look at the Owusu-Ansahs in the Kumase section. Maybe you'll find them there."

"Boafo," I said, "That was really thoughtful of you. But 1994. My father must still have been wearing short pants then."

I tried the thinner volume first. It was a mess but at least the page with the Owusu-Ansahs was intact. There were twenty-seven of them.

"When do think this directory might have been published?" I asked.

"I can only guess," he said. "Perhaps around the millennium, as they called it. As far as I know this is the last telephone directory ever published in Ghana. Treat it with respect. It's valuable."

"Shit," I said. "The entry wouldn't have been in my father's name. He must have been a schoolboy still. I should be looking for my grandfather's entry. And I have no idea what his first name was."

"Well, you could start phoning, in alphabetical order," said Boafo.

"You must be joking," I replied.

"Sure thing," he said.

I thought, he must have picked up that expression from me. Or was he kidding me?

"The telephones haven't worked for thirty years," he continued. "We've set up a new system recently, but it's only for emergencies and the like. We're still manufacturing every exchange and every phone laboriously by hand."

"I see there's an address against each name," I said.

Boafo brought out his map and marked the location of each Owusu-Ansah on it. The map didn't show many street names but he seemed to have a street name directory in his head.

"Don't expect too much," he told me. "Many buildings were destroyed in the civil war. Many of our people were killed or died of hunger or disease. And most of the survivors have been displaced, gone back to their villages. But it's worth a try. We'll have a lot of walking to do. Or let me see if I can find a bike for you to use."

Then he said, "Look, I'm still suffering from last night. What say we get some more sleep and get started when it's cooler outside? Shall we say four o'clock?"

That suited me fine. I had other plans.

I waited twenty minutes. Then I went up to the roof and left a brief message for Bud. I told him that I had unconfirmed intelligence that William Franklin and his party were imprisoned in Kumase Fort. I told him I was on my way to attempt to check this out. I told him that in no circumstances should he call me—to do so might compromise me and endanger the whole project.

I went back to my room and hid the wristcom. I locked the door. I put my ear to Boafo's door and seemed to hear his regular breathing.

Downstairs our old Lebanese landlord was puffing at his hookah. I wondered whether I should offer him a bribe not to tell Boafo I had gone out. But that would have been pointless. All Boafo had to do was to knock on my door.

I didn't have much time. Fortunately the Fort was only a short walk away. There was a man stretched out on a watchman's chair in the shade of the mango tree which stood in front of the red brick building. He was dosing, a conical straw hat over his face. I went to the heavy studded door and knocked. There was no answer. I tried again, with the same result. I looked at the guard, if such he was, but he still seemed to be asleep. I tried the door handle. The door was locked.

Without removing his hat, the watchman asked, *"Oburoni, na wo pe den?"* meaning white man what are you after? It seems he was more efficient than I had given him credit for. I went over to him.

"Wo te Brofo?" I asked him, meaning do you understand English?

He took off his hat.

Without getting up, he said, *"Oburoni, wakyea me anaa?"* meaning white man have you greeted me?

I had to apologize for my bad manners. Again I asked him whether he understood English. He said no, but why did I want to speak English when I spoke perfectly good Asante. I was flattered. I wanted to say that my Asante wasn't up to explaining what I wanted, but my Asante wasn't up to explaining even that. He asked me again what I was after.

"Me hwehwe Amerikafoo no," I said hoping that he would understand that I was searching for the Americans.

He understood very well.

"Wo koo," he said, meaning they have left, *"Wo koo akye,"* meaning they left a long time ago.

I didn't believe him. I considered confronting him with the accusation, *"Wo boa,"* meaning your are lying. I decided that he was unlikely to succumb to that kind of pressure. Should I offer him a bribe? I kicked myself that I hadn't got hold of some of the local currency, such as it was. I decided to ask him where they had gone, but I wasn't sure how.

"Ehefa na wo koo?" I tried, intending where did they go?

"Me nnim," he replied, *"Wo tuu kwan,"* meaning I don't know; they traveled.

I was more than ever convinced that he was lying, but I already had a headache from trying to devise questions that he could understand. I looked around for an interpreter but there were no likely candidates in sight. I had to get back before Boafo woke up and met my absence, as they say there.

Stopping at the first junction to wait for a gap in the bicycle traffic, I turned and looked back at the Fort. The security man was banging on the door. I saw it open. He went inside.

I passed *Christmas in Egypt* on the way. The proprietor was outside in the street supervising some loading or off-loading from a cart. I greeted him.

"I was here last night," I told him. "Do you remember me?"

"Of course," he replied. "Didn't I mix you a dry martini? Was it OK?"

"Fine," I said. "Were you told that there was almost a fight after you left the bar?"

He didn't look surprised.

"It happens," he said.

"The man who caused the trouble was pretty drunk. Do you know who I mean?"

"I think so," he replied.

"Do you know who he is and where I can find him?" I asked.

"Sorry," he replied. "He's not a regular. In fact last night was the first time I saw him. Did he pick your pocket or something?"

"No, nothing like that," I said.

I considered asking him whether he knew anything about the Americans and decided against.

We exchanged goodbyes.

As I walked on he said, "Give my greetings to Kofi Kanea."

I took it that he meant Boafo.

I replied, "He will hear," and it struck me at once that the Asante language was affecting the way I speak English. I would never have said that at home.

The landlord was dosing with the hubble-bubble pipe stuck in his mouth. I went up and let myself in. There was no sign of Boafo. I guessed that he was still sleeping. It was a quarter before four, so I knocked on his door before going to my room.

I felt a sense of unease. Something was wrong in the room but I couldn't make out what it was. I lifted a corner of the mattress. The wristcom was where I had put it. Nothing seemed to be missing. Had I left the sheets on the unmade bed in just that state of disarray? I told myself I was being stupid and lay down to think while I waited for Boafo. I had nothing new to tell Bud so I decided to postpone my call.

We tried the three nearest Owusu-Ansah addresses before dark, all without a hint of success.

"Where shall we eat?" Boafo asked.

It was a stupid question. Or perhaps not. There was only one answer available to me.

"How about *Christmas in Egypt* again?" I suggested. "The fufu and snail soup was good. But no drinks for me. I'm getting too old."

I thought the drunk might be there again, but he wasn't.

Boafo met a friend who joined us in the courtyard. They talked football; they meant soccer but they called it football. There was a big match on the next afternoon, Sunday. They agreed to meet at the Stadium and insisted that I should join them. I would have preferred to have gone off on my own, scouting around the back of the Fort, or searching for my parents, but Boafo would have none of it.

He woke me early.

"Would you like to go to church?" he asked.

"Only if it's Presbyterian," I said and handed him the Pastor's grubby card. "This man was at Abono last Sunday and promised to make inquiries about my parents."

Boafo looked at the card and handed it back to me.

"Too far," he said. "and too long. Those Presbyterian services go on and on and on. We'd miss the football."

"Which church did your parents go to?" he asked me.

"I really don't know. Why?"

"I thought that that might be a good place to start," he replied.

"Seems a good idea," I said. "I'm A. M. E. Zion. Pa and Ma Ferguson had me baptized there after my parents left. That's where I met my wife."

"African Methodist Episcopalian," I spelled it out for him.

"A. M. E. Zion are here too," he said. "They're near Asafo Market. That's on the way to the Sports Stadium. We could say our prayers, inquire about your father, have a bite somewhere on the way and meet Joe. A good, lazy, leisurely Sunday. How about it?"

Back home Millicent drags me and the kids off to church every Sunday morning without fail. The services are too long. I usually fall asleep during the sermon. Millicent keeps prodding me in the ribs. Millicent, for all her undoubted virtues, doesn't have a forgiving nature.

Apart from the uncomfortable seating, there was nothing remarkable about the service, except this: I remember the subject and at least some of the content of the sermon. The subject was the words of despair which Christ is reported to have spoken from the cross, *Eli, Eli, lama sabachtani?* My Lord, my Lord, why hast Thou forsaken me?

"In these days," the preacher asked, "is there one of us here who has not felt the same despair? We ask ourselves, what did we do wrong, that the Lord should punish us with such suffering, not only our generation, but those of our children and grandchildren? Our ancestors believed in heathen gods. The white man, whatever bad things he visited upon us, did bring us the greatest gift, the knowledge of Christ and the only true God. We accepted that with hope; we deepened our faith. Is it charity we have lacked? Or is it that we allowed ourselves to become dependent on the charity of others?

"The workings of God's mind are beyond our understanding, puny human beings that we are. So my message to you today, my brothers and sisters, is that we must have faith in God's wisdom and mercy, even in the depth of our suffering and misery."

Then he launched a blistering attack on Anokye. He said he was feeding false information to the Asantehene. He said that Anokye was determined to destroy the churches by demanding that they send the proceeds of their collections to the local Peoples Councils; and that this proved that he was the agent of the Devil himself, indeed that he was the Devil in human form, the Devil incarnate. He liked that last phrase so he said it again, "The Devil incarnate." The congregation liked it too.

He said that Christians must demand a Constitution and free and fair elections to a Parliament. He said that God demanded that every member of his church should support the new Constitution Party. It sounded more like a political speech than a sermon, though he managed to lace it with supporting chapter and verse.

At the end of his sermon, he reminded the congregation that the clergy were dependent, as ever, upon their generosity. Since the currency of the former state had no value, all gifts in kind would be appreciated and should be brought to the front for display.

"Rabble rouser," Boafo said.

"I want to go and have a word with him," I said.

"Reverend," I said and he held out his hand for me to shake.

"I see a new face amongst us," he said, "My young brother, you are welcome."

Young? I'm over forty. His eyesight must have been defective.

"Reverend," I said when I had thanked him, "I wonder if you might make an announcement for me?"

I explained what had brought me to the country. I wondered whether there might be anyone in the congregation who could give me any news of my natural parents. My father's name, I told him, as Pa and Ma Ferguson had told me, was Owusu-Ansah, John Kwadwo Owusu-Ansah.

His announcement caused something of a sensation. Everyone wanted to shake hands with the visitor from America. Then one old man, bald, quite bald, in a shiny dark suit and frayed tie, pushed his way through the crowd, pulling an equally old woman after him.

"Your father was at Achimota School with us," he told me. "Class of two thousand and three, is that right, Gloria?"

Gloria, it seemed, was his wife; and had been his school-mate.

"If it's the same John Owusu-Ansah," said Gloria. "His father was a diplomat, something in the United Nations, I think. We went to the university at Legon. John's father sent him to study in the United States. I remember how jealous we all were."

My heart missed a beat and then started pumping double-time.

"Do you know where he is now? He and my mother? Are they still alive?"

"Sorry," said the old man. "Haven't seen him for years. Last time, I think, was at a funeral in Accra. That must have been in the twenties, before the troubles, you know."

And that was that.

As soon as we entered the football stadium I saw its virtues. Bosomtwe paled in comparison. Here was an ideal landing site for the Thunderbirds. The armored vehicles could roll down the ramps and be at the Fort in minutes, break in, collect Franklin and his team, drive back to the Stadium, roll up the ramps and be away within an hour of arrival. I was so excited, picturing the scene and working out the details that I paid little attention to the game.

Now I really needed to talk to Bud. We stopped for a meal on the way back to the apartment. I took no liquor.

"It's against my religion," I told them. "I don't drink on the Lord's Day."

Tongue in cheek, Boafo accused me of blasphemy. It struck me that he was an atheist.

CHAPTER 6

I WENT UP to the roof at midnight and called Bud. I reckoned he would be home by then. He started his usual rant as soon as he came on-line. I wanted to shout at him but I was scared of waking Boafo down below.

"Bud, you asshole," I whispered to him, "Will you shut your fucking mouth and listen for once?"

I told him I had located William Franklin and his team with 95% certainty, enough, I reckoned, to warrant a rescue mission. I told him about the Sports Stadium. That calmed him down.

He said he'd pass on my report and call me back with zero date and hour. I told him that on no account should he call me. I'd call him at midnight GMT every night for instructions.

As I opened the door to the corridor I thought I saw a crack of light under Boafo's door, but then it was gone. I put an ear to the door. I could hear nothing but the whirring of the ceiling fan. Get a grip on your nerves, I told myself and went to bed.

Our search for my lost parents kept us occupied. Each day the houses we sought were further and further away and each day we drew a blank at each.

The next time I spoke to Bud he read the game plan to me. This time I didn't go to bed. I slipped out of the front door, taking the wristcom with me. It was pitch dark and there was no one about. I recorded my position and the time. Then I set out to walk to the Stadium. There was a security guard at one of the gates, asleep. I selected another gate and scaled it. I made my way to the center spot and took an accurate fix. Then I spoke to Bud again and fed the data through to him.

There was no moon and the sky was overcast.

I closed the door behind me and then paused to make sure that I was unobserved.

The air was still and the city asleep. I retraced my earlier route. Soon after I set off, I thought I heard footsteps some way behind me. I stopped and the sound stopped too. I looked back but there was only darkness. I set off again. The sound was there again though softer now. I decided that I was hearing an echo.

After twenty minutes I had scaled the same gate as before and was back in the football stadium. I groped my way to a seat in the bleachers, opposite the center spot and sat looking out into the darkness, waiting for the game to start.

I called Bud, whispering into the wristcom.

"I'm at the stadium," I told him.

For a change he was cool and professional. The three Thunderbirds were sitting on the deck of the Half Assini No. 5 off-shore oil platform, just a hundred and fifty miles south west of Kumasi. The count-down to take-off was in progress. He confirmed our mission: snatch the hostages; no casualties. I let him take me through the plan but I already knew it by heart: it was based on my own first draft. I checked my wristcom against his time. Then he wished me good luck and signed off. I'd like to believe that that was the real Bud.

I had an hour to wait with little to do. I tried to pray, but though I do go through the motions in church, I'm not much of a praying man. I gave up and focused my mind on Millicent, Millicent of the good days, when we were courting. I tried to create a virtual wristcom, with a mental telepathy button; and willed her to come on line. I failed. She would have been fast asleep already. Or maybe her will to shut me out had more power than mine to reach her. But Fergus was there; and Marilyn, too. Both eager to hear me declare my love. I told them that it was for their sakes that I was carrying out this dangerous mission and that I would be home soon, soon, soon.

There had been an owl about, hooting occasionally. Now there was a different sound, more like a cough, somewhere behind where the net would have been, over to my left. I screwed up my eyes, but it was too dark. I made a mental note that I should have brought a pair of night vision glasses. Then I thought I saw a red spot of light. It could have been the glow of a cigarette, or a tobacco pipe. Suddenly I was nervous. What if there were someone over there? Or was it only my imagination?

I kept watching and listening. At the same time I forced myself to concentrate and analyze the situation. If there were somebody there, who might it be? It might be a single security man, a night watchman. I tried to imagine any circumstances in which his presence might sabotage the operation. I couldn't. At worst (for him), he might get himself shot. At best he might live to tell a pretty good tale. But by that time the force would have come and gone, and I would be gone, too. Another possibility was that some local had got wind of the plan and that there was a reception committee waiting out there behind the goal. I discounted that almost at once. I was the only person in Kumase who could conceivably know anything about the plan. Even if I had unwittingly given myself away by speaking in my sleep, there was never anyone else in my bed to hear me. Could somebody have been hiding on the roof, listening in to my whispered conversations with Bud? Impossible. There was no place to hide on that roof.

I toyed with the idea of walking over to investigate. If there were anybody there, a night watchman, say, and he saw or heard me, he would certainly regard my presence as irregular and might take some action which might prevent me fulfilling my duties. I was the key man in the whole operation. First my wristcom was to act as a beacon during the descent to the field. Second I was to guide the party to the Fort. We couldn't afford either to have the steel birds blundering around looking for somewhere to land or, that done, to have the vehicles getting lost in the maze of Kumase streets.

"Crash," I told myself, "get a grip. There's no one there."

There wasn't another cough, nor another lighted cigarette glowing in the dark. They were figments of my imagination. That's what I told myself.

A thought floated up unbidden from my sub-conscious mind: what if the hostages weren't in the Fort? I reckoned I had convincing circumstantial evidence that they were there. It was certainly the most logical place in Kumase to keep them. But the fact remained that I hadn't seen them in person. Perhaps I should have made an attempt to scale the wall at night? But what if I had been caught in the act? That would have been the end of the whole mission. My decision turned on a balance of risk. I was the man on the spot, the only man on the spot. I had to make my own best judgment and act on it. That's what I had done.

These were useless, unproductive thoughts and I forced them straight back where they had come from. This was no time for doubts.

I used my body to shield the light of the wristcom from the ghostly watcher on the spectators' ramp. At precisely thirty minutes before kick-off I sent a signal and received a brief acknowledgment. Everything was going to plan.

I ran a fast-forward into the immediate future and watched the upcoming movie. I saw in my mind's eye the fearsome beauty of the Thunderbirds, descendants of the Ospreys which had fired my imagination as a boy. I admired the sleek precision of their design and their faultless operational efficiency. I saw the consummate skill of my Marine colleagues, each man knowing his job, many times rehearsed, going to it, working as a well-oiled cog in a magnificent human machine. This was going to be like a game of soccer, with the world's best eleven playing against a team of novices. It would be a push-over, the game won before half-time.

I thought briefly about Pa and Ma Owusu-Ansah and

wished they were there with me to enjoy the show. Sadly I recognized that the personal part of my mission had been a failure. In an hour or two I would be airborne, on my way to the rig and then, after debriefing, on to a hero's welcome, firstly in Saint Thomas and then back home. I might even have an audience with the President. But Pa and Ma Owusu-Ansah would be lost to me forever.

Fifteen minutes to kickoff I sent another message. Then I headed for the field, climbing through one of the gaps in the spectator fence. Now the adrenaline began to pump. I calmed myself by concentrating on the task ahead. As I reached the center spot, the stadium was illuminated in a sudden flash of lightning. It was so unexpected that I didn't have time to look towards the ghostly spectator I had invented. Who would be there anyway, at 2 a.m., I thought as I waited for the clap of thunder.

Scanning the sky, the mythical story of the beautiful Ankyewa Nyame, founder the Asante nation, descending from heaven on a golden chain flashed into my mind. I laughed. The Thunderbirds would soon do just that; but the Thunderbirds were no myth.

At minus five minutes I sent my last signal and received a strong reply. At minus a hundred seconds I switched the wristcom to full power and began a count-down. At eighty I thought I heard the roar of the approaching force. Dead on time; trust the U.S. Marines, I thought; and said a silent prayer that the rest of the exercise would run as smoothly. In my mind I pictured the turboprop nacelles rotating from horizontal to vertical, always a fascinating, almost miraculous, performance. At a height of a hundred foot the Thunderbird down-lights came on, flooding the field. I braced myself against the blast of air from the engines, screwed up my eyes and put my hands to my ears.

"Let the game begin," I said aloud.

I turned the wristcom on to delayed action photography, set at five second intervals. Then I pointed it at number three. Just seconds later, I knew, Bud would be watching the action in Washington.

Numbers one and two came to rest, precisely as planned, at the corners of one penalty box; and number three right on the opposite penalty spot. The prop-rotor blades slowed. The engines switched to idle. I was overcome by an enormous sense of pride and elation. At that moment it felt great to be an American.

Almost simultaneously the three ramps folded down all facing me at the center spot. The three armored vehicles already had their lights on for the descent. The crews would have seen me in their powerful headlights. I started to move towards number three. The plan was that I would guide the driver of the first armored car out of the stadium and towards the fort, just ten minutes away. The other two vehicles would follow. By the time the Asante had rubbed the sleep out of their eyes, we would have broken down the gates of the Fort. Half an hour later we would have rescued the hostages and returned to the stadium, ready for take off.

Then through the rumble of the idling turboprop engines and the revving of the vehicles on the ramps, I heard another sound, this one totally unexpected. As I turned, one of number one's prop-rotors had already been destroyed, I guess by a grenade. A moment later, numbers two and three suffered a similar fate. There was no cover on the open field so I dived and lay flat. I must have been just ten yards from the center spot. Instinctively I switched the wristcom to video mode and aimed it at the action, aware that I was creating a unique historical record. But of what? I had no idea. At that moment I was utterly confused.

I saw the crews begin to gather in a defensive formation, taking cover behind the Thunderbirds. That was part of their standard drill, poor guys. They must have been driven by instinct.

Then all hell rose up upon them, erupting from the bowels of the earth. The first explosion threw number three twenty foot up into the air, all fifteen tons of it. It must have torn the fuel tanks because there was a mighty secondary explosion while the Thunderbird was still airborne. It hit the remains of the armored car as it fell and the two became a single blazing skeleton. All around me balls of molten metal were descending from the sky. I pulled my knees under me and dropped my head to the grass, covering my ears with my hands, minimizing my exposure to the firestorm and to the terrible noise. That was just the first holocaust. The destruction of Thunderbirds one and two followed, seconds later. I didn't watch, just kept my eyes tight shut, waiting for my end. Terrified.

I'm sure the crews never knew what hit them. That is one consolation. There couldn't possibly have been any survivors. Every single Marine on that football field was cremated alive that fateful day. Except me. I was just plain lucky. Only God knows why He spared me.

After a while the explosions subsided. For a minute there was only the quieter sound of the flames. And my convulsive sobbing. Then there was another sound. It must have been a generator starting up, for moments later the stadium lights came on. I felt some mad instinctive drive to escape. I tried to stand up but my knees buckled. I tried again and this time I succeeded. I could stand but I had no confidence that I could walk, let alone run.

Then the stadium loudspeakers crackled and a voice boomed out. I recognized the triumphant war cry, *"Asante Kotoko, kum apem, apem beba,"* Asante porcupine, kill a thousand, another thousand will rise up.

Drums followed, mimicking the tones of the voice. Even in my befuddled state, I thought: talking drums. I had heard of them but this was the first time I had heard them. The drums came again; and then the voice, again and again.

I took one step, and then another, stumbling, weak, but determined somehow to make my escape. I had no plan, just a driving determination to get away. Without thinking, I headed for the players' tunnel, the nearest exit. I picked my way through the scattered fires, one step at a time, conserving my damaged physical resources. Up to this time I hadn't seen a single foe. I didn't have long to wait. A troop of Asante warriors emerged from the tunnel, barefooted, clad only in loin cloths, their bodies and faces decorated in white and red patterns, dancing, chanting. Bizarrely, each carried an ancient AK47. One of these was soon sticking into my back. They felt me for weapons. I had none. I was still clutching the wristcom. They took that off me. Standing behind them was a man dressed in an African smock, what they call a *batakari*, plastered with small leather purses. He seemed somehow familiar but his face was also decorated with paint and I couldn't make him out. The wristcom was handed to him. As soon as he had it, he left the scene.

I was stripped to my underpants. My hands were tied behind my back and my ankles were strapped together.

Someone said, "*Oburoni*, now you see Asante power."

They hoisted me above their heads, horizontal, face up; and carried me around the stadium on a lap of honor. Their honor, perhaps. My everlasting shame.

The Asante had prevailed in the best American tradition of hygienic warfare. No casualties on their side, one hundred percent, less one, on ours.

Back at base they would have seen only the first few seconds before the destruction of the on-board video cameras. But they might also have received a confused series of images from the wristcom. My last thought before I lost consciousness was what would they do next?

CHAPTER 7

WHEN I CAME to, I was lying in a bed, under a clean white sheet. There was a tube taped to my left arm, connected to a drip-feed bag hanging on a stand. There were thick curtains and the room was dark except for a lamp aimed at my head and shoulders. A woman in a white coat sat on a chair holding my wrist, a doctor, it would seem, taking my pulse. My body ached, every inch of it, every joint and every muscle.

The woman spoke in Asante.

"He's conscious," I guess she said.

I closed my eyes and tried to think but I must have been sedated. All I wanted to do was hide myself in sleep.

When I woke again, there was a man sitting there. I couldn't make out his face in the dark and I didn't recognize his voice.

"Captain Crash Ferguson," he said in English, "you are under arrest."

He gave me the customary warning. Anything I said might be used in evidence against me. I closed my eyes and tried to focus my mind. I was so drowsy.

"Right now," the man said, "there is one thing we want to know from you. How you answer my questions will have a substantial bearing on how we treat you. It will be in your best interest to be totally honest with me. Do you understand? If I think you are lying, things may go hard with you."

I nodded. I desperately wanted to go back to sleep.

"I am not going to waste time asking you to identify yourself. I know who you are and who sent you here. At the Kumase Sports

Stadium the other night our forces inflicted a humiliating defeat on the expeditionary force your people sent to invade our country. We know very well that the United States does not lightly accept humiliation. History tells us that you set out to kill at least three, sometimes as many as ten natives for every American killed. What I want to know from you is this: what plans do your people have for a follow-up? What retribution can we expect them to visit on us for the humiliation you and they have suffered?"

I couldn't help him. I didn't know the answer to his question. If there was a plan B, no one had told me.

Over the next twenty four hours they put me through the works. Nothing illegal, mind you, but exhausting.

"We are a humane people, by and large," one of the interrogators told me. "We don't use torture. In fact the only law-breakers we imprison are those who might be a danger to themselves or to society at large. We have had to make special arrangements for you, for your protection. We wouldn't want to give any of our wilder young men the opportunity to lynch you."

Then he entertained me by playing a recording of Billy Holiday singing *Strange Fruit*. He played it over and over.

Their good cop bad cop tactics didn't work. The truth was I had nothing useful to tell them. In the end they seemed convinced of that.

They put me in a small cell. The guards brought me food twice a day but said nothing. Their hostility was palpable. My clothes had been taken from me, leaving me only my shorts. I supposed that they reasoned that there wasn't enough in them for me to fashion an instrument of suicide. There was nothing in the cell except a straw mat, a plastic water bottle and a plastic bucket. In the morning they took me to shower under close supervision. At least I had the cell to myself. Indeed, it seemed that apart from my guards, I had the whole prison to myself. I neither saw nor heard another prisoner while I was there.

I broke up the day by doing stretches. The rest of the time I spent contemplating my future. It seemed bleak.

At worst they would execute me, with or without prior torture and with or without a show trial.

I prepared myself for an interrogation. I might refuse to talk, citing the old Geneva Convention or what have you. I could imagine the response. I asked myself what purpose my silence would serve. Nothing I might say could place the members of the attack force in jeopardy: they were surely all dead. If I were to tell the whole unvarnished truth, who would suffer? The objective of the attack had been to free the prisoners in the Fort. Could the Asante hold them—the prisoners—responsible for the attack? What about my government and my colleagues in the Corps? Would they ever know if I spilled the beans on them?

Then again, hadn't the Asante called the attack down upon themselves, imprisoning U.S. citizens? If I were to accuse them of that, would they take offense?

I reviewed my options.

One. Escape. Impossible. I had nothing left but promises to use as a bribe. And these guards were clearly under instructions not to allow me to try to establish any sort of relationship with them. Even if I were to get away from Kumase, what chance would I have of reaching the coast? And then? Even if, by a miracle, I were to succeed in recovering the spare wristcom which I had buried with my other kit, would the U.S. government be happy to issue instructions to rescue me? I wrote off option one.

Two. Hold my tongue. Refuse to talk. They would surely execute me.

Three. Try to strike a deal with them. Offer to tell them all in exchange for my life. That might just work. Indeed that was probably what they had in mind, the interrogation, the extraction of useful intelligence from me. That was surely why they hadn't already executed me. But what guarantee was there that after hearing all I had to tell, even believing it, they would not then decide that I was expendable, an embarrassment, that it would be to their advantage simply to wipe my name from history?

If I were lucky though, they might let me join the other

Americans in the Fort. Would the U.S. make a second attempt at rescue? They would still have the benefit of all the intelligence which I had transmitted through the wristcom; but on the other hand that was already stale and devalued. Since the Asante had clearly somehow got wind of the details of our plan, insofar as it concerned the Sports Stadium, they must have known what our objective was. And in that case they would have removed Franklin and his team from the Fort.

Washington would certainly know that the mission had failed, but would they know how? They would have been watching the live transmissions from the Thunderbirds and armored cars until the explosions destroyed the transmitters. After that they would have had only a confused series of images from my wristcom. Would they regard my rescue or that of the other Americans as worth the exercise of the overwhelming force which might be necessary to achieve it? Did they know I was alive? Where I was being held?

My cell had a small window, without glass and heavily barred. Through it I could catch a glimpse of the sky. Since the attack it had been overcast, so their satellite imagery would have told them little. They might have learned something though, from radar or infrared. I speculated. My days were filled with speculation.

I must have been suffering from delayed shock. Once a day a doctor came to examine me. His manner was appalling. A doctor's job is to keep human beings alive: this one would clearly have been happy to see me dead. He said he found nothing physically wrong with me. And if he had found that I was suffering from post-traumatic whatever, that would only have given him pleasure. So he had me sent back to my cell.

The shock must have affected my thinking because it was some time before I began to wonder how they had got wind of the attack. Clearly they must have known about it well in advance. Take a minor point first: the stadium floodlights. I doubt that they had worked for years. Clearly there had been a time in the past when they had played soccer at night;

otherwise the towers wouldn't have been there. But that would have been long ago. They would have needed time to organize a generator, get fuel, find and install the lamps. God almighty, where did they dig those up? Perhaps they had some old stock in a store? I have to give it to those Asante engineers, when it comes to improvising; they have us beat, hands down.

It was clear that they knew exactly where the Thunderbirds would touch down. They must have dug pits at those precise locations and filled them with explosives. They couldn't have guessed the positions, they must have known.

They might have had a mole at the American end of the operation, somehow feeding information to them but that seemed, and seems, far-fetched.

There was only one other explanation. It took me a long time to accept this, but eventually I had to face up to the facts: someone must have been listening in on my conversations with Bud. Kofi had left for Mpoanokrom: it couldn't have been him. The old Lebanese landlord? No way. That left only Boafo. He said he was a writer. He never did invite me into his room, but once I glimpsed the contents before he shut the door. There seemed to be more gadgetry there, electronic gadgetry, than one would have expected from a mere writer. The lock on my door was new. I was given only one key. Boafo might have had the duplicate. He might have gained access that day when I slipped out to reccy the Fort. He had warned me to leave valuables behind and I had left the wristcom with my dollars and gold under the mattress. What if Boafo were some sort of electronics whiz-kid and if he had borrowed the wristcom and discovered enough about the way it works, radio frequency, encryption and suchlike, to intercept my transmissions right up there on the roof? That stretches the imagination, I thought. But what if he had set up some powerful miniature microphones in, say, the grapevine? He could have recorded every word I spoke to Bud. That would have given him at least half of the picture. The operational plan was basically mine. All Bud had done was to refine the draft I had recited to him. And if Boafo was indeed responsible,

Kofi must have been involved too. Had Kofi sent Kwabena to climb that coconut tree to spy on me? Had Kwabena seen and overheard me speaking into the wristcom and reported back to him? Was Kofi an Asante spy? That might account for the delay in getting me to Kumase. He might have been giving them, Boafo and his bosses, time to prepare for my arrival. Come to think of it, my room still smelled of paint when I moved in. The walls could have been bugged and then re-plastered before painting.

It seemed a plausible theory. I felt miserable when I thought about it, almost suicidal. I did consider suicide, but I didn't have the means, no poison, no blade, no hangman's rope; so my resolve wasn't tested.

Whatever the explanation, there was clearly a total failure of intelligence on our part. I take most of the responsibility for that. I guess that I underestimated their intelligence, intelligence in the sense of brain power, I mean. Some of the blame though must lie with Bud and his planning team. They had been working on the scheme of my mission for months before I was selected to carry it out. They had clearly overestimated the advantage that our technology would give me. The wristcom is without question a magnificent piece of miniaturization. That said, it didn't turn me into Superman.

My natural parents might have come from this country and that was clearly a major factor in selecting me. But I didn't by some miracle imbibe the culture and language with my lost mother's milk.

It is true again that my foster parents hailed from this place. But in spite of their efforts, I grew up as an American, an African American yes, but before that, an American.

I had to face up to it, I was ill-fitted for this mission. These folk were on their own ground and they were just too clever for me. I didn't understand them. I was that proverbial ugly American. I am no fool; but I am not all that smart either: it took me time to learn. And as I learned, I became more and more aware of the complexity of this society and how little I understood it.

So the debacle was my fault, but not all my fault. If you put me in the dock you must put Bud there, too, Bud and his team and those who authorized what I now see as a crack-brained scheme from day one.

After I had been in this cell for a week, they returned the clothes I had been wearing when they caught me, neatly laundered and ironed, complete with one or two burn marks. As usual, they told me nothing, just barked orders. Those guards really hated my guts. I thought, this is the end. They want me to look decent at the firing range.

"Where are you taking me?" I asked.

"Shut your mouth," one of them told me.

They took me to a house in the old European quarter of Kumase, a solid old bungalow built in colonial times, in the early nineteen hundreds perhaps. The prison guards handed me over to a new set who were just as cool and distant, but just a little less unpleasant about it. They stayed outside, keeping a watch on all the exits. They let me walk in the garden as long as I didn't venture too near the fence. At six, as it got dark, they switched on a generator to run the security lights. As a bonus I had the luxury of electricity in the house all night. The generator disturbed me at first but I soon got used to it. At least it drowned out the cicadas.

There was an elderly man in the house who introduced himself.

"My name is Kwadwo, Sir," he told me. "I am your cook-steward. May I show you round the house?"

He was dressed in starched khaki shorts, down to his knees, and a clean white shirt, somewhat worn at the collar.

"The clothes are for your use, Sir," he said as he opened a wardrobe. "You may select whatever you need. Those are my instructions."

I resisted the temptation to ask him who it was who gave him his instructions.

Kwadwo spoke two varieties of English. For me it was stiff and formal and with only an occasional grammatical lapse. When he spoke to the guards, it was in pidgin and in a manner in which he managed to convey his view of their inferior status. Quite without justification, I pigeonholed him as a house nigger.

The bathroom fittings matched the age of the house, but since there was no running water, it didn't really matter. I had long since learned to bath with a bucket and a jug. The water Kwadwo supplied was hot; and there was soap, a loofah and a shaving kit. I had a shave and scrubbed myself from head to toe. That night I slept in a four-poster bed between clean white sheets, protected by an old-fashioned mosquito net and with a ceiling fan, a working ceiling fan, to keep me cool.

No one woke me and I slept late.

"What time is it?" I asked Kwadwo, but he didn't have a watch.

He served me an excellent English breakfast, fresh orange juice, papaya (or pawpaw as they call it), pineapple slices, porridge, fried eggs, bacon, and coffee. The coffee wasn't quite up to standard but I could forgive the chef for that. And there was no toast. The food he dished up in the following days was just as good, tasty, interesting and varied.

"As for we Ghanaians," Kwadwo told me, "we have excellent cuisine."

He loved that word and took every opportunity to introduce it into the cooking lessons he gave me. There were no books in the house, so learning to cook was one way to pass the time. I soon established a friendly relationship with Kwadwo, who had an insatiable appetite for stories of life in the United States. Once we had become friends I tried to extract from him some information about my situation. Why was I being kept in such relative comfort? Who was giving the orders? What did they plan to do with me? Kwadwo pleaded ignorance. He was only a humble cook-steward and nobody told him anything. He had tried to eavesdrop on the guards' conversation, he said, but they seemed equally ignorant.

As we became friends his English slipped from its initial formality into a more relaxed mode.

"Master Crash," he called me now. I tried but failed to get him to drop the offensive title, telling him, "Kwadwo, my brother, I am not your master. Please stop calling me that," but to no avail.

"Master Crash," he asked me as I was peeling a yam for my evening meal, "Master Crash, you no get family in your country?"

Millicent's picture came to me. She was a stranger, in another country, another world. I felt ashamed.

"I get one wife," I told him, falling into his vernacular, "One beautiful wife and two children, a boy called Fergus and a baby girl called Marilyn."

Kwadwo's wife stayed with him in the servants' quarters at the back of the house. Their children were all grown but they had a grandson with them.

"You no miss um?" he asked.

"Sure I miss them," I replied, "What do you think?"

He continued to quiz me about them and I answered as best I could, elaborating to meet what I judged to be his expectations.

The next morning there was a single sheet of paper, an envelope and a pen on the breakfast table. I began to turn over in my mind how I might make use of them.

"Write," Kwadwo commanded when I had finished eating.

It was unusual for him to order me around like that.

"Write what?" I asked.

I had forgotten our conversation of the previous evening.

"Write your missus and your piccin," he commanded.

"What shall I write?"

He shook his head in disbelief.

"Kwadwo mus tell Master Crash wettin he go write his wife? Tellum you alive and well. Tellum you living in fine bungalow. Tellum Kwadwo teaching you African cooking. Tellum maybe you see um soon."

I did more or less as he instructed. I folded the letter and put it in the envelope. When I was about to lick the flap, he stopped me.

"Just write address for front," he commanded and when I had done that he took the unsealed envelope and the pen from me.

"Are you telling me that you are going to put a stamp on that and put it in a post box and that it will turn up in Washington,

D.C.?"

He just smiled a secret smile and went off to deliver my letter to one of the guards.

One day when I had been there about three weeks by my reckoning, putting on weight from the good food and lack of exercise, I was sitting in the shade on the veranda, wearing only a pair of shorts and sucking a ripe mango when Kwadwo returned from his regular trip to the market.

"Bad news, Master Crash," he told me when he had offloaded his purchases onto the kitchen table. "Bad news."

I could see that he was shaken. There had been a demonstration, he told me, demanding my blood. The demonstrators, "young men" as he described them, had evidently learned where I was being held and had set out for the old European quarter with the intention of lynching me. The militia had diverted them and they had then gone off to the Asantehene's palace to register their discontent.

"They say you are a spy, Master Crash, and a mercenary. They say that you tried to bring Americans to capture Kumase, or to burn it down, like Sargrenti."

He didn't tell me who Sargrenti was and I was too shaken to ask. I had been tranquilized by the pleasant lazy life I was leading. Suddenly I was once again aware of the danger I was in.

As I considered what answer I should give, a squad of men armed with ancient automatic rifles marched up and stationed themselves at the two ends of the street. It was clear that their orders were not to prevent my escape—that was the job of the guards in the garden—but to protect me from enemies unknown.

I slept an uneasy sleep that night. The next morning, when I had bathed and eaten, Kwadwo told me to select some of the clothes in the wardrobe which he then proceeded to pack in small valise.

"You're leaving," he told me. "Too dangerous here."

"Leaving for where?" I asked.

He just shook his head. Clearly he had no idea.

CHAPTER 8

BLACK MERCEDES Benz drove up. The guards unlocked the gate and it entered the driveway. I was astonished. Many bicycles passed by the bungalow every day but I hadn't seen a single car in the month that I had been there. I had time to notice that the bodywork was in excellent condition for a car which must have been fifty years old. Its tires were a little worn, but who was I to complain about that; or about the fact that it had no number plate? I shook hands with Kwadwo and apologized for my inability to tip him for his excellent service to me. The guards in the garden waved, friendly for the first time since my arrival. They must have been pleased and relieved to see the back of me. Soon I was ensconced in the ancient leather seat, sandwiched between two men. I greeted them but the tone of their reply hardly encouraged conversation.

I forced myself to concentrate on reviewing my situation. It seemed unlikely that they were taking me to a place of execution for, if they were, why was I being conveyed in a car which looked as if it might be reserved for the use of the Asantehene himself; and why would Kwadwo have been instructed to provide me with some changes of clothes? Had the U.S. government managed somehow to ransom me? Was I on the first stage of a journey home? Or was I just being moved to more secure quarters while the authorities, whoever they were, decided what to do with me?

We drove. An old signboard said Manhyia: *Oman-hyia*, the nation meets. We were approaching the palace of the Asantehene.

Bewildered, I closed my eyes and tried to concentrate on… nothing, to clear my mind, ready for a quick response to whatever was to happen. Ma Ferguson used to sing an old song, a hit she told me, in her parents' time, back in the last century. *Che sera, sera,* she sang, what will be, will be.

The car pulled into the drive of a large, modern house and stopped under a covered entry. I noticed armed guards in the garden. A young man dressed in *ntama,* the Asante toga, opened the door for me. For a moment I imagined I was being treated as an honored guest.

Another young man, similarly attired, addressed me with a weak smile, "Mr. Crash?"

I nodded, said, "That's me, brother," and held out my hand.

He ignored the gesture and told me to follow him.

Briefly, not for the first time, I considered making a break for it. It would have been an act of suicide and it didn't take me long to reject the idea.

He led me to a large waiting room, furnished with armchairs around the walls and several rows of upright chairs in the middle.

"Please wait. Nana will see you shortly," my escort told me.

Nana? Nana who? Was it Nana Asantehene himself who was to see me?

I counted the seats. There must have been a hundred. Room for a hundred people to wait? But to see whom? Today there were less than ten waiting, scattered around the room. There were several doors, all shut. Were they all waiting to see the same Nana as I was, my Nana? Or were there many Nananom, one to each door and the room to which it gave entrance?

A man brought me a bottle of water and a glass on a tray. He filled the glass and I thanked him. I wondered whether it would be safe to drink. Thirsty as I was, I decided against. They might have drugged it, I reasoned, to lower my resistance. There were three fans hanging from the ceiling, spinning so slowly that you could follow the blades around. The place was hot. I was sweating. I took a sip from the glass. It tasted OK, so I drank it all and refilled the glass from the plastic bottle. I examined it: a relic from the days when they had sold drinking water in sealed bottles.

The armchair was comfortable. I dozed; and dreamed. Yaa at Bosomtwe. Another world. I woke with a hard on and looked around guiltily in case someone had noticed.

There were pictures on the walls. I got up to take a look. Oil paintings, many of them. Some seemed to be portraits from life. Royalty, I guessed, judging from their finery: heavy *kente* robes and plenty of gold, on their fingers, their heads, their arms, their ankles.

"Mr. Crash," a voice behind me said.

It was the same young man.

"Our ancient kings," he explained, pointing to the portraits. "Some from life but most are the creations of the artist's imagination. Of course, no one knows exactly what Nana Osei Tutu the First really looked like."

"Of course," I replied.

"Nana will see you now. Please follow me," he said.

My Nana sat behind a large, ancient wooden desk, which stood on a low carpeted dais at the far end of a long room. He was writing and paid no attention to us. I could see that he sported a full beard and perhaps a mustache, too, but not much else. His face remained in deep shadow throughout our interview.

My young man coughed.

"Mr. Crash, Nana," he said.

Nana didn't look up but made a gesture with his free hand which my young man understood to mean that he should offer me a seat. There was a row of upright chairs facing Nana's desk. I took one near the center, directly opposite the writer. It was upholstered in leather, dark old red leather held in place by brass headed nails.

The windows were hung with heavy curtains. Nana had a reading lamp, but the rest of the room was dimly lit. I could hardly make out his features. The room was cool and I guessed that it was air-conditioned. Since Nana was too busy to deal with me, I felt free to look around, peering into the gloom. The walls were paneled in dark wood. Mahogany was the word which came to my mind. I looked up at the ceiling. There was a row of spots, in whose light I sat. Nana was going to get a better view of me than I would have of him.

"Mr. Crash," Nana interrupted my reconnaissance.

Then he noticed that my young man had not left.

"Akwasi," Nana said. "Did I ask you to stay?"

"Nana?" replied Akwasi.

"I said you may leave," said Nana and then said a few sentences in Asante which he spoke so rapidly that I understood not a word.

I heard the door close behind me.

"Mr. Crash," asked Nana, "is that your real name?"

"No, Sir," I replied. "My name is Ekem Ferguson. But Crash is what I have been called since I was a child."

"So: Ekem Ferguson. With such a name you must have connections with this part of the world. George Ekem Ferguson was a dedicated servant of the British Empire in the Gold Coast colony. Were you named after him? Are you a Fanti?"

"Sir," I told him, "I was born in the United States of America. I am a citizen of that country."

Then I outlined what I knew of my family history. The questions he asked were so accurately on target that I began to suspect that he knew more about me than he was letting on.

"So you came to this country to search for your natural parents who had abandoned you in infancy, leaving you in the care of the Fergusons?" he asked.

"Yessir," I replied.

"Tell me then, Ekem Ferguson, how you came to be standing on the center spot in the Kumase Sports Stadium in the early hours of the morning of…no doubt you recall the date?"

Up to that point his manner had been, if not friendly, at least neutral. I should have been on my guard and I wasn't. All I can plead is wishful thinking. I was lulled by a dream that the U.S. government had done some sort of deal which would lead to my being shipped back home.

Now this question, descending on me like a tropical cloudburst. There was no way it could be avoided. Though I had reviewed my options during the past month and resolved to tell the truth, I hesitated.

"Crash," he asked, "Do you know who I am?"

Stupidly, I guessed.

"Nana Asantehene, sir?" I asked.

He laughed.

"Not quite," he replied. "They call me Anokye. That is not my real name, as Crash is not yours, but it will do for the time being. I am the Asantehene's *Gyasehene* and his *Okyeame*, his chief advisor, his spokesman, and the head of our national political movement. At this point in our history, I am (and I say this without false modesty) I am the most powerful man in this kingdom, excepting only Nana himself, who invariably chooses to delegate his powers to me. There are many calls on my time. Do you have any idea why I have sent for you?"

"No sir," I replied.

"Do you think I am toying with you, as a cat does with a terrified mouse, before delivering its coup de grace? Satisfying some sadistic quirk in my character, perhaps?"

"I don't know, sir. I mean, no, sir," I mumbled.

His tone softened.

"Crash, let me tell you a story," he said. "Some seventy odd years ago, Asante was still part of the post-colonial independent state which its founder, Kwame Nkrumah, had named Ghana. The political structures which the new rulers had inherited from their colonial predecessors were deeply flawed and totally unsuitable for our people. A succession of leaders, many of them drawn from the military, proved incapable of breaking the chains. At the time of my story, the ruler was a young air force man. Those were the days before the world's supply of oil ran out and this young man spent much of his leisure flying the planes of the country's tiny air force, at the expense of the poor, of course. His initials were J. J. and it was by these that he was known. Our forefathers spread the word that J. J. stood for Junior Jesus. Now Junior Jesus had a bosom friend who went by the name of Nii. They were like brothers, twins even. They had been at school together, poor academic performers both of them, always involved in wild escapades of one sort or another and barely scraping through their examinations. Nii had something in common with you: his parents were from the United States, blacks, African Americans as they were called in those days. They had met Kwame Nkrumah when he was a student in your country and had come here to help him build the new Africa. They were both dedicated professionals and I have no doubt that they made a substantial contribution to the welfare of our people. They no longer regarded themselves as Americans: they had come to stay, to spend the rest of their lives here. But Nii was their cross. He was incorrigible and nothing they could say or do had the slightest impact on him.

"After school, Junior Jesus and Nii joined the air force. Junior Jesus was always the leader and even in those days would give vent to his half-baked political ambitions. These led him, in the course of some years, to the seat of power. Once there, he found a job for his friend in the security apparatus, where Nii soon acquired a reputation for unthinking brutality."

Anokye rang a bell and ordered iced water for both of us.

"One day, some civilian who didn't know Nii, or his reputation, crossed his path. Nii was in uniform but unarmed. He went to his parked car, fetched a gun, returned and shot the man, killing him on the spot.

"Although Junior Jesus had some popular support he ruled largely by intimidation and fear. He might have saved his friend but it was risky. He had him arrested and tried for murder. Nii was convicted and sentenced to death.

"At this stage, friends of Nii's parents, my grandparents amongst them, hurriedly collected signatures for a petition to Junior Jesus, begging for mercy for Nii on the grounds of his parents' contribution to the country and the devastating pain which his execution would inflict upon them. The petitioners hoped that their petition would offer Junior Jesus

90

a way out. He could commute the sentence and explain that his mercy in this particular case arose not from his widely known friendship with Nii, but from the issues raised by the petitioners. Confident that their action would result at least in a postponement, some of the petitioners, my grandmother included, joined the parents on a visit to Nii in the condemned cell.

"Nii was executed by firing squad that same night. His parents were not informed either before or after the execution. The first they heard of their son's death was the announcement on the one o'clock news on the state radio the next day. Their son's body was never given to them; and they never discovered where he had been buried."

He paused. I sat with my head bowed, trying to gauge why he had chosen to tell me this story.

"What do you think, Crash?" he continued, "Did Junior Jesus do the right thing? Is it a sign of weakness or strength when those in power choose to temper justice with mercy? In Junior Jesus's position, what would you have done?"

I thought I understood. He was challenging me to sit in judgment in my own case.

"In my country," I told him, "No one is punished without due process of law."

"Ah, yes," he replied. "In your country. I have never been there but that doesn't mean that I know nothing of the United States of America. You see, my parents studied there; and but for economic circumstances beyond their control, they might still be there. My father believed that your country was the greatest in the world. Of course he was right in terms of power; but he believed that it was the greatest in every other respect too. He would not hear a bad word spoken about your country. My mother was not so sure. I remember her telling me a story about the man who was President when they were there, the great grandfather of the present incumbent. That President had previously been Governor of the State of Texas. During his term of office he had broken all records for executions. If I remember correctly, there were over a hundred and fifty. In those days, she told me, there were more than three thousand Americans sentenced to death and awaiting execution, on 'death row' I believe you would say. Fifty years later, there are three times as many; and half of those are young men whose ancestors came from this continent.

"So, yes, due process of law; but what kind of law?"

"You have to understand," I explained to him. "Society must be protected. Those people are criminals, enemies of the state, murderers…"

"Crash," he interrupted me. "During the ten years since our present Asantehene, Nana Osei Tutu III, was enstooled, there has not been a single judicial execution. In this country we value human life. Yes, we have murders. We regard a murder as an accusation. As a society, we failed the victim; and we failed the murderer, too. We have only one prison in this country, you know. There we keep only those deemed criminally insane, people who are sick, mentally ill, unable to control themselves and thus a danger, to society, yes, but also to themselves.

"Of course, if you go back into our history, two hundred years back, you will find that we once believed that when our big men died, they needed to be escorted to the village where our ancestors reside. Then we killed many, both convicted criminals and unfortunate innocents. But we have redeemed ourselves as a society in recent years and now we can look our past unashamedly in the face. Today you know, every Asante child is an historian. You have to understand your past, warts and all as you say, to deal with the problems of today and those which will surely arise tomorrow."

During this digression I prepared my reply.

"Only one prison?" I asked. "What about the Kumase Fort, then?"

"Ah," he laughed. "The accused turns accuser. What about Reverend Ramseyer's Fort, then?"

The man was clever. During my Marine training I participated in simulations of capture and interrogation. The mock interrogators invariably came across as both malign and stupid. I don't know whether it was the actors, or the parts they were assigned; probably a bit of both. It was so easy to outwit them. Intellectually, I mean. One came out of those sessions feeling proud to be an American and supremely confident in one's competence as a Marine to face all odds. But this guy was different. Most of the time he was relaxed and pleasant, even friendly. As if he were on my side. It was hardly like a real interrogation. And yet I have to admit it, he caught me on the wrong foot time and time again. I can only plead that my training was inadequate.

But this time it was he who was wrong. He thought he needed to explain who he was talking about.

"Reverend Ramseyer," he explained, "Was a missionary my forebears kept under siege in that Fort, together with a number of British soldiers and their African mercenaries. That was in the nineteenth century. We made a mistake. We should have killed them all and cooked them.

"Ramseyer's revenge was sweet. We eventually succumbed to the superior fire power of the Brits and the Reverend was given a free hand to convert us all to Christianity. A hundred and fifty years passed before we could begin to liberate ourselves from his mental clutches.

"But I digress. I have a weakness, you will have noticed, for our history.

"Kumase Fort then. A prison. Was that, then, the real objective of your mission, to free the prisoners whom you believed we held in the Fort against their will?"

I had fallen into his trap. What could I answer? Invent some transparently cock and bull story? I had already decided that there was no option but to tell the truth. So far, he had been careful not to put the question directly. Now I could see that he had been doing no more than softening me up.

I said nothing. I wasn't being stubborn. I knew that I would have to give a full account of myself. But I was at a loss where to start.

"Crash," he said, perhaps understanding my silence as a refusal to answer, "It seems to me that you are living in a dream world. Let me bring you down to earth. A few weeks ago your government attempted to invade our country. Fortunately for us, we had advance notice of the invasion and were able to wipe out the invading force. By your presence at the site of the invasion you demonstrated your key role in this project. We have attempted to conceal the invasion from our people. We know that a follow-up is probable—Uncle Sam does not allow himself to be humiliated by upstart nations like ours—but we have no wish to spread alarm and panic. However, in spite of our best efforts, rumors about the incident and about your presence have circulated. Yesterday there was an unruly demonstration in the course of which calls were made for your blood. You may not know it, but you were in danger of capture by what I have to call, with regret, a mob. Amongst my own colleagues there is a demand that you be put on trial without delay. I can assure you that due process, as you call it, will be observed but I cannot see any outcome but a verdict of guilty. I would expect strong demands for your execution, demands which it would be extremely difficult for Nana to resist, whatever my advice to the contrary.

"If you are to have any chance of having your life spared, it is essential that I have your full cooperation. I am going to send you away now. Think about what I have just told you. And don't do anything foolish. I will see you again in the morning. I shall expect you then to tell me your whole story, concealing nothing, from beginning to end. Remember that we know a great deal already. If I have the slightest suspicion that you are trying to deceive me, I shall have no option but to…"

He rang his bell and I was shown to a guest room in the same building.

I spent a restless night, troubled by dreams, violent dreams inhabited by Millicent and the kids and exploding Thunderbirds and armored cars. I woke up sweating and took a cold shower. After a good breakfast I was taken back into Nana Anokye's office. He was behind his desk, lurking in the shadows again. It struck me that I had yet to get a good look at his face. What was he hiding? There were two young women present, fiddling with wires and equipment, both strangers to me. They turned out to be audio technicians, in charge of recording my deposition.

I told my story, or stories: my natural parents' temporary abandonment of me as an infant, which had turned out to be permanent; my adoption by the Fergusons; my education and enlistment into the Marine Corps; my marriage to Millicent and the birth of our children; and my long-standing plan to try to locate my natural parents, particularly after the death of Ma and Pa Ferguson. I also outlined my career in the U.S. Marines and my gradual rise to the rank of Captain. I said that I had seemed to get stuck at that level and that my failure to earn promotion for several years had introduced some stress into my marriage.

Nana Anokye listened attentively, interrupting occasionally to ask for clarification. After a while he called a halt, switched off the recorder and checked the playback. Then he asked me to continue..

"Some months ago," I said, "I was called in by a senior officer. He told me that he been looking for a good man to carry out a special mission. He had come across my file and it seemed to him that I had all the desirable qualifications for the job. He told me that the mission might be dangerous; how dangerous he could not say. Success would not only earn me the gratitude of the American people and many American families; it would also be a strong factor when I was next considered for promotion. He wanted to give me the opportunity to volunteer for this mission. Of course I volunteered.

"He told me that he was aware that my natural parents had been Ghanaians as had my foster parents. The mission would be located in the territory of the former Republic of Ghana, which had collapsed and disintegrated and was now designated, like many other former African states, as a failed state, that is to say there was no central government. He told me that to a greater or lesser extent anarchy ruled throughout the territory.

"He then gave me a brief review of the state of the world

and the place of the United States in it. He referred to our two wars with China and our loss, in the Second China War, of access to the oil and other resources of Central Asia and the Arabian Gulf. He mentioned the critical importance to the U.S. economy of the resources of the African continent. He explained the decision to take over the island state of São Tome, now Saint Thomas, as an American colony, by saying that the state of anarchy and corruption there constituted a threat to America's national interests. Our bases on Saint Thomas, he told me, were a key factor in maintaining U.S. control of African resources. Fortunately, he said, West Africa is a long way from China.

"He revealed to me that the Central Intelligence Agency was actively investigating and identifying all the remaining economic resources of the African continent that might be of interest to the United States. He emphasized that such resources would be exploited for the mutual benefit of the U.S. and the people of Africa.

"He said that the U.S. Office of Aid to Africa had some months previously sent a civilian mission to the former Republic of Ghana as part of the broader program of investigation. The mission had been led by a distinguished African-American professor, by name William Franklin. The members of his team were young experts in a range of fields, geologists, surveyors, economists, mining engineers and so on. The Aid Office had thought it wise, in view of widespread hostility to the U.S. in the area, that all the members should be African Americans. One of their principal tasks was to assess the remaining gold resources in the Ashanti region of the country.

"The team had made contact with such center of authority as remained and had managed to reach a town called Obuasi, the site of what was once, he told me, the richest gold mine in the world. Professor Franklin had sent back regular reports via satellite. Then, suddenly, his reports had stopped. Nothing had since been heard from other members of the team except some letters to members of their families which had been mailed in the U.S. Analysis of the content of these letters revealed them to be of a highly suspicious nature. Our Intelligence Services believed that they had been written under duress. They had received unconfirmed reports of the establishment of some sort of communist regime in Kumase and thought it likely that the team had been arrested and imprisoned. That was a situation totally unacceptable to the U.S. government. However, Washington was not in contact with any authority in the territory to which it could address a demand for the release and return of the members of the team.

"My mission would be to enter the country disguised as a native, locate the American hostages and, if the circumstances warranted it, act as a beacon for an expeditionary force which would be sent in to rescue our people."

Nana Anokye said, "OK, take a short break."

He put on earphones and again checked the playback. The equipment looked archaic to me but he seemed satisfied with the result. He told me to continue.

"They brought in a professor to give me a crash course in Asante language, history and culture," I said. "I quickly discovered that, like me, he had been born in the United States of Ghanaian parents and had never been in Africa. That didn't give me much confidence in him and I have to admit that I didn't pay as much attention as I should have. It was all very strange to me. I realized quite quickly that I wouldn't be able to pass myself off as a native-born African. We then agreed that my declared mission would be to locate my natural parents. That suited me fine since it would be the fulfillment of a dream I had long cherished.

"To cut a long story short, I was flown from St. Thomas to one of our deep sea oil platforms called Half Assini. A tanker heading back to St. Thomas sent me ashore at night in a small boat. In the morning I presented myself at the nearest fishing village. It is called Mpoanokrom. There I engaged a man called Kofi Kom to act as my guide and bring me to Kumase."

"And where is this Kofi Kom now?" asked Nana Anokye.

"He handed me over to a man called Boafo and returned to his village soon after we got here," I replied.

I told him of my activities in Kumase and my conclusion that the hostages were being held in the Fort. He cross-examined me in some detail as to how I had come by this knowledge. I was totally frank in my reply.

"Why," he wanted to know next, "did you not simply approach Nana Asantehene and request the release of your countrymen whom you believed he had arrested?"

"That would have blown my cover," I told him. "My handlers in Washington were of the view that the head of what they believed was a communist regime would almost certainly turn down such a request and arrest me. They believe that you are all deeply hostile to the United States. To approach you would have meant, in effect, to abort my mission. Moreover, it would have put you on the alert and made it just so much more difficult for a follow-up mission to achieve success. So they specifically instructed me not to reveal my primary mission to anyone here."

That seemed to satisfy him. He had one more question, about how I communicated with Washington. I told him about the wristcom, which seemed to fascinate him.

"And where is this wristcom, as you call it, now?" he asked.

I told him that it had been taken from me at the Sports Stadium and handed to a person wearing a *batakari.*

He nodded.

"Ah yes," he said, "that would be our electrical genius, Professor Saman."

Then we were finished for the day.

There were several more sessions, some of them with other interrogators present. We went over the events at the Sports Stadium in detail, but as I have already described them, I won't repeat myself here.

Then I was left alone for several days, days full of speculation about my future.

CHAPTER 9

THE NEXT FRIDAY morning I heard the sound of drumming. Guards led me into a courtyard full of rows of benches, all occupied. A full house, I thought.

The drumming had stopped. There was a murmur as some spectators caught sight of me. The view of others was impeded by the canopies under which they sat and they rose to their feet and moved to one side to get a better view. The murmur rose to an angry clamor. One man raised his fist and called out an insult I could not understand. Some sort of official banged a gavel on his table and called the assembly to order, but without noticeable effect. I was led to a chair at a table, with a guard seated on either side of me, the hostile audience behind us. I was scared. Such was the animosity of that crowd that I thought I might well be dragged away and lynched. Billie Holiday was inside my head, singing *Strange Fruit*.

I looked up. Before me there was what the Asante call *odampan*, a room with only three walls, open on the side facing the courtyard. It had a proper roof, not just a canopy; and its floor was raised a step. On it was a long table. Behind the table there were three empty chairs; and on each side of these, another six, occupied by mostly quite elderly men and women. To the left there stood a small group of drummers with their huge drums, the kind they call *fontomfrom*; to the right six men holding ornately decorated elephant tusks before them, some large, some smaller. All of them, the officials and the musicians, wore the traditional Asante toga, what they call *ntama*.

The drumming began again. I could hear that the drums were talking but I couldn't understand what they were saying. The crowd went back to their seats and became silent. Then the horn players blew. Each tusk had just one tone, but the tone of each was different. It was as if the six players and their tusks were part of a single musical instrument. Somehow the sounds that came out transcended the limitations of the individual horns. Together, they also seemed to speak a language, a harsh language and one, again, that was beyond my understanding.

In the silence which followed, Nana Anokye led a man and a woman into the *odampan* from a side entrance. I guessed that they were the Asante King, the *Asantehene* as they call him, and the Queen Mother, the *Asantehemaa*. Everyone present rose and I rose too. They took their seats and so did I.

The King was simply dressed in a plain green ntama, without any mark of his office. The Queenmother wore the traditional dress of women here, called *kaba*, a long skirt with a blouse and head wrapper of the same material. Her cloth was a print, a little more elaborate than the King's but the overall impression was of simplicity and dignity.

Once they were seated, Nana Anokye rose and moved to the front of the table. He wore wrap-around shades as though his eyes needed protection from the glare of the tropical sun. His height was like mine, about five six but he was stockier in build. He too wore ntama.

He produced a square green bottle and poured libation, asking, insofar as I could understand him, the blessing of the ancestors for the proceedings of the day.

"Nana," he said then, speaking to the Asantehene, "I request your permission to address the accused directly."

The King nodded his assent. Anokye asked the two ladies operating the recorders if they were ready. Then he turned to me.

First he asked me to identify myself, which I did.

"Captain Ferguson," he said, "the proceedings of our courts are normally conducted in our own language. However, in view of the fact that Asante is not your mother tongue, we are willing to use English for this trial. Is that your wish?"

I said that it was and thanked him for his consideration.

He continued, "Since you are a stranger amongst us, I am going to explain to you the practice of this court. We are the inheritors of a failed state, the Republic of Ghana. That state was in its turn the inheritor of a British colony called the Gold Coast. Ghana took over British law and its practice, including the wearing of white wigs by judges and lawyers and similar ridiculous foreign customs. We have scrapped them all, together with the adversarial system which you also practice in your country.

"The purpose of our court hearings is to determine the facts of the case and then to effect a reconciliation between the parties, including, if appropriate, some form of compensation. We do not impose fines which would tend to impoverish the guilty party and we do not use imprisonment as a form of punishment. Indeed we have only one prison and that is used only to house the criminally insane, who we deem to be a potential danger to others as well as to themselves. We run it more as a secure hospital than as a place of punishment.

"We no longer practice the barbaric form of punishment which is so common in your country, that is, judicial murder.

"This does not mean that if you are found guilty you will be allowed to go free. Our law has been developed with the interests of our own citizens in mind. You are not a citizen and we reserve our right to impose upon you any punishment which we regard as appropriate for your offense, if proven.

"The court will hear and see all the evidence which we have gathered. Only then will it decide on the charges. You will be given ample opportunity to dispute the evidence and cross-examine any witnesses. Do you have any questions?"

"With respect, Sir," I said, "all this is strange to me. Might I request the services of a lawyer to advise me?"

"Lawyers, in the sense that you know them," he said, "have no role in our courts. In our new dispensation we do not recognize them. It is an obsolete profession."

"Hell," I thought, "if ever there were a kangaroo court, then this is it."

"However," continued Anokye, "long before our ancestors ever saw the face of a white man, our courts used the services of an *adamfo*. Adamfo, Captain, means friend. The adamfo is the friend of the accused and at the same time the friend of the court. So, if you would like to choose a friend to speak for you, the court would have no objection."

I racked my brains: Kofi Kom and Boafo clearly belonged with my accusers. Who else was there? I knew no one. I said so.

Anokye went over to the King and consulted him, *sotto voce*. Then he spoke to one of the other judges. Finally he walked down into the courtyard and spoke to a white-haired man dressed in a gray Western style suit, sitting in the second row.

"We offer you a choice of two," he told me.

"Nana Odoom," and here he indicated the judge he had spoken to, "was a distinguished jurist in Ghana. He would recuse himself as a judge in this case and hold himself available to advise you.

"Dr. Maxwell," and here he pointed out the man wearing a suit, "Dr. Maxwell is the leader of the Constitution Party. You might say he is the Leader of the Opposition in Asante."

The cheers of a few supporters were drowned by loud catcalls. The court clerk hammered angrily with his gavel. That, it struck me, must be a survival from the colonial courts.

"Dr. Maxwell has a doctorate in law from a well known university in your country and he, too, practiced in the courts of Ghana. You may make your choice."

I thought, if they are paying, why not chance my arm?

I said, "Might I have both?"

Anokye frowned. There was laughter, at my impudence, I suppose. I had second thoughts.

Before Anokye could reply, I said, "Dr. Maxwell, please."

During the recess Maxwell came to see me. He told me about his time in the States, many years before; and how much he admired our country. That took him ten minutes. Then the guards came.

"Tell them nothing without talking to me first," he said as they led me back to the court.

"Too late," I thought to tell him, but I was distracted by the scene before me. Two loudspeakers had been brought in and there was a white screen in the deep shade behind where the Asantehene had been sitting. He and his elders had moved to either side. There was a buzz of anticipation behind me.

" Captain," said Anokye, "You will be shown a series of moving and still images. When you have seen them I shall ask you whether you regard them as an authentic visual record of the events at the Kumase Sports Stadium."

Maxwell had come to sit next to me. He stood up.

"Objection," he called. "Nana Okyeame…"

"Objection overruled," Anokye interrupted him and continued, "Maxwell, sit down."

The movie started with a black screen. Then two circles of scruffy grass were revealed as the descending Thunderbirds switched on their flood-lights. I guessed the camera must have been high up on the stand opposite me. The planes landed, the downward blast of the turboprops stirring up clouds of dust. The camera zoomed in to show the ramp of the nearer plane hinging down. In the background we could see the same action at the other Thunderbird, almost perfectly synchronized. Three armed Marines ran down the ramp of each plane and took up defensive positions. As the two armored cars began to roll down, the camera pulled back so that we could see both planes. I knew that a pilot and a flight engineer remained in the cockpit of each and that one man was at the wheel of each car. With the three already on the ground, that would make a crew of six in each plane, eighteen men in all. With me, nineteen.

Then we—the audience, that is—saw the glint of one,

two, perhaps three grenades arching almost simultaneously through the air towards each idling prop-rotor. The Marines, to their credit, reacted within split seconds of the first explosions, diving under the body of their planes, guns blazing into the darkness behind the goal line.

Before they had a chance to take any further action, two blinding balls of fire rose out of the ground, one from under each Thunderbird. Both planes were thrown into the air, the armored cars with them. The Thunderbirds' fuel tanks exploded and by the time they hit the ground each was a raging inferno. The camera zoomed in on a frightening image of a Marine burning alive.

The audience reacted as if this were an entertainment movie. The bad guys had got their comeuppance. There was excited applause and cheering. Someone shouted above the din in Asante in which I thought I made out the name Jack, repeated several times. Each time the audience roared with laughter.

The camera panned, gloating over the detail of suffering and destruction.

I could hold it no longer. I stood up, opened my legs, bent over and vomited. Then I was on my knees, retching uncontrollably.

I heard Anokye call out, "Stop the movie."

Then he was beside me, bending down with his hand on my shoulder. My eyes were full of tears. Anokye let me finish my business. Then he took one elbow and a guard the other. They helped me up and the guards led me away.

Anokye was there when I came out of the bathroom. Maxwell, too, arguing with him in Asante. I felt too sick to try to follow what it was all about. The guards led me to my cell and helped me to lie down. One poured me a glass of water and I drank deeply.

"I'll have a doctor come and examine you," Anokye said.

When I returned they started again from the beginning. After the part I had already seen the camera panned to the center spot, found me lying nearby and zoomed in on me, a figure clearly terrified.

I guess that I had suppressed the memory of that experience. Reliving it now I just shook my head in dismay.

The scene switched to the blazing skeleton of the third plane, a crematorium for its flight crew, who had remained inside. Then it panned back to show the charred remains of the assault crews of the first two Thunderbirds, who now lay scattered, their uniforms stripped off them by fire, their corpses scorched, blackened, charred, incinerated. This time the audience was silent.

Then the soundtrack boomed out the Asante Kotoko war cry and I was shown again, captured, raised above the heads of my captors and carried round the stadium in a lap of triumph. The bleachers had been empty; but the court was full now and the spectators' cheers and applause and echoes of the war cry filled the air, accompanied by the drums and horns. I had never before felt as small and lonely. At that moment I wished the earth would swallow me.

The camera lingered to watch the sunrise and survey the wreckage. The bodies were loaded onto stretchers, one by one, and taken away. Silence descended again upon the audience.

Finally there was a shot of the corner of a cemetery, evidently taken later, eighteen white wooden crosses in three neat lines of six, with well cut grass.

The movie had come to an end but the performance wasn't over yet.

A slide show followed. The pictures were mine. They had managed to extract them from my wristcom's memory. There was nothing there that the movie hadn't shown, yet the succession of images somehow reflected my change of mood from initial pride and a sense of triumph to the anguish of defeat as the pictures became blurred, off-target and crooked. Judging from the talk behind me, the audience had begun to lose interest.

Anokye asked: "Captain Ferguson, do you have any

objection to these images being entered as part of the record?"

Maxwell put a restraining hand on my arm, but I stood up all the same and said, "No, sir."

The Asantehene beckoned to Anokye and they had a short conversation. Then Anokye adjourned the proceedings.

CHAPTER 10

I HAD SPENT the day sitting, yet I was exhausted and fell at once into a deep sleep. The next morning I was still completely drained. I tried not to think of the proceedings of the previous day but the images I had seen kept invading my conscious mind.

There was no court that day. One of the guards told me that the King and his Elders had gone to their respective farms to work.

"In Asante today," he said, "only the very old and the sick are excused. If the Asantehene himself spends at least one day every week using cutlass and hoe, who can refuse to do at least the same? As for me, I am also a farmer. If it were not for your case, I would be at my farm today."

I tried to read the bible that I had found in the room. My eyes saw the words on the page but my mind made no sense of them.

In despair, I tried to pray. It was no use. The words wouldn't come. It struck me that I might have more success if I got down on my knees. That didn't work either. It was a long time since God had heard my voice and it was clear to me that he didn't recognize it.

I pictured the Asantehene on his farm, weeding with a hoe, perhaps clearing the bush with a cutlass. That's what I needed, some demanding physical activity, hard labor. I lay on the concrete floor and did some push-ups.

Maxwell came to see me at noon. I soon wished he hadn't. The man had an agenda of his own. I featured only insofar as my case could advance his private ambitions. I think he saw himself as President of a republican Asante, somehow modeled on the America he had known, or thought he had known, in his student days. He told me he hoped that Uncle Sam would send another force soon, if only to rescue me. He wanted me to see myself as a hero in his struggle for democracy, the rule of law and the free market. When the United States punished Asante for its effrontery, I would recommend him, Maxwell, as its true friend.

"Dr. Maxwell," I told him politely, "I am tired. Please let me take some rest."

"Of course, of course, my boy," he said. "Just remember not to agree to anything they ask you to do without consulting me first. You didn't bring any American cigarettes with you by any chance? No? Pity. I gave up smoking years ago. By force, you know: we no longer have cigarettes in Asante. But meeting you has revived an old hunger."

I expressed my regret.

"Never mind, never mind," he told me as he took his leave.

My sleep was disturbed by fractured dreams. My throat parched, I groped for the water bottle. It wasn't there. I opened my eyes. My vision was blurred. There was a bearded white man with a dog collar sitting on the bench.

"Your sleep was troubled," he said. "Shall we pray together?"

I found myself on my knees again, elbows on the mattress.

The pastor led me in the Lord's Prayer.

He spoke English with a guttural accent, German perhaps.

"Deliver this young man from the yoke of the heathen despots in whose clutches he finds himself and give him peace," he prayed. "Soften the hearts of his oppressors. Open their eyes to the only true way. Direct their ungrateful souls to the path of wisdom. Incline them to hear Thy commands and humble themselves before Thee," and so on.

On Monday morning the guards came for me.

They led me into a living room furnished with comfortable

armchairs. Nana Anokye rose to greet me. He was wearing the same shades. I wondered whether he suffered from some eye disease.

There was another man with him.

"You know the Professor, of course," Anokye asked.

It was Boafo, or if it wasn't him, it was his twin.

"Boafo?" I asked.

"The same," he said, shaking my hand.

They had been drinking palm wine. Anokye asked if I would join them, or would I prefer something stronger. I said palm wine would do very well thanks.

"Crash," said Anokye, "we have what might turn out to be a serious problem and we need your help."

I said nothing, but my face must have shown my puzzlement.

"We are worried that your government will decide to send a mission to rescue you and to punish us. We want you to send a message to your President through your handler in the hope that it will persuade them against. Will you agree to cooperate?"

I leaned back and took a sip of the palm wine. It seemed months since I had sat in such a comfortable arm chair. I wouldn't have minded drinking myself silly and falling into a drunken sleep in that chair. I tried to focus on their request. I realized that I wasn't thinking too clearly. The court hearing had unbalanced me.

"You took my wristcom," I said. "How would I send it?"

"Wristcom?" Boafo asked, pulling the thing out of his pocket and holding it up. "So that's what you call it?"

"What would you want me to say?" I asked, carefully wording my question so as to avoid committing myself.

There was a sheet of paper lying on the center table. Anokye handed it to me.

"It's a draft," he said. "You know your people better than we do. If you want to suggest changes, feel free."

It was a good draft. Whoever had written it had evidently given it a lot of thought. I penciled in some additions and alterations and handed it back.

Anokye said, "That's fine. You would have to read it. No ad-libbing, mind. Do you understand?"

"I'd like to talk to Dr. Maxwell about it before I agree," I said.

I think that was the only time I ever saw Anokye lose his cool.

"Maxwell!" he said. "That nincompoop! No way! That old fool would welcome an American invasion. The idiot believes that his Yankee mentors would install him as their puppet President of Asante."

"As for Maxwell," contributed Boafo, "he thinks the sun shines out of Uncle Sam's asshole."

"Kofi!" Anokye reprimanded him.

Boafo looked surprised. Then it dawned on him that I might be offended.

"Crash," he said. "I'm sorry. For a moment I had forgotten you were an American."

Anokye had regained his composure.

"Crash," he asked, "what do you say? But no Maxwell."

"OK," I said, "I'll do it."

"When?" the two of them asked in one voice; and laughed.

I looked at the clock on the wall.

"If I do it right now," I said, "he'll still be asleep and I can leave the message on his machine. If we leave it until later, he'll be awake and might ask questions that could be difficult for me to handle."

So Boafo handed me the wristcom and I called up Bud's machine and read the message.

"Bud, this is Crash. I'm alive and well. Please tell Millicent and the kids and give them my love.

"The Asante arrested me and have put me on trial. They don't have capital punishment here and they have promised that if I tell them the truth they will not execute me. They might even let me return to the States some time.

"They confiscated my wristcom but they have given it back just to send this message.

"I want to say how deeply sorry I am about the loss of

our brothers who died in the disaster at the Sports Stadium. Some of the fault was mine. I grossly underestimated the Asante intelligence. It seems that they managed somehow to intercept our conversations. How they did it is still beyond me.

"They tell me that I got it all wrong. Professor Franklin and his team weren't in the Fort as I had been told. That is the only prison they have in this country and it is used only for the criminally insane. William Franklin, they tell me, is dead. According to them he died a natural death. The young experts he brought with him are all alive and well. The Asante tell me that they agreed to stay behind here of their own free will and that they may return to the U.S. any time they choose. They are scattered around the country but they all have a chance to gather in one place two or three times a year. Some of them have married and have Asante children. All this is what I have been told but I expect to have a chance to meet some of them at least before I return to the U.S. I do intend to return, if and when I am released from custody.

"The Asante have allowed me to send this because they have a message which they want to address to our President. This is it.

"'To the President of the United States of America.

"'Sir,

"'Asante is a proud country, with a history going back at least as far as that of your own. There the resemblance ends. In the aftermath of a civil war and other disasters, we are desperately poor. Our economy functions barely above the level of subsistence. We have practically nothing to send abroad. You seized our remaining offshore oil resources. Most of our gold has been mined out. Little remains of our tropical forests. Once we led the league of world cocoa exporters, but you have developed genetically engineered temperate varieties as substitutes. And you use synthetic chemicals to make your chocolate.

"'Our country has no material resources of interest to

the outside world. In difficult circumstances, following the collapse of the Republic of Ghana, Asante is trying to build a new society. All we ask is to be left alone to get on with it. We are not a threat to your country or any other.

"'You sent Professor William Franklin to us with a team of young experts. Their altruistic task, the professor told us, was to identify new resources which we might exploit for the benefit of our people. Professor Franklin, regrettably, suffered a heart attack and died. In the course of our investigation to determine the cause of his death, we examined his documents and discovered that he was an agent of your Central Intelligence Agency. He was, in short, a spy. The resources which were of interest to him were those of a strategic nature, which your government or its agents might exploit, for your own benefit, not ours.

"'The members of Franklin's team were unaware of this: they satisfied us that they had been duped. We offered to let them return to the U.S. Every single one of them preferred to stay and help us. We imposed no conditions upon them and they are not under any duress. Each one of them is free to leave tomorrow. We have helped all of them to send letters home telling their families of their decision.

"'You may have believed that their letters were fabrications. Perhaps you were unable to understand how they could have chosen to live and work in such a poor country when that meant foregoing the opportunities open to them at home?

"'You sent Captain Ferguson here to find them and to anchor a rescue mission. We discovered your plans in advance and were able to wipe out the invaders within minutes of their arrival. We did this without malice but to protect our national integrity. Our ancestors succumbed to one superpower; we do not want to give history a chance to repeat itself.

"'We have no standing army. Our voluntary militia is poorly equipped. The United States is infinitely more powerful than Asante. If you so choose you could send bombers from Saint Thomas to annihilate us tomorrow.

"'Mr. President, we beg you not to do so. After all, what would you gain? You already control all West Africa's remaining oil resources, onshore and offshore. We have no onshore oil. If Professor Franklin had lived, he would have had to report to you that we have no material resources that might be of use to you. So all we ask of you is this: please leave us alone to live in peace.

"'I am, with the greatest respect, Dr. Yaw Mensah, aka Osei Tutu III, Asantehene.'

"Bud, that is the end of their message, I am signing off now. Once I have done so, I shall return the wristcom to my captors."

We sat and chatted for a while and Anokye handed me some old books he had brought for me to read, novels by African authors, political stuff by Kwame Nkrumah.

When it was time for me to return to my cell, I said I had one question, just one, for Boafo.

"What is your real name?" I asked him.

They laughed.

"Let me introduce you formally," said Anokye, "Captain Ekem Ferguson, U. S. Marines, also known as Crash. Professor Kofi Boafo. Boafo, as you know, means 'helper.' Kofi was once professor of electrical engineering at the Kwame Nkrumah University of Science and Technology, for which reason he is also sometimes called Kofi Kanea (that is to say 'Kofi Light,' or 'Kofi Electricity.') He is also known, to his embarrassment, as Mansa (which is a girl's name, the name of a girl whose part he played years ago in a play at the boys school he attended) and sometimes as Saman (which is an anagram of Mansa and which means 'ghost,' a title conferred on him by his friends to honor his skill as a detective.) Like many Asante, he is a man of many names."

Again they both laughed; but all I could muster was a weak smile.

Later that day I sent a message to Anokye as a result of which Boafo came back with my wristcom. I tried to reach Millicent but the channel had been blocked.

As a rule the Asantehene's court sat only on Fridays. When I appeared for the next session, the following week, the judges were back in their original positions. I noted with relief that the screen had been removed. No more movies.

The customary introductory proceedings having been observed as before, Nana Anokye addressed me.

"Captain Ferguson," he said, "in today's session we are going to play back certain recordings to you."

The court clerk handed me a sheaf of papers; and gave another to Dr. Maxwell.

"That document," said Anokye, "is a transcript of what you are going to hear. Please follow the recording carefully and mark any disagreements you may have with the accuracy of the transcript. At the end of today's session I shall ask you to sign a copy, a corrected copy if that proves necessary, agreeing that it is a true reflection of the recordings. Do you understand? Dr. Maxwell?"

Maxwell objected. He objected to everything. All he managed to do was to antagonize the judges. I pulled at his jacket but he wasn't going to miss a chance of making a speech. Eventually Anokye managed to persuade him to sit down.

The first recordings covered all my Kumase conversations with Bud, at least those from the roof of Cedar House. Bud's contributions were there as well as mine. That meant that Professor Boafo, alias Mansa, alias Kofi Kanea, alias Ghost, had done a more sophisticated job than just rigging up some hidden microphones: he must have cracked our codes and intercepted the radio waves. A clever guy. I wouldn't have credited anyone living in this backwater with the capacity to do that. A clever guy indeed. I no longer doubted that the man had been a real professor.

The second set of recordings covered my answers to Nana Anokye's questions in his office.

Maxwell tried to persuade me to refuse to sign the transcripts, but they had been professionally done and I had to agree that they were accurate. Again the idiot stood up to make a speech.

"Maxwell, sit down," I told him and then, when he refused, "Maxwell, you're fired."

I hate to think what my fate might have been if the tables had been turned and Maxwell had been the Chief Justice.

I signed the document.

"Captain Ferguson," said Nana Anokye. "That is the end of the court's evidence. Do you want to call any witnesses? No? Is there anything you want to say?"

I said, "With respect, Sir, I still don't know that the charge is."

"At the next sitting," he said. "Everything will be tied up at the next sitting."

"Nana Asantehene, Nananom," said Nana Anokye, "You have seen and heard all the evidence in this case. I would now like to address you on two interrelated issues. Firstly, who is the accused; and secondly, what offense has been committed?"

He began by reminding the court of the case in which it had convicted Professor William Franklin (deceased) of espionage and of the acceptance by all the members of Franklin's team of the Asantehene's invitation to them to stay and work in Asante. They had all written letters home telling their families of their decision.

"The U. S. government seems to have believed that these letters had been written under duress and planned to send an expeditionary force to rescue the writers. That plan was doomed from the start, firstly because the Americans were here of their own volition and secondly because they were living and working at widely dispersed locations.

"At this stage a boat brought Captain Ferguson from an American oil tanker to the Fanti coast. Our brothers working on the Americans' Half Assini oil platform had warned us to expect him and Fanti night fishermen monitored his arrival. The rest of the story you have heard from the Captain's own mouth, as captured on tape during my examination. He has accepted the transcript of the tapes as an accurate record of what he said. I believe that he has told us the unblemished truth."

He paused to drink water.

"It is clear to me, as I hope it will be to you, Nananom, that the principal culprit in all this is the Government of the United States of America under the leadership of its current President. Our generation has witnessed the Americans' recolonization of the African island of São Tome, and its renaming as Saint Thomas; together with their de facto, if not de jure, colonization of large tracts of our continent's western seaboard and of inland islands of territory in the Congo, Nigeria and elsewhere.

"The defeat of the Americans in what they call the Second China War; and their consequent loss of access to the oil and gas supplies of the Arabian-Iranian Gulf, left their economy in a fragile condition. Africa has had to pay the price. A few African traitors and collaborators have benefited while the majority of our people have been impoverished to an extent unimaginable at the turn of this century.

"Nananom, we are fortunate, I believe, that though we in Asante are potentially rich, we have no resources that are of interest to the Americans. William Franklin, if he had lived, would have had to take home a report that said just that. Our potential wealth is in our people, in our capacity to create a new society, based not, as in America, on an insatiable greed for power, money and luxuries, but on the satisfaction of our simple human needs: food, clothing, shelter, security, companionship and solidarity.

"I wish the Americans could be satisfied that all the seams of gold which once lay beneath our land have been mined out and that the mines have been flooded beyond economical recovery, even if there were anything useful left down there. My fear is that they might be driven now by an irrational need to punish us for our audacious response to their invasion. We know from our study of history that Uncle Sam does not gladly suffer the taunts of those whom he regards as insolent upstarts. Think only of Cuba, Viet Nam, Paraguay, Guatemala, Nicaragua, Afghanistan, Iraq, Iran, to name just a few. And think of Kwame Nkrumah's Ghana."

He took another sip of water.

"Nanamom," he continued, "forgive me for my digression. I would like to propose the Government of the United States of America as our first accused. The charges would be, firstly, espionage; and secondly waging undeclared war. I believe that the facts before you would warrant a verdict of guilty.

"Unfortunately, the U. S. President and his collaborators, and those gray eminences who manipulate them, do not lie within the limited bounds of our judicial power. To try them would be an exercise in futility.

"That being the case we are left only with the unfortunate Captain Ekem Ferguson who sits here before us. He did not initiate the acts for which he has admitted responsibility. His handlers did not even judge him worthy of making him privy to all the intelligence available to them concerning his mission. Perhaps they thought that if they had shown him the letters received by the families of our American guests that might have sowed seeds of doubt in his mind.

"Nananom, I propose that we charge Captain Ferguson firstly with espionage and secondly with being an accessory to the crime of unjustified invasion of our territory with aggressive intent. I request Nana Asantehene to order that the court be cleared to give Nananom an opportunity to consider my proposal in camera."

I sat in my cell, thinking.

Espionage. I hadn't thought of myself as a spy but now that I did come to consider the matter I had no doubt that I was one. Guilty as charged.

Accessory to unjustified invasion of Asante with aggressive intent? Invasion, yes: there had been an invasion, even though it had failed. Accessory, yes: my role had been a key one. Unjustified? If my countrymen had decided to remain of their own free will, there was no justification for my mission. Yes, unjustified. Aggressive intent? If there had indeed been prisoners and our force had freed them and got away without casualties on either side, would that have been meant that there was no aggressive intent? How could we have rescued the hostages without using force to break into the prison?

I was led back into the court two hours later and took my seat.

The court clerk said, "The accused will rise," and I rose.

Nana Anokye stepped forward and read the charges.

"Captain Ekem Ferguson, do you plead guilty or not guilty?"

I asked, with proper humility, whether I might have some time to consider my plea. Anokye asked me how long I needed. I said two hours. He gave me one and adjourned the court.

Back in my cell, I wrote him a short note, asking whether I might talk to him in private. One of my guards agreed to deliver it. The guard returned and took me to the same room where I had met him before.

"What is it, Crash?" Anokye asked.

I thought I sensed some impatience in his voice.

"I hope you won't think me obstructive," I said. "You know that I have dispensed with Dr. Maxwell's services. So I must do my own thinking."

He seemed to soften, and nodded.

"In the U.S.," I said, "we have a process called plea bargaining. The accused might agree to plead guilty in return for an undertaking by the prosecutor to request a reduced sentence."

"I've heard the term," said Anokye. "Crash, there will be no bargaining. The judges have already considered the evidence and decided the verdict and the sentence. Your plea is a mere formality. However, if you were to be so misguided as to plead not guilty, we might have to reconsider. Do you understand?"

I bowed my head.

"You don't have to worry," he said. "We are not going to execute you. We are not even going to imprison you. But you will have to stay in Asante for at least a year. During that period you will have to work for us."

"Work for you?" I asked.

"Work for us; and for yourself, too," he replied. "Now don't ask me what work. You'll find out soon enough. Now let's get back to the court and get this over with."

I pleaded guilty as charged. Then, for reasons I could hardly fathom, I was accorded a singular honor. The Asantehene himself stood up and came to the front of the platform. He gathered his ntama and threw it over his left shoulder. Then he addressed the assembly. His subject was my sentence.

"*Nananom, agyanom, enanom,*" he said, "citizens of Asante, Captain Ferguson has pleaded guilty to the crimes with which we charged him. There were other charges which we considered adding: terrorism for one; but we thought that would serve no purpose. The crimes to which he has pleaded guilty are serious enough. In his own country they would almost certainly have warranted the death penalty. In his country they practice murder by the state, by poisoning, as our ancestors did, and by electrocution. His sentence, most likely, since he is a military man, would have been death by firing squad.

"But, as you well know, we do not practice judicial murder in our new Asante. Indeed when I was persuaded to take the office of Asantehene, one of the conditions I set was that we would in no circumstances, I repeat, in no circumstances, practice capital punishment in our country.

"You know, too, that we have, as a people, given serious consideration to the nature and purpose of punishment for criminal acts. We initiated a countrywide discussion of this issue which led to a consensus that we cannot afford to waste scarce resources building, and equipping, and staffing, and maintaining prisons. A majority of our people agree that imprisonment is a futile response to crime. In

Ekem Ferguson's country, which barely fifty years ago, was the only super-power on this Earth, they had the largest prison population, per capita, in the whole world; and my guess is that they still enjoy that dubious honor. Yet there is no evidence that the practice of imprisonment has reduced the rate of crime.

"We Asante regard crimes committed in our midst as evidence of the malfunctioning of our own society and as occasions for self-examination and self-criticism. One important aim of the type of punishment we practice is to reform the criminal, to draw him (or, much less often, her) back into our fold as a fully functioning and contributing member of our society. Another is to compensate the victims of the crime.

"All this you know.

"The convicted criminal in this case, Ekem Ferguson, is an American but he is also one of our children. He is our son. His parents, he tells us, were our fellow citizens; and when they effectively abandoned him in the United States, he was brought up by a caring Fanti couple who had settled there. Can we attribute his behavior to the fact that his parents abandoned him, as he himself tells us? Before the United States shut its gates, it was the cherished ambition of many of our young people, particularly our young men, to emigrate to that country. Those who could did so. Why? Were we, I mean our parents' and grandparents' generations, not to blame for the fact that when the youth of the time thought of their own country, it was only of how to leave it? We have to face the facts of our history. We sold many generations of fine young men and women to the white man to transport across the Atlantic as slaves. Later, we dissipated our energies in futile civil wars and so let the white man in at our back door. We let them kidnap Prempeh I and exile him to the Seychelles. By the time he returned he had been thoroughly brainwashed, turned into a white man, wearing white man's clothes and thinking the white man's thoughts. He had become a Christian. That was the ultimate victory of the British. And we, who had stayed behind, most of us had also been brainwashed. It was only after the time of 'Things Fall Apart' that some of us began to think for ourselves again. The popularity of our message, throughout our country, and the social revolution which our people have begun to accomplish, is evidence that the seeds of our greatness as a people were only lying dormant.

"My sisters and brothers, if I have digressed, I have done so with a purpose. My purpose has been to sketch in the thinking which led to the sentence we have devised for Ekem Ferguson.

"We have decided that he must stay in Asante for a year. After that period he will be free to go; but he will also be free to stay with us, provided we are satisfied with his conduct.

"We are going to make a movie, a documentary. In it we shall tell the story of Ekem's arrival in this country and what he did after he arrived here. Those of you who have attended the earlier sessions of his trial will have seen some of the footage which we filmed ourselves and some of the material which Ekem himself shot. We will supplement this with interviews with those of our people who kept watch on him throughout his stay and made it possible for us to destroy the invasion force without any loss of Asante life. The movie will honor our heroes. It will expose the Americans, I mean their government, for what they are: arrogant, greedy, power-hungry, irresponsible and, dare I say it, stupid. It will invest our people with pride and self-confidence in our capacity to shape our own destiny. It will warn them of the dangers we may face and give them courage to face those dangers. Our enemies might call it propaganda. But propaganda is lies. We shall tell no lies in this movie, that I promise you.

"Ekem will feature in this movie. Not as a hero, but also not as an unvarnished villain. Rather as a victim, a victim of those who sent him, and William Franklin before him, on a malign mission. We shall include interviews with him and expect him to tell the truth, as we believe he has done in his pre-trial testimony.

"Once the movie is ready, we shall send it round the country, to every town and village. Ekem will accompany the film and after it has been shown, those who have seen it will have the opportunity to ask him questions, in public. We expect this experience to have a profound effect on his thinking. He will also have an opportunity to see our problems, as we do, from below; and he will see what we are doing, as a people, to solve them and make a better life for ourselves and for our children.

"Finally, we shall expect him to earn his keep. Like every one of us who is physically capable, he will have to do two or three days physical labor every week, on a farm or in a workshop.

"*Me nuanom*, my brothers and sisters, I have finished. I am going to return to my seat and hand the proceedings over to Okyeame Anokye."

There was loud applause. The people rose from the benches and called out the praise names of their king. Then someone started to sing their national anthem, *Yen ara asase ni* and everyone joined in.

When they eventually calmed down, Anokye addressed the assembled citizens.

"Our final Court of Appeal has considered the evidence. Our Elders have deliberated," he said, "and arrived at a consensus. A verdict has been agreed and the sentence has been pronounced. Nana has spoken. A conclusion has been reached. The matter is closed."

He paused, allowing his words to sink in. Then he continued.

"Or is it? Is the matter closed? That is how things were in the courts of the colonial times and after, when the courts were the preserve of professional lawyers and judges wore little white wigs on their heads. But times have changed. We have regained our independence. In our towns and villages, ordinary citizens serve as magistrates and judges. They do not search huge libraries for decisions made many years ago in the British House of Lords. We have scrapped all that. We are building a new legal system, based on consensus amongst ourselves. Our law is no longer a domain of mystery and the province of corruption. It is a people's law.

"So Nana invites you to ask questions and state your views on the evidence, the charges, the verdict and the sentence. If you wish to contribute, please raise your hand."

I turned. The assembled citizens of Asante were slow to react. Except, that is, Dr. Maxwell, whose hand uncoiled and shot up like a child's Christmas toy. With a tone of resignation, Anokye named him.

"Three minutes, Dr. Maxwell," he said.

"This court is totally lacking in legitimacy," declaimed Maxwell in English. "Its self-appointed head, the so-called Asantehene, was neither selected nor enstooled in accordance with time-honored traditional practice. The Constitutional Party demands that a National Convention be called to draft a democratic, multi-party, constitution and a bill of rights for this country; and that that constitution be put to the people in a referendum conducted in the presence of foreign observers…"

He was standing only a few paces from me but I heard no more: his voice was drowned out by roars of protest. Anokye tried to persuade them to give Maxwell a hearing, but they would have none of it.

The next speaker identified himself as a fitter from *Suame Magazine*. He spoke in Asante.

"What you have just heard is a voice from the past. We the common people have had enough of crooked lawyers and politicians speaking English in suits. If Maxwell doesn't like the new Asante he should emigrate to a place where they speak his language and wear his clothes. The verdict and the sentence are a manifestation of the humane wisdom of Nana and the Elders. We should be proud of them. I propose that we endorse their decisions."

There was another roar, this time of approval. The verdict and sentence were endorsed by acclamation. I felt a burden lifted from my soul. At least now I had some idea of what the immediate future held for me.

CHAPTER 11

WHILE THE SCRIPTWRITERS worked on their screenplay, three tutors kept me busy, at Anokye's behest. One worked on my Asante language skills, though to scant effect; one coached me in the intricacies of Asante culture and philosophy; and the third gave me a crash course on Asante and Ghanaian history, from which I prepared the notes which follow.

Man probably makes his first appearance in this part of the world, in small numbers, a thousand years before Christ, perhaps earlier. Three thousand years ago West Africans about whom little is known start producing the remarkable Nok terracotta sculptures. Fifteen hundred years ago the first great state is established in the savannah country south of the Sahara: Ghana; to be succeeded by Mali and then Songhai. A thousand years ago new immigrants begin to bypass the tropical forest in the area where the savannah reaches down to coast along the line of the Volta River. Some few brave souls begin to penetrate the forest, hunting and beginning to discover, by trial and error, which plants are edible and capable of cultivation or have medicinal value. Some of the pioneers stake out territorial claims and begin to establish small centers of population. Some begin to mine surface deposits of gold and to sell the metal to savannah traders, through whom it eventually reaches the Mediterranean coast and Europe. In the fifteenth century Portuguese explorers begin to edge their way down the West African coast, seeking to short-circuit the trans-Saharan caravan trade. They discover and colonize off-shore islands, including São Tome (now the U.S. colony of Saint Thomas); and, in due course, Brazil, where they start to cultivate sugar.

Around 1700, Osei Tutu, the "king" of Kumase, unites his own state with those of Dwaben, Kokofu, Bekwai, Nsuta, Mampong, Asumegya and Kumawu, whose leaders are all eager to escape the hegemony of the king of Denkyira, to whom they have been subject and who has exacted heavy tributes from them. They name their new united state Asante. Osei Tutu is advised by a priest, an *okomfo*, called Anokye. Okomfo Anokye proves to be a brilliant psychologist and politician. In the Akan tradition, the stool has become the symbol of legitimate state power. Anokye conceives the idea of having a golden stool descend from heaven into the lap of Osei Tutu in the presence of the other leaders. Henceforth the golden stool comes to embody the soul of the Asante union. Kumase is recognized as its capital and Osei Tutu becomes the first Asantehene.

Osei Tutu's first task is to conquer Denkyira. That done, he and his successors set out to consolidate and expand the Asante state, by trade and by conquest.

Osei Tutu's Asante has three principal exchangeable resources. The first is kola, the mildly narcotic seed of a tree which is indigenous to its forests. The kola nut is in high demand all over the Muslim world.

The second resource is gold.

Its last resource is enslaved human beings.

This is how the institution of slavery arises in Asante. The harvesting, collection and transportation of kola to markets in the north requires much labor. The mining of gold likewise, as also the clearing of the forest and establishment of farms to provide food for the population. There is a serious labor shortage in Asante. Part of the proceeds from the sale of gold and kola is used to buy firearms from the Europeans. These firearms are used to conquer adjacent territories. Prisoners of war are enslaved. Asante treats them humanely and in the course of one or two generations they are absorbed into the population. This process is encouraged by a law which makes it an offense to reveal or discuss the origins of any citizen.

Over the years, the Asante empire expands until it covers practically the whole area of what will one day become the Republic of Ghana.

The Portuguese, Dutch, British, French and Danes (and some other minor players) have by this time conquered the Americas. They have also acquired a taste for bitter drinks: cocoa, coffee and tea; and need sugar to sweeten them. They establish vast estates to grow sugar cane. The American natives prove unamenable to enslavement and their populations are decimated by imported diseases. The Europeans turn to Africa for labor.

Sometimes the supply of slaves to Asante exceeds demand. They sell the surplus to the Europeans.

Anokye stops by, listening in on my history tutor's peroration.

"So here," he comments, "in greed for wealth and power, we have the origins of the trans-Atlantic slave trade. Over a period of four hundred years some twelve million Africans were forcibly transported across the ocean. Our royal ancestors were undoubtedly accomplices in this nefarious business. However I have to say in mitigation that they can hardly have been aware that the Europeans would treat their slaves as cruelly as they did. We treated our slaves as human beings and had no reason to believe that the Europeans would do otherwise."

The sale of slaves to the Europeans grew to become a major source of income for the Asante and the British decision, in 1807, to stop the slave trade was an economic disaster for them. They had to find other goods to export. The rubber tree and the oil palm which grew wild in the forest filled the gap.

Towards the end of the nineteenth century, British imperial ambitions expanded. They were determined to carve out space for themselves all over Africa. In 1874 they invaded Asante. Exhausted by the march from the coast, their expeditionary force stayed just two days but that was long enough for them to burn Kumase. In the peace agreement which followed, they forced the losers to agree to bear the cost of their aggression. This war, the Sargrenti War as the Asante call it, led to schisms in their society. Years of civil war and disintegration followed. In 1888 a new Asantehene, the young Kwaku Dua III, better known as Prempeh I, was enstooled and immediately set about rebuilding the Asante state. This was anathema to the British on the coast. Prempeh tried to bypass the hostile governor by sending a delegation to London to negotiate with Queen Victoria. However Joseph Chamberlain, the Colonial Secretary, was not amenable to reason. He was determined to crush Asante and refused to see its envoys. In 1896, the British again invaded. Prempeh and his advisers, their confidence damaged by years of civil war and rumors of the destructive power of the Maxim gun, were persuaded that it would be folly to resist. Received in peace, the British at once made demands on Prempeh which they knew he could not meet, principally the immediate payment of 50,000 ounces of gold. When, as expected, he failed to deliver, they arrested him and sent him into exile, first at Elmina Castle, then in Sierra Leone and finally in the Seychelles. It was not until 1924 that they allowed him to return to Kumase.

So ended my tutor's lesson. He took my leave advising me that Okomfo Anokye himself, Okyeame to Otumfuo, Nana Asantehene, would conduct the final session.

"Nana," I said, "I am just a common criminal, a convicted common criminal. Why are you devoting your valuable time to giving me an education? Even at our top universities in the States, few students ever get to enjoy a one-to-one session with a professor."

He laughed. He was in a relaxed mood that day.

"*Abotare ye,*" he said. "Be patient. All will be revealed. In the course of time. Now let's see if we can dispose of the twentieth century."

"The British kidnapped Prempeh in January 1896. By April

they had approved the grant of a mining concession covering a hundred square miles at Obuasi. The following year, the £1 shares of the Ashanti Goldfields Corporation which had been set up in London to exploit the concession, were selling for £18. Within a few years the colonial government had built a railway from Sekondi to the mine. By mid-century that mine had yielded over 6 million ounces of gold."

I said, "Not a bad return on Prempeh's unpaid debt of 50,000 ounces."

He nodded.

"The kidnapping and exile of Prempeh in 1896 was a watershed: Asante was decapitated.

"Our people made one futile attempt at resistance, led by a courageous old queen-mother, Yaa Asantewaa of Edweso.

"Once the British had crushed it they had no difficulty in finding collaborators prepared to allow themselves to be bent to the British plan: exploit the country's gold and other resources for export; get the natives hooked on British goods; educate them to the extent necessary to accomplish those ends; and, finally, and ultimately perhaps most damaging, infect their minds with the virus of Christianity, undermining their confidence in their own culture and their capacity to resist.

"English became the language of power. Initially, many Asante refused to send their children to school, fearing the consequences of indoctrination. But as they saw Fantis from the coast master the English language and take the wages and material goods which jobs in the changing economy offered, their resolve weakened. On entering mission schools our children were given English names. One favorite was Maxwell, in honor of a British governor.

"Our music and our arts were dismissed as pagan and barbaric. Christians had to deny the supreme being, *Onyankopon*, worshiped by our ancestors, and pray to a new god, called God, whom we were required to approach through God's white son Jesus and Jesus's mother Mary, symbols of European power.

"Prempeh put his royal seal on this program when the British brought him back to Kumase in 1924. While in exile he had been converted by Anglican missionaries. On his return to Kumase he advised our people to emulate him. So there were two Prempehs: the young man fighting to retain Asante independence; and the older man, the returnee wearing suit and Homburg, recognizing the reality of defeat and agreeing to accept the left-overs from the colonial master's table, the trappings, without the power.

"The British could at last relax. They had long since conquered the minds of the coastal people; now Asante too was theirs.

"We learned to grow cocoa and prepare the useless beans for export. Useless to us because you cannot eat them, nor turn them into oil or rope or thread. But the white man had some use for them. And we needed their money to buy their alcohol and tobacco; their cloth; and their hoes and ax heads.

"In the course of time we became world champion cocoa exporters, both in volume and in quality. Two thirds of our export proceeds came from cocoa. The rest came from other unprocessed raw materials: timber, gold, diamonds, manganese. Now we hungered for flour and sugar cubes, corned beef and sardines in tins; trucks and tires and fuel; cement and corrugated iron roofing sheets; but we made none of these.

"Throughout the twentieth century, this process of incorporation in Western markets continued. Even the struggle for national independence can be seen as part of it. For one thing, the thinking of our leaders was strongly influenced by Western ideas.

"In the second World War the British recruited our young men; but when the survivors came home and reminded their masters that they had been sent to fight for freedom and democracy, they found that the noise of the guns had made the white man deaf. Our upstart politicians, many of them lawyers trained in Britain, hastened to place themselves at the head of the discontented ex-servicemen. However, since they were all busy with their own affairs, they sent for the young Kwame Nkrumah, who had been studying in America and Britain, to manage their campaign. Nkrumah soon proved himself too radical for their liking and they sacked him. He seized the moment, started his own party and stumped the country, cadging lifts from town to town and village to village, sleeping rough. The many women who fell for his charms fed him and became party activists. The old guard called the young men who rallied round him "veranda boys."

"The British Governor saw Nkrumah as a dangerous agitator and had him shut up in one of the old slave forts. Stupid move: it only enhanced his support. The Brits were few and we were many. There were no white settlers with vested interests as elsewhere in the continent. The anopheles mosquito had seen to that. The Brits decided to take a chance and allow an election. They expected the old elitist party to win the day, but it was Nkrumah's CPP that prevailed. The Governor had little option but to release him from prison and appoint him Prime Minister, with a promise of full independence to follow."

I applauded. My sympathies were entirely with Nkrumah. Independence! The concept wasn't strange to me. I had been celebrating July 4 with fervor ever since I could remember. But Anokye raised his right index finger.

"Wait," he said and again, "Wait."

"The state which Nkrumah inherited was a colonial state. He was aware of his weakness. Economic independence for Ghana was not on the cards. However he hoped to use Ghana's political independence as a stepping stone to the creation of a united Africa. The odds were stacked against him. For one thing the leaders of the newly independent African states had no intention of giving up the powers of patronage which they had inherited from their former colonial masters. He was forced to narrow his ambitions to the industrialization of Ghana.

"The model he chose was the command economy. Since there was no time to build a working class he would build socialism from above, relying on the support of his veranda boys.

"The Brits had bequeathed him a nest-egg, the cocoa receipts they had kept in London to prop up sterling in the post-war years. Nkrumah used this to embark upon an ambitious program, building roads and schools, hospitals and health centers. He found the funding to build the Volta Dam at Akosombo by agreeing to sell cheap electricity to an American aluminum company.

"In a short space of time he created the nucleus of a new managerial middle class. What he hadn't taken into account was that these inexperienced new managers and bureaucrats had their own agenda. Their first priority was not to build Ghana but rather to build their own wealth. The state enterprises Nkrumah established were mismanaged. Our word for government is *aban*, literally a stone house, such as the Brits built. We had never had any compunction about robbing the colonial aban and we continued to do so. It was a hallowed tradition. It is only in our time that we have been able to abandon it."

"How did you do that?" I asked.

Anokye looked at his wristwatch.

"Aban was destroyed by Things Fall Apart," he said. "We have resisted the temptation to rebuild it. There is nothing to rob."

"Nkrumah was reckless," he continued. "He insulted the U. S., calling it Imperialist. He ignored the one abiding rule of the international politics of the last century: no one was permitted to cock a snook at Uncle Sam with impunity. That is why we are so nervous about our success in defeating your mission; why we had you send that message to your President.

"The price of cocoa slumped, whether as a result of market forces or through manipulation by the U.S. is not clear. The kitty was empty. Imported goods were in short supply. The people were unhappy and ungrateful. Concentrating on the tasks of building a modern state and advancing African liberation and unity, Nkrumah had squandered the goodwill of those who had propelled him to power. While he was abroad on a peace mission, his own military overthrew him with the active support of the American government and its agents."

This was news to me. I found it difficult to believe.

"Why would they do that?" I asked.

"I've mentioned one reason: sheer exasperation with his insolence," Anokye replied. "Here is another. It was the time of what was called the Cold War. The Americans believed that Nkrumah was a communist who would steer Africa out of the Western sphere of influence and deprive them of access to our raw materials. That was nonsense. Nkrumah was an African nationalist pure and simple; and he lacked the power to harm the U.S., even if he had wished to do so.

"After the coup d'etat, the American ambassador, a black man, went round the country handing out gifts of a dozen bags of cement here, half a dozen there. Washington retired him soon afterwards. He was never given another diplomatic post. He had done his job.

"The basic fault in Nkrumah's political and economic analysis was its top-down, outside-in nature. Politics was conducted through the medium of English, a language foreign to most of our people, particularly to the poor. Educational policy was designed to create the black westerners whose job it would be to build and staff the institutions of a state based on a Western model. Schools and hospitals were indeed built but Government became increasingly centralized and more and more devoted to serving the needs of the new middle class. Colonialism had enmeshed Ghana in the web of global capitalism. The West could not permit an attempt at real independence to succeed.

"In the years after Nkrumah was overthrown, the most energetic of our youth came to discover that the neo-colonial system had little to offer to them. Salvation, for them, lay in the West. They dreamed of emigration to *Aburokyiri*, the white man's country, or, second-best, to the obese diseased cities, particularly Accra and Kumase. Meanwhile the shrinking output of our export commodities and falling international prices made it impossible to satisfy the expectations of a growing population, increasingly conditioned by the perceived glamor of foreign soap operas and television advertising for imported goods in glossy packaging. The West kept things going for a while with what was called 'aid.' Their agenda was to sustain the supply of the raw materials they needed; and the market for their own exports. Accra became a city of vast warehouses, devoted to the storage of imported rice and sugar and consumer goods. The situation was unstable and unsustainable. It didn't occur to our politicians, brainwashed black westerners all of them, that there might be alternative scenarios. They certainly did not plan for the consequences of the end of our timber and gold and the substitution of synthetics for cocoa; nor for the spiraling price of oil, as world supplies ran down. Discovery of oil on our offshore continental shelf delayed the evil day but that was all. And even that oil was mortgaged to the foreigners who had discovered it.

"Nkrumah was followed by a succession of alternating military and civilian governments whose leaders' names are best forgotten. What distinguished them was their inability to balance their budgets. They became increasingly dependent upon the so-called 'aid.' Their debts grew and so did the interest they owed to their foreign creditors. Ghana was working for its Western bankers. The middle class grew too, identifying itself by large cars and ugly mansions surrounded by high walls with coils of barbed wire on them. Those who could, sent their children to universities abroad. Many Ghanaians, educated and otherwise, emigrated, their skills contributing to the growth of Western economies. Few returned. Their remittances to family back home became a significant factor in the national economy. Alms, conscience money."

"My grandparents and parents were amongst those who went," I said, "but they came back."

He nodded but there was no stopping Anokye's passionate flood of words.

"Poor and uneducated youngsters tried to follow in their footsteps, inventing claims for political asylum or attempting to bypass the legal points of entry. The Europeans and

Americans reacted by erecting virtual walls around their territory. Now they would accept only the most highly qualified, or workers in professions such as nursing, which their own natives were reluctant to enter. They preached free trade but maintained high tariff barriers and introduced new regulations to protect their producers from competition from the foreign poor. At the same time they persuaded our corrupted leaders to open our borders to their produce. They told us that in return for our concessions, foreign investment would flow in to build new factories and provide jobs for our steadily increasing population. It never came.

"For a while the West subsidized our budget deficits. The value of our currency declined steadily, as did the real incomes of most of our people. Class differences, once mitigated by strong ties of kinship, began to emerge."

He stopped to take a sip of water.

"I hope you are not overwhelmed by my potted history," he said.

"Such foreign investment as did come in, was directed at the continuing extraction of our raw materials. The mining companies dug deeper and deeper until no more gold could be extracted economically. Then they left. When all our useful trees had been cut down and exported as lumber the saw-millers followed. Our cocoa sector died when genetic engineering produced cocoa trees that could survive temperate climates; and the chemical industry learned to synthesize chocolate.

"When we had nothing left of value to the West they lost interest in us and the budget subsidies dried up. Meanwhile the world's oil resources were approaching exhaustion. Your people fought two wars with China over access to the Gulf. You lost the second and turned your attention to the extraction of West African oil, under the protection of military control from your new island colony of St. Thomas.

"Crash, a great Nigerian author of the last century, Chinua Achebe, wrote a fine novel called *Things Fall Apart*. He took the title from the work of an Irish poet. The full quotation is:

'Things fall apart; the center cannot hold.'

"That describes what happened to us. We had nothing left to sell. We had no resources to fund the maintenance of our existing assets. The foreign benefactors of our ruling class abandoned their clients. With nothing left to tax and no subsidies, the government lacked the resources to provide any services to our people; they couldn't even pay wages to their civil servants, nor, ultimately, to themselves. Those of the remaining middle class who could, emigrated.

"For a short while the political and military classes succeeded in using coercion to squeeze the poor but in the end that failed. The country was taken over by the rump of the national armed forces and rapacious gangs, criminals who had escaped from the prisons. They looted the abandoned homes of the rich. Then they descended upon the rural areas, surviving by stealing foodstuffs from subsistence farmers. Without medical services, diseases spread, decimating our population. Then the gods, or God, the kindly Christian God, who had quietly presided over this holocaust, sent us a major earthquake which left many dead, ruined many buildings and permanently disabled the hydro-electric plant at Akosombo, subjecting us to an almost universal light-off. Those who could, fled abroad. Others returned to their ancestral villages to live on a diet of cassava. Ghana disintegrated. Brigands ruled. It was our good fortune that they soon ran out of ammunition and could not afford to replenish their stocks.

"Those of us who had stayed, learned to live without the small luxuries we had become accustomed to. No toilet rolls, no toothpaste or toothbrushes, no blades to shave with; no sanitary pads for our women; no condoms for you know what and no talcum powder or nappies for the babies that resulted. And in our vestigial health centers, no drugs, no rubber gloves, no disposable syringes. And, to cap it all, no shoes. That was serious, proper serious, because, without fuel, our cars were morphing into piles of rust in our backyards and there was, of course, no public transport. We had to learn to make our own shoes from old car tires."

"If I had been in your position," I said, "I would have emigrated. Why didn't you?"

"I'm coming to that," Anokye replied.

"Eventually the village people began to organize their own defense. And as the brigands ran out of ammunition and lacked the means to replenish their supplies, they lost their power to terrorize the population. Their guns, too, began to rust."

"What did they do then?" I asked.

"My guess is that, in order to survive, they crawled back to their home villages and resumed their grandparents' rôle as subsistence farmers."

"So, no arms or ammunition, no terrorists?" I asked.

Anokye nodded sagely.

"The ultimate terrorists, you know, are not those who wield the weapons."

"Who then?" I asked.

"Those who manufacture the guns and ammunition and profit from doing so. And those who sanction that manufacture. And we have none of those here."

"Gradually," he continued, "some sort of peace returned to the country. During the Things Fall Apart life expectancy had halved, but the hardiest and luckiest had managed somehow to survive."

"You amongst them," was my superfluous comment.

"Crash, those were traumatic times, times of constant fear, times of hunger. We were witnesses to terrible and terrifying acts of violence, to outrages which every one of us would prefer to forget. I'm not sure which is better for our sanity: collective amnesia or forcing ourselves to face up to the past; you know: remembrance as a healing process. Right now, though, we seem to have opted for amnesia, wiping the past from our memories and concentrating on making something of our future. My guess is that the ghosts of our past will continue to haunt us. One day we shall have to confront them. One day. Not now. Not yet."

There was a knock at the door. I recognized the young

woman as one of the audio technicians who had recorded my deposition in Anokye's office. She apologized for interrupting us.

"Nana, you asked me to call you. They are ready to start," she said.

"OK," he said, "we'll finish the history lesson some other time."

He didn't get a chance, at least not until much later.

"Come on Crash," he said. "Let's go to the theater."

CHAPTER 12

A S WE MADE our way to the courtyard in which I had been tried, Anokye explained.

"Every year," he said, "we have a drama competition. It starts in the villages and works its way up to the national level. The winning troupe is rewarded with a holiday for themselves and their families. And it is my privilege, as patron, to select a cast of the most talented actors to perform a play of my choice. This afternoon we are going to a private dress rehearsal. Next week we'll have a national premiere, with Nana Asantehene and the theatric-loving public of Kumase in attendance. Then the troupe will set off on a national tour."

"What's the play?" I asked, though I knew the answer already.

"I'm sure you know it in English, but I'm not going to tell you what it is," he replied. "This afternoon it will be performed in Asante. Let's see if you recognize it; and how much you understand."

So that's how I sat through a command performance of Shakespeare's Julius Caesar, translated into Asante by one B. Forson, in the palace of the Asante King, with only the King's Chief Linguist and a few technicians for company. I was to see the play several times, but it is this first performance that I remember best. I am not a theatre critic so I am not going to attempt a review. Let me just record that the sets were elementary, the acoustics no more than passable, and the costumes extravagant, Kente cloth serving as an excellent substitute for Roman togas. The performances were entirely convincing and it seemed as if the story might have been extracted from some episode of Asante history. I remembered the play from my school days so I could follow the action. Here and there I could make out a complete sentence and that added to my enjoyment. I spent two hours completely absorbed, transported from my present predicament into another world.

At the end of the performance, Anokye rose to his feet. I followed and together we gave the players a two-man standing ovation. The players applauded us in turn and then called for their producer to join them. This, of course, was the man Opoku, who had explained to me at Bosomtwe why Anokye had selected Julius Caesar for them to perform.

I stood back diffidently while Anokye congratulated him. Then Opoku came to me and embraced me.

"Crash," he said, standing back, "is it you? I never expected to meet you again. Certainly not here. Well, how did you find our show?"

Yaa Amponsah, the feminist agitator, who had played Portia, came over and shook my hand shyly. Anokye came to join us.

"So, Crash, you already know these people?"

I explained and he nodded. Then he clapped his hands for attention.

"My brothers and sisters," he told them. "You have done an excellent job; much better, I am ashamed to tell you, than I expected. Next week you will be performing for Nana Asantehene. This theatre will be full. The people of Kumase will be here to see you. I know that you will do yourselves credit.

"When I selected you for this task and challenged you to do this play, I gave you some inkling of what was in my mind, why I had chosen it. At the time you might still have been unfamiliar with the work and you might not have understood fully what I was talking about. So I want to remind you. After the play is over and you have taken your bows, I would like you to invite members of the audience to come forward and discuss the relevance of Julius Caesar to our present-day concerns. They might at first be shy, but you all now know the play in your bones. So please get things moving. Raise the questions and be free to tell us all what you think. Don't allow yourselves to be inhibited by Nana Asantehene's presence. I can assure you that he will be as interested in a good debate as he will enjoy a good performance of the play."

The next morning I was called to a meeting. We sat around a large conference table, about ten of us. Opoku, the producer of Julius Caesar, was there; so was Boafo. Anokye was in the chair. He had called the meeting, he told us, to discuss the production of a documentary movie based on what he called the American aggression against Asante. He said the aim of the film was to celebrate the Asante victory and so to build up the people's self-confidence.

He asked each of us to introduce ourselves briefly.

When it was my turn, I said, "My name is Ekem Ferguson. I am generally known as Crash. I am a Captain in the U.S. Marine Corps. I was arrested as a result of the part I played in the recent American action. I was tried and found guilty but received a light sentence in return for my agreement to participate in the making of this movie."

"Let me make one thing quite clear at the outset," Anokye said. "This is not going to be a Hollywood blockbuster. Our budget is extremely limited. We will have to decide how to use the existing video footage of the invasion and the dramatic shots which Crash took with the gadget he calls his wristcom. We have the audio tapes of Crash's various statements to me, but no video footage. We have already transcribed those tapes. Those are our basic resources. I am going to resist the temptation to tell you how I think we should proceed. Instead I propose a collective brainstorming leading, I would hope, to a consensus."

It was a long meeting. Boafo was nominated to lead a small team of script-writers. Since much of the screenplay was to be based on a transcript of my statements, I was appointed consultant to this team. Opoku was the natural choice for director, but he was tied up with plans for the national tour of Julius Caesar. The names of others were mentioned but none were received with enthusiasm. The truth of the matter was that there was no one in the country with any experience of making movies. The older generation had emigrated or died out during the Things Fall Apart period.

It was I, Crash, who resolved the issue.

"How about Yaa Amponsah?" I suggested, making my first and only contribution to the debate.

I could see the cogs turning, as if those skulls were made of Perspex.

"Why not?" said Anokye, and "Why not?" they all echoed.

They sent for her.

"She's a talented actress," said Opoku while we waited, "and what she lacks in experience she'll make up with ambition. Good for you, Crash. I hope you won't regret your suggestion."

I did. I did. I lived to regret it.

Two months later the documentary had been completed. The premier was to be at Edweso, on the 150th anniversary of the start of Yaa Asantewaa's War.

Yaa Asantewaa was the Queen Mother of that town. Just a few years after the Brits abducted the young Asante king, Prempeh I, and exiled him to the Seychelles, Queen Victoria's man on the spot demanded that the Golden Stool of Okomfo Anokye and Osei Tutu I be delivered to him. He planned, as representative of the Queen, to demonstrate British sovereignty over Asante by sitting on it. The cream of the Asante aristocracy had been exiled with Prempeh and the remaining chiefs, all of them men, were hesitant. It was the old lady, Yaa Asantewaa, who shamed them into taking up arms against the Brits. So the movie was to be premiered at Edweso in honor of her memory.

The show was due to start at nightfall. There is no cinema, no Saturday night at the movies, at Edweso. Not surprising: there are no cinemas today anywhere in Asante. So they sought out the widest, highest expanse of plastered block wall in the town and gave it a fresh coat of whitewash. That was our screen. Many of the audience had brought their own stools and chairs. The children sat on the ground at the front.

Before the show, there were speeches. The Asantehene spoke, and his chief Okyeame, Nana Okomfo Anokye, did too; as did the elected chief of Edweso and the current queen-mother. An interpreter sitting next to me told me what they were saying but I don't recall a word. I was too nervous, anticipating what was to come. Though no one had seen fit to show me the rushes, I knew enough already.

Boafo and his technical team achieved a wonder of improvisation. They had collected an army of fully charged batteries to provide power and had loudspeakers rigged up on the trees which surrounded the open-air theater.

There was a great cheer as the screen lit up and we watched a countdown, 5, 4, 3, 2, 1. Then the title and credits in Asante and English. The title: 'Asante Kotoko, Kum Apem, Apem Beba' and the sub-title, "A Documentary of the American invasion," against a still of the burning Thunderbirds; and the credits, just: "Directed by Yaa Amponsah and starring Captain Ekem Ferguson, U.S. Marine Corps, aka Crash, Professor Kofi Boafo ('Kofi Kanea'), Kofi Kom."

Behind the credits, there was a view of the ocean taken from the shore. Then the camera panned round, showing first the coconut palms which line the beach and then, in the middle distance, Mpoanokrom. There was a voice over commentary, of which I understood little. Then there was an interview with my old friend Kofi Kom, telling the story of my arrival from his point of view.

The bulk of the script was based on an edited version of my deposition to Anokye. On screen, what we saw was a question and answer session. Yaa Amponsah had taken it upon herself to be the interviewer. I had been given my part in advance with instructions to commit it to memory. Since the original words were my own, I had overcome my reluctance and done what I was told. I had little choice. This was an essential part of my sentence. On screen they had overlaid the English of the original with voices over, Yaa playing herself and some fellow I didn't know speaking my part in Asante. Visually, it was pretty boring stuff, mainly two alternating talking heads. The background did change, though. Parts of the interview had been conducted on location: at Cedar House, in what had been my room there; in Boafo's room, complete with his electronic gear; and up on the roof, where I had had to show how the wristcom worked; at the Fort and in the Stadium.

As an actor, I didn't do too badly: plenty of animation in my expression. As a viewer I got the impression that Crash, the actor, was telling the truth.

Boafo took over for a while, demonstrating his equipment. Then the scene shifted to the Stadium and we watched the holes being dug and charged with explosives.

I made a further appearance, describing how the Thunderbirds would have risen from the deck of the oil platform with their turboprop nacelles aligned vertically, the rotation to horizontal for the flight to Kumase and then back to vertical for the descent into the stadium. I explained my role in guiding the Thunderbirds to their landing targets.

Then, action: the arrival and destruction of the invasion force. A collage of the footage which I had already seen during my trial, together with the shots I had taken with the Wristcom. Then, my capture and the triumphal parade of my inert body around the stadium. The stadium had been empty of spectators, but the audience at Edweso made up for their absence in the volume of their excited cheers.

144

So far, my role had been to offer a factual account of the events, seen from my own point of view. Up to this point, Yaa had stuck pretty well to the script which I had been told to memorize. So far, in my own judgment, I had acquitted myself well, both as an actor and as a prisoner of war. Of course, I was cast as the villain of the piece, but on screen I came across as just another guy, a nice guy indeed. Now, sitting in the front row at Edweso, I began to sweat.

When we had reached the end of the prepared script, Yaa had continued.

"Crash," she had asked, "your natural parents were Africans and so were your foster parents; but you were born in the United States of America. Do you see yourself as an African or as an American?"

"Hey, hold on," I had protested, the camera still running. "That's not in the script you gave me."

At her signal, the camera had panned round to her talking head.

"Crash," she had told me. "I am the Director of this movie. You may be the star but that's as far as it goes. I have a number of questions to ask you. Please answer them as best you can. And I hope you will be truthful. Now I repeat my question, are you an African or an American?"

I won't repeat my stuttering reply here: it's there to be witnessed in the finished movie as is the interview which followed.

Yaa had clearly done her homework. Or someone had done it for her. Anokye? Boafo? I wonder now. At the time I thought she was out to humiliate me. I had an inkling of her strong pro-woman views and I felt then that she was setting me up as part of some strategy, perhaps feminist perhaps not, of which I was only dimly aware. My evasive answers on screen show my nervousness. I was frankly scared of saying anything which would compromise me if and when I returned to the States. The scripted part of the interview dealt with facts. Now my views were being probed.

She recited a list of countries where, she alleged, the United States had indulged in what she called adventures, most of them military, during the past century: Cuba, Haiti, Nicaragua, El Salvador, Grenada, Sudan, Congo, Angola, Libya, Palestine, Iraq, Iran, Korea, Viet Nam, São Tome and Principe, Venezuela, Nigeria . . . I don't remember them all. History never was my strong point. She put me on the spot: was I or was I not in favor of this "adventurism"? Why, she wanted to know, did the United States insist on interfering in the affairs of other states? I was a member of the U.S. armed forces, she reminded me, and a volunteer at that. Did that mean I endorsed the actions of the U.S. government which she had just enumerated?

I wasn't prepared for this onslaught and, frankly, I buckled. I pleaded that I was just a career soldier, that in the Marines we observed the highest standards of conduct, that we were required to learn parts of the old Geneva Convention off by heart, that in our democratic society, political decisions were made by elected politicians; it was the job of the military to implement the orders of the politicians.

"Without question?" she asked.

"Without question," I replied.

Sitting there at Edweso, I saw my performance in this interview for the first time. I began to sob. I don't know why. I felt humiliated. I felt that I had betrayed my country and the Corps. My knowledge of our own history had been put on display and there was only one word to describe it: ignorance. The case she built up against us seemed incontrovertible. Certainly Ekem Ferguson lacked the equipment to contradict it.

Up to this point the audience's reaction had seemed pretty neutral. There had been an occasional hostile cry from some joker, but on each occasion that had elicited no more than a howl of laughter. Now, my on-screen answers began to attract hoots and jeers. I noticed Anokye call aside a group of tough young men. I trusted him implicitly. It struck me that he was taking precautions, acting to protect me in case of trouble. As far as I could see, the men were unarmed. I was scared. As the interview progressed, the hostility of the crowd was palpable. A picture of a lynching, of the corpse of a black man hanging from the branch of a tree floated up from the depths of my memory: *Strange Fruit* again. If I could have run, I might have done so. But where to? On-screen my humiliation went on and on and on.

In the earlier part of the interview, Yaa had addressed me as Crash. Now it was Captain Ferguson. Had I ever killed a man, she wanted to know. How many? What about women and children?

"I want you to tell me the circumstances of each killing," she demanded.

Then she switched to the domestic scene in the U.S. She wanted to know about the Abandoned Territories, how they were run, who lived there, what rights ("if any") the inhabitants had. She asked me about our political system, about who controlled elections, about what she called "the dynasty." She tried to get me to agree that our country is not really a democracy, that it is run by unelected corporate bosses, what she called "gray men lurking in the shadows, oil barons, arms manufacturers, drug dealers." It seemed it would never stop. I sensed that the audience felt she was overdoing it. They seemed restive, even bored. This might have been good politics, but it was bad cinema. But I had underestimated her. Just at this stage she brought the questioning back to Asante.

"You know now that Professor William Franklin was sent here by your government to spy on us, to report back on whether, in the wake of the colonial plunder, we had any material resources left, resources which your corporations might like to exploit. And I believe that you know that the team of African American professionals and experts he brought with him, were innocent dupes."

"That is what I have been told," my alter ego on the screen replied.

"Now what about you," Yaa continued, her face a dark mask, "what was your hidden agenda?"

And so it continued, until the final sequence, run behind a repeat of the credits.

Led by a single drummer, six solemn figures clad in birisi, the deep indigo Asante funeral cloth, carry a wooden coffin at shoulder level; and then another; and yet another. The procession enters the small walled garden which will serve as the final resting place of my brave colleagues. The credits end and the moving picture stops. We are left with a still, a view of a well maintained lawn with an array of eighteen small white crosses, surrounded by walls clad with creepers and a border of crotons, the neatest and prettiest cemetery I have seen in Asante.

CHAPTER 13

THE NEXT MORNING, Sunday, Anokye gave the sermon at a church service. Well, it wasn't exactly a church service; rather it was instead of a church service. And it wasn't exactly a sermon either, although it is true that Anokye's speeches did tend to the didactic.

He started with the customary respectful greetings to the Asantehene (who was present) and the Nananom of Edweso, who, unlike the King, no longer held their titles by virtue of royal descent. Then he paid homage to the memory of Yaa Asantewaa, courageous old woman, anti-imperialist, freedom fighter; but also, as he pointed out, a firm believer in the ancient institution of slavery.

The formalities over, he went on to confront some of his critics.

"A few years back," my interpreter whispered his translation, "on a Sunday like this, the Christians of Edweso would have been worshiping in their separate churches, the Catholics at Mass, the Anglicans and Methodists singing their hymns, the Presbyterians listening to long sermons like mine (laughter), the *Action* and *Lighthouse* people singing and dancing and praising the Lord with Hallelujahs and Amens. Who have I forgotten? *A.M.E…?*"

A voice called, "*Cherubim and Seraphim.*"

Another called, "*Tigari.*"

That brought the house down. I have no idea what kind of

church *Tigari* is or why its name caused such amusement.

Other voices volunteered more names. Anokye tried to keep up, as if taking bids at an auction. He was hamming and the crowd loved it.

"If you measured the size of a town by the number of different denominations of Christianity in it, Edweso would indeed be a large city," he told them. "Perhaps as big as New York."

There was much laughter. My interpreter found it difficult to contain his amusement.

"My brothers and sisters in Jesus Christ," Anokye asked, "can you tell me what it was that divided you? Is there any difference between a Roman Catholic and a Methodist, between Anglicans and Seventh Day Adventists? I mean a difference of importance to us as Asante, as Africans, indeed as human beings? And again, is there any fundamental difference between Christians and Muslims; or between those who find their beliefs in the Bible or the Koran and those of us who pour libation to commune with the spirits of our deceased parents and with our other ancestors?

"Today we are all here, practically every citizen of Edweso, young and old, female and male, and we are united. Oh yes, I know we have our differences and disagreements but we are united in our determination to follow our age-old custom of arguing matters out until we reach a consensus.

"And today nobody will be passing a box or bag around, demanding contributions. Contributions for what? Do I need to tell you?"

"No, no," came the response, but then there was a loud call from the back, "Tell us, tell us."

"I beg you," Anokye responded, "excuse me. There are ministers, pastors, reverend ladies and gentlemen amongst us today. I welcome them. The last thing I wish, is to say something which might embarrass them. Indeed, before we finish today, I plan to invite those of them who so wish to say a short prayer. The Imam too, of course. And I hope that my

150

fellow Okomfo will pour libation.

"In the old days our people used to pour libation at the start of proceedings like this, telling the ancestors what they were doing and asking for the blessing of the unseen ones. The Christians took over the essence of our custom, except it was God whose blessing was sought.

"I deliberately did not do any such thing. And my reasons were two. The first is: it would be divisive. If a Catholic father were invited, the Protestants might be upset. And vice-versa. My second reason: we have many problems. I do not believe that God or Allah or, indeed, our ancestors, are going to help us solve those problems. We are men and women, women and men, each gifted with natural intelligence, each, even our younger brothers and sisters and, indeed, children, with useful experience, each with individual ambitions and desires."

He was serious now and the audience was listening with hushed attention.

"I believe in my own abilities," he said and paused, looking out at us.

Someone began to applaud. He held up a hand for silence. The applause stopped.

"I believe in my own abilities," he repeated, "but I believe just as strongly in the abilities of every single one of you."

"If God, or gods, exist and if they have any business in our daily affairs," he said, "it is because they live amongst us. It was not for nothing that our ancestors gave their supreme being a familiar name. Kwame Nyame, they called him, Onyankopon Kwame, God born on Saturday. Called Kwame just as we call every boy child born on Saturday Kwame. And they called the spirit of the earth, so important for those of us who are farmers, who till the soil and depend on its fertility, they called her Asase Yaa, Thursday's girl-child of the earth."

What emerged from his lecture (for that is what it was) was his lack of faith not only in organized religion but also in representative democracy. He urged every citizen, young and old, to get directly involved in some way in the government of their town, in determining policy, in agreeing priorities. No outside agency, he told them, was going to bring them "quote aid unquote." They could build themselves a better life but they would have to do it themselves, indeed they could only succeed if they were determined to do it themselves.

He did his utmost to instill self-confidence into these people. In my judgment they sorely needed such a pep-talk. Even in their Sunday best they were clearly desperately poor. They showed deep scars of the time they called Things Fall Apart. I could only judge the general standard of education by the English of the few who made pathetic attempts to speak it; and if evidence was needed of how limited their technical skills were, it was there to be seen in the poor quality of their material surroundings.

And yet ...

When the speakers and pray-ers had done their thing, the drummers took over and there was a brass band and the people flocked to dance in the open grassed quadrangle around which they had been sitting; and they danced with such joy and such dignity and such pride, *adowa* and *sese* and highlife, young and old, with such pride, that watching them I was moved almost to tears, considering what I had lost, growing up far away from the land of my natural parents. And I began to think about them again and wonder what had happened to them. Would I ever find out, I wondered.

And then Millicent. I longed for her presence, to show her what I had learned in that place, to lead her out on to that field and dance the steps of my ancestors and hers, too, surely, if she would only acknowledge them. And Fergus and Marilyn. Had they received my letters which Anokye had promised would be posted in the U. S.?

I was sitting all alone now and in my loneliness reflecting on my abysmal performance in Yaa Amponsah's documentary.

Anokye was surrounded by a crowd of people who wanted to talk to him, or listen to him, or just touch his cloth. My interpreter had gone to dance. I could see no one that I knew. I was in no mood to approach a stranger. What if I were recognized as the Crash of last night's movie? I felt deeply depressed. Yaa had asked me who I was. I remember feeling at that moment that I was very much an American, an ugly American, lost in a sea of Africans.

Just then I caught sight of Boafo, dancing expertly, with grace and animation in the company of a pretty young woman, no more than a girl, really, perhaps sixteen or eighteen. Some people have all the luck, I thought. Then he saw me. At once he stopped dancing, took his partner's hand and led her to me.

"Crash, old fellow," he said, very British, "we can't have you acting the wall flower. On your feet and start shaking your body this very moment. Adwoa, this is Crash. He comes from America so you'll have something to talk about. Crash this is my daughter Adwoa, who would be the apple of my eye if she didn't love your country so much."

He took me by my hand, pulled me to my feet and steered me onto the grassy dance floor.

"Uncle Crash," Adwoa asked, in perfect English, "do you know how to dance highlife?" and proceeded to give me a lesson.

Out of the corner of my eye I saw Boafo pushing his way through the crowd surrounding Anokye.

By the time the music stopped, my depression had lifted. Dancing is a wonderful cure for the blues. Adwoa led me in search of her father.

"Crash," said Anokye, taking charge of me, "I have neglected you. Come and stand by me."

He took the microphone and penetrated the buzz of conversation with a call for attention, *"Agôô! Agôô!"*

"Amêê!" came the answer from the crowd.

"My brothers and sisters," he said, speaking in Asante, but

slowly and choosing his words so that I would understand, "I have been guilty of a serious oversight. Most of you will have seen that remarkable film last night. Standing here beside me is my brother, Crash, who was the star of that film. What you saw was a true story and Crash was, in real life, the central performer. He was tried in Nana Asantehene's court and found guilty. He admitted his guilt and told his story without dissimulation. We were lucky and he was lucky: none of our people died in the American invasion. So Nana and his elders chose a relatively light punishment. They required him to act in the film you saw, *Kum Apem, Apem Beba*, and travel round the country with it, answering any questions that might be asked him. We have forgiven him and, on behalf of Otumfuo, I charge you to do the same."

There was some rather unenthusiastic clapping.

"Here too," continued Anokye," is the man who was responsible for the brilliant technical improvisation which enabled us to inflict such a resounding defeat on the invaders, Professor Kofi Boafo, a man of many names. Take your choice: Kofi Kanea, Mansa, Kofi Saman. A man of many names but even more skills: he it was, too, who led the team which wrote the screenplay of the film."

The applause was more enthusiastic.

"Last but definitely not least, I want to introduce you to a very remarkable young woman. As if you didn't already know her. Yaa, where are you?"

Yaa made her way through the crowd, followed by a light-skinned fellow, with a little girl on his shoulder. Anokye took her hand and raised it high.

"I give you Yaa Amponsah, citizen of Edweso," he said, "Winner last year of the national best actress award. Director of *Kum Apem*, in which she also played a leading role as interviewer of Crash. Could we ask for a more distinguished successor to her ancestor, Nana Yaa Asantewaa?"

This time the reaction was deafening: drums, brass, ululations and shouting drowned the hand-claps. A sea of white handkerchiefs fluttered above the heads. Those on the platform gathered around Yaa, raised both hands and pointed their index fingers at her. She beckoned to the light-skinned fellow to stand by her side; and took the little girl from him. Then she held up her free hand for silence.

Her speech was brief. She thanked Otumfuo and Anokye and Boafo and the actors, including me. Then she thanked "my husband, Akwasi Oboadi, formerly known as Robert Service."

Robert Service, I knew the name. A poet. I'd had to learn a piece of his by heart in the eighth grade. It told the story of a *Soldier of Fortune,* 'the last living of my slaughtered band,' who is offered his life by his savage captors if only he will agree to deny his God. An unbeliever, he nevertheless decides to die rather than succumb to dishonor. The last lines came back to me now,

"...Strike! Strike, you dogs! I'll not deny my God.

"I saw the spears that seemed a-leap to slay,

"All quiver earthward at the headman's nod;

"And in a daze of dream I heard him say:

"Go, set him free who serves so well his God!"

And I wondered then whether, in agreeing to lend myself to Anokye's plans, I had sacrificed my honor and that of my country. Perhaps, if I had refused to cooperate, they would nevertheless have released me and let me go home.

My mind was far away as I struggled to recall the words of the poem. There I was again, standing at the front of my class, basking in the applause of my fellows; and, yet again, alone on the stage at the annual school concert. A different world.

Service stood out. It was not his light skin color; there were a few others as light as he; perhaps it was his extremely casual dress and his body language. I knew at once that he was an American.

"Hi," he greeted me. "I'm Bob. And this is Akua. Akua shake hands with the uncle."

Akua, on his hip, held out a shy hand.

"Crash," I introduced myself, though of course he knew my name already. "I'm surprised to hear an American accent here. You are American, I take it."

"Sure thing," he replied, "I'm surprised to hear that you're surprised. Do you have time to talk?"

"I guess so," I said, looking around.

Anokye and Yaa and Boafo were all occupied. Bob caught Yaa's eye. They exchanged signals.

"Do you recognize the music?" Bob asked.

A brass band was playing a catchy highlife tune. I didn't recognize it.

"It's called Yaa Amponsah," he told me. "Nothing to do with my Yaa, though. Hit tune of 1926 or thereabouts. It still gets them dancing. Can you believe it?"

We entered an open-air bar, a ramshackle sort of place with canopies of bamboo and plantain leaves.

"Do you take palm wine?" Bob asked.

We sat down on benches facing each other across a crude wooden table. The palm wine was served in a calabash. As foreigners, I guess, we were privileged to drink out of glasses.

He summoned the proprietor's daughter, handed Akua to her and asked her to take her home to someone called Maansa; and to tell Maansa that there would be a guest for lunch.

"You will eat with us, I hope?"

I nodded. We each took a long draft of the palm wine.

"Your daughter?" I asked.

Bob smiled and nodded.

"Pretty girl," I said and he smiled again.

Bob couldn't have been more than twenty five. He wore khaki shorts, a batakari, the northern smock, and a baseball cap, which he put down on the table. He mopped his brow. We opened our mouths to speak simultaneously.

"You first," he laughed. "Be my guest."

"Well," I said, "you've heard my story. How about yours? How do you come to be in Asante?"

"You mean Nana Anokye hasn't told you?"

"Not a word," I replied.

"I hope this isn't a breach of security, but then Nana saw you with me, so I guess it's OK."

He sipped the palm wine.

"I'm one of the guys you came to look for," he told me.

He must have seen the genuine surprise on my face.

"Robert Service?" I said. "Stupid Crash! I thought I recognized the name, but it was your namesake the poet who came to mind."

"Ah, him," he replied. "But tell me the truth: Nana Anokye gave you no inkling that you would meet me here today?"

I shook my head.

"Well, it seems that he intends you to hear my story, our story, out of my own mouth," he said, "so here goes."

He paused.

"But tell me first. Didn't they give you our names; I mean those who sent you here?"

They had, but the names were in the wristcom and I hadn't taken the trouble to commit them to memory.

"You must have been briefed as to what brought us here. What were you told?" he asked.

I couldn't see any harm in disclosing the briefing I had had in D.C.

"You were a group of twenty scholars," I told him, "mostly recent PhDs, mainly men but with a few women, three or four, I don't remember. Most of you were from M.I.T, a few from other colleges. Your leader was Harvard professor William Franklin. All of you were African Americans. So was Franklin. The Agency presumably thought that blacks would be more acceptable to the Asante. Your mission was to survey Asante's raw material resources and advise its government about export potential.

"You disappeared without trace. My mission was to find

you and advise the best way to bring you all back home."

"An humanitarian rescue mission?"

"If that proved necessary."

"And you thought we were all imprisoned in the Fort in Kumase and that's why you set up the abortive invasion?"

"I didn't set it up," I told him. "The decision was made in Washington. All I did was act as a beacon to guide the force in to the Kumase Stadium."

Bob shook his head in what I took to be disbelief.

"Cretins," he said.

I must have looked puzzled.

"The noble leaders of our nation," he explained, still shaking his head.

"What did they tell you about Franklin?" he asked.

"Distinguished Africanist," I replied. "Historian. Also a linguist with a passing command of Asante. Many friends here, from Ghana days. That's about it."

"The shits," Bob said. "The fucking shits. The fucking malign shits."

"Hold on, hold on," I interjected. "Isn't that a bit heavy?"

"Heavy?" he asked. "Generous, rather. Listen, Crash. If you are being straight with me, they suckered you."

"That's what Anokye told me, but I still find it difficult to believe."

He shook his head again, slowly this time.

"Just listen to me," he said. "As you were told, there were twenty of us, all single except for one couple. We had been selected from a larger pool of volunteers. We had a variety of skills: geologists, mining engineers, surveyors, an agriculturalist, economists. There was supposed to be a doctor on the team but he dropped out at the last moment.

"Our base was to be Obuasi, site of what was once one of the world's richest gold mines. Franklin had underestimated the problems and we had a tough time getting there. The drugs we had with us proved ineffectual and we all suffered from the whole range of tropical diseases. That slowed us down. The idea was that once we got to Obuasi, Franklin would go on to Kumase and clear things with the Asantehene, whom he claimed had once been a buddy of his.

"Soon after we arrived in Obuasi, Franklin died suddenly. Most likely a heart attack. He had had the only computer with a satellite connection. None of us knew the password. After some discussion, we decided that we would all meet, in a school room as it happens, inviting the townspeople Franklin had been dealing with, and collectively examine his files to see if we could find a clue as to how to report home.

"Amongst his possessions we found a small electronic device, no bigger than a wrist watch, which one of our chaps thought he recognized as a gadget used by intelligence. He said it was called a wristcom. One of the girls said that one day, during our trip up, she had come across Franklin unexpectedly, speaking to himself, or dictating, or talking into a satellite phone, she wasn't sure. Seeing her, he had stopped talking at once and tried to cover up. His behavior had struck her as peculiar. She thought she might have seen him putting the wristcom into his pocket. We passed the thing round. It struck us all as some miracle of super-miniaturization but none of us had the foggiest idea how to use it, or, indeed, what sort of technology it was based on.

"Thanks to you and Kofi Kanea, we know a little more now.

"The local Omanhene (that's an elected post now so there's some argument about the title; anyhow: the head of the town committee) took possession of it. He was a retired mining engineer. It seems he sent it up to the University, or what remains of it, in Kumase. We joked amongst ourselves that they'd probably take it apart and then find that they couldn't put it together again."

"Next," he continued, "we went through Franklin's papers, reading each document aloud to those assembled. Then, his computer. Access was password protected, but with twenty of us making suggestions, we soon made the right guess. We read those files aloud, too.

"I'm not going to tell you the details of what we found. I couldn't, since my memory of them is patchy. But our conclusion, our unanimous conclusion, was that Franklin was an intelligence agent, a spy, and that we were the unwitting dupes of his bosses. His mission was indeed to survey Asante's resources, but not to help Asante. The question he was to answer was whether there was anything here of sufficient value to justify the establishment of an American base and what action would be required to achieve that."

"That's more or less what Anokye told me," I interrupted. "But it still sounds far-fetched. We are not, never have been, an imperialist nation."

"Come off it, Crash," he protested. "That might be the version of history they teach you in the Marines. Believe me, it is far from the truth."

He paused and then apologized.

"Look, I'm sorry. You're my guest. I didn't mean to insult you. Yaa has already given you a hard time and the record of that is cast in stone; or its digital equivalent. Anokye asked us to go easy on you."

I inclined my head. Had Anokye set up this invitation? I wondered why he would have done that.

"Getting back to my story," Bob went on, "the Obuasihene and his elders had heard it all and it was their view, not surprisingly, that Franklin's material put us under suspicion. They helped us to bury the professor and then sent us all to Kumase under armed guard."

"To the Fort?" I asked.

"That's right," he replied.

So my drunken friend wasn't just fantasizing, I thought.

"They treated us OK," he continued. "The conditions were Spartan and it took us a little time to get used to eating African food, morning, noon and night, but all in all we had no complaints. They even gave us books to read, including some on American history which you might find interesting.

"They interrogated us, individually and in a group, but without aggression. Nana Anokye was one of the interrogators, though we didn't then know who he was.

"My guess is that our quarters were bugged but we had nothing to hide, so that was no sweat. We had plenty of time to get to know one another. The single girls selected their partners, to the regret of those of us who didn't make it.

"We talked and talked and talked. There were clear political differences amongst us. We fell into three broad camps. One group was inclined to excuse Franklin and his handlers on the grounds that they were acting in America's best interests. The second lot had had little previous interest in politics but were outraged at the cynical way our trust had been abused. Franklin was a man for whom they had had deep respect and they were now completely disillusioned. The last group I call the secret radicals. Secret, because if the selection panel had been aware of our views we would never have been included in the party. Radical, because we go along with the view that American politics is a sham. We see the American government as serving the interests of the big corporations, transferring dollars from the pockets of poor and middle class tax payers into those of the corporate bosses and others of their class.

"We were all surprised that Franklin had allowed himself to be bought, but beyond that all the evidence fitted into the broad picture as we saw it. Those in the other two groups found it impossible to contradict the evidence and even the 'Americans' eventually came round to our point of view.

"The Asante invited us to write one letter each, just to tell the folks back home that we were alive and well. They read them in our presence but didn't ask for any changes. They undertook to have the letters delivered but I still don't know whether they did, since none of us have had replies. But then there is hardly a courier system as we know it working here.

"After a couple of months, the enforced idleness and uncertainty about our future began to work on us and we began to quarrel. It was at this stage that Nana Anokye…"

The proprietor's daughter returned carrying Akua, Bob's daughter, on her back

Screwing up her eyes in concentration, she recited the message Yaa had sent her to deliver. Lunch was ready.

Bob put Akua on his back and I followed them down eroded alleys between adobe walls.

Bob's house was a simple single-story building arranged around a square open courtyard. The entrance door was open.

"Akua Maame, we are here," Bob called, putting his daughter down.

Yaa came out into the courtyard, wiping her hands on a cloth, and curtsied. She must have been pulling my leg, doing that. I put out my hand and she took it.

"My name's Crash," I said.

She smiled. A warm genuine smile which suggested to me that she had worked through her outrage and anger. Guiltily, I recalled my dreams of her.

A table had been laid in the shade.

Maansa, who turned out to be Yaa's younger sister, brought us water to drink and then a basin with soap and a slice of lemon to wash our hands. Bob invited her to join us but she declined.

"Maansa doesn't have much English," Bob said and then said something to her in Asante which I didn't understand.

"I hope you eat fufu," Bob asked as Maansa brought the bowls. "Now where was I?"

"Anokye," I helped him.

"Ah, yes. Nana Anokye came to talk to us. He told us that their investigation had shown us all to be innocent parties who had been used in a shameful manner by our government, with the active complicity of the late Professor Franklin. There were voices, he told us, that maintained that in spite of the not-guilty verdict, we were a potential security risk and should be kept in detention indefinitely; or sent home.

"When some had protested that this would be both illegal and unjust, others had brought examples from history to prove that the American government itself had set precedents in the past, detaining perceived enemies without trial on the grounds that they would be a threat to the state if allowed their freedom. On the other hand, he told us that one of their number, an historian, had suggested that Asante was in some way indebted to us, since it was their ancestors who had sold our ancestors to the Europeans as slaves.

"Anokye reviewed all these arguments at some length and then asked us whether we had anything to say. I spoke for our group. I apologized for what our government had done and condemned Washington for using us in the way it had. I said we put ourselves in the hands of the Asante government and would agree to do whatever they proposed. I didn't really have a mandate to say that, but I decided on the spot that we really had no choice.

"Nana then said that he had a proposition to make to us. He said, 'We recognize you as our long-lost brothers and welcome you home to Africa. On behalf of Nana Asantehene, I invite you to make your homes here, either for a temporary, open-ended period, or indefinitely, until,' he said with a laugh, 'you meet your six feet.'

"He said, 'I recognize the positive effect of having people from a different culture in our midst. You might help to stimulate new thinking and suggest solutions to problems which now seem intractable.'

"He told us that they had initiated a bold social project in Asante, in which every single citizen was encouraged to participate, without regard to gender, ethnicity, family origin, age or disability. It was a project based on a realistic appraisal of Asante's poverty following years of epidemics, disasters and war; but also of its potential to provide every citizen with a modest level of life-long security. It was not, like the so-called free-market capitalism in which we had grown up, based on the worst aspects of the human psyche: greed, a hunger for power, extreme individualism. On the contrary it was based on mutual support; on cooperation rather than competition.

"He said that he recognized the wide range of skills which we had to offer and he asked us to agree to put these at the disposal of Asante. He said he didn't have the resources to offer us American style salaries; and even if he had the resources he wouldn't make such an offer because it would undermine the principles upon which the new society was being built.

"He suggested we go into caucus and subject his proposal to a tough, critical appraisal before accepting or rejecting it. He warned us frankly against adopting a romantic view of Africa. He said that he was aware, from previous experience, that there could be serious problems in communication between Africans and African-Americans. Where Africans found themselves in America, they had to adapt themselves; no one questioned that. He asked us to recognize that if we were to accept his proposal we might have to pass through a difficult and frustrating process of adjustment; and that there might be times when we felt homesick and just wanted to get the hell out.

"He thought that if we accepted his offer, it would help us to integrate into Asante society if we were widely dispersed, the only exception to this being, of course, couples who were married or intending to marry. But, he promised, we would have the opportunity to gather at regular intervals to discuss our several experiences and to share them with our Asante brothers and sisters.

"That was one of the most moving speeches I have ever heard. I can tell you that I was in tears as I listened to him. At the end he took his leave, saying that he preferred postponing answering questions until we had had an opportunity to discuss his proposal amongst ourselves.

164

"Several meetings later we all agreed to accept Nana's offer. He travels the country regularly, encouraging good work, pointing out deficiencies and, most important, stimulating the widest possible participation in the political process. He asked us to be patient so that he could take us along with him on these trips and introduce us personally to the people who would be our hosts."

Maansa had joined us and Akua came to sit on her lap. Yaa mimed tears at her daughter's preference for her young aunt. Akua climbed down and went to comfort her mother.

"I was the last to leave the Fort," said Bob. "Now, with the help of Yaa and Maansa and Akua and their extended family, I'm half-way to becoming an Asante."

"What do you do here?" I asked.

"I trained as a geographer and land surveyor," he replied. "During the fighting, the Survey Department in Accra was burned down. The country was left virtually without maps. My job is to survey this district. Technology has moved on since the original maps were made. Fortunately I brought a good system with me and I have an old but usable computer; and a good team of local advisers who tell me the meaning of what I see on the ground.

"In the old days, there was no private ownership of land here. The Edwesohene held the ownership of all land in his domain in trust. He had the right to allocate land, but for use only. With the westernization of the economy that gradually changed. However they never had comprehensive maps tied to boundary pillars on the ground showing who owned what. Now that has become irrelevant. Under the new dispensation ownership of the land has reverted to the Edwesohene. The only difference is that that has become an elective post and the incumbent has to submit himself to re-election at every monthly town meeting. Re-election is usually a formality, but if we slipped up and gave the job to the wrong man, we would have plenty of opportunity to change our minds and our Chief."

"Sounds unworkable to me," I said.

"Well, there's a town meeting tomorrow. If you can stay over, you'll see how things work. And they do work, after a fashion, an African fashion. It can be frustrating for a westerner, used to our standards of efficiency, but provided there is no urgency, and there seldom is, it seems tuned to their needs. Or should I say our needs?" and he smiled at Yaa.

Akua had fallen asleep and Maansa went to put her down.

"Let's go and look for Nana and see what plans he has for you," Bob said.

CHAPTER 14

THE TOWN MEETING was held in a church, a simple building, designed for the tropics, dark and cool inside, with window openings on the shady north and south facing walls, window openings without glass.

The chief called the meeting to order and an elder poured libation. The secretary read the agenda and the minutes of the previous meeting following procedures which I suppose are common all over the world. The chief intervened to note the presence of a visitor and to tell me that I was welcome and should feel free to participate.

Then the elected elder responsible reported on the successful arrangements for the events of the past weekend. Another elder reported on maintenance work on the town's public buildings and a third on problems in implementing urgently needed improvements to the town's water supply and sanitation.

The chairman of the committee of school principals bemoaned the shortage of school furniture and urged the chief carpenter to speed up manufacture and delivery. He announced that Nana Anokye had promised to send them a stack of old correspondence files salvaged from the Ministries offices in Kumase.

"The printing is only on one side of the paper, so our children can write on the back," he explained.

The chief intervened to say that Anokye had told him that university people were working with the fitters in Suame

Magazine to develop a machine which would manufacture paper from agricultural waste.

"In the old days," he said, "we imported all our paper. Now we have no choice but to find a way to make our own."

The elder in charge of sports was next. He was heavily criticized because of the poor performance of the town football team in a recent match against the neighboring town Dwaben.

Bob reported on the progress of his mapping team.

"What use will these maps be to us?" someone asked from the floor.

I ribbed Bob after the meeting, suggesting that he had set the questioner up to give him a chance to deliver a lecture. He just smiled.

And so it went on, much like the meeting of a local council practically anywhere. Pretty dull stuff if, like me, you knew nothing of the background. If there was a striking difference perhaps it was that this one was open to all the citizenry. It was well attended and several of those present showed no inhibitions about making complaints and offering suggestions. Nothing special; just grass roots democracy at work. The only difference I suppose was that at the end of the meeting the chief submitted himself and each of the elders to a vote of confidence.

The sports minister was voted out of office and replaced by his strongest critic.

My traveling days began. Opoku had gathered a team of technicians to set up the solar panels to charge the batteries. The batteries were heavy and transport was a problem. Until we acquired our own horse a month later, we had the push and pull a cart loaded with our gear from village to village. Opoku would cycle to the next village a few days in advance and get the chief and his people working on the preparations for our arrival and the film show. I kept as low a profile as possible.

Every able-bodied person, young and old, is expected to do some agricultural work or other manual labor every week.

In theory at least, none are exempt, not even the Asantehene himself, not even Anokye. Not even Crash. Often, when I was stuck in some place, idle, waiting to move on, or waiting for a weekend show, I would be the subject of a mild argument. Some, often older folk, would argue that the rule didn't apply to me. Others would insist that there was nothing special about me that entitled me to a free meal at their expense. I soon learned to cut the talk by volunteering. Doing so earned me respect and acceptance. Then when some old greybeard persisted in referring to me as Oburoni, one of his fellows would reprimand him.

In the months that I spent traveling around the country I became a jack of all trades. The simpler ones, like manipulating a cutlass to clear undergrowth or a hoe to weed, or harvest cassava or yam, I mastered at no more cost than aches in muscles I hadn't known I possessed. Where the tasks required more training, I learned, at least, to recognize my own limitations and to admire the skills of the experts. Both my successes and my failures, I have to say, were treated with great good humor. I learned to make the mud balls used in the technique of building house walls which I believe we call *pise-de-terre* or adobe and they call *atakpame*. I operated a leather bellows for a blacksmith and hammered the red-hot steel on the old engine block which he used as an anvil; and I operated a smaller bellows for a goldsmith who was making brass buttons using the lost-wax technique. Once I joined a gang smoking out a swarm of bees which had established a hive in the wrong place. I helped to gather kola nuts and carry a head-load back to the village. That was one of the hardest tasks. These people have carried buckets of water on their heads from early childhood, boys and girls, both. Their neck muscles are made of steel. I soon discovered that, fit as I was, mine were made of jelly.

Most often I used an ax to cut firewood or a pickax to dig ditches. At first my hands got badly blistered, but that, too, passed.

Much of the most strenuous physical work was accompanied by song. I have stored away in the computer in my skull a whole repertoire of Asante work songs. And now I understand, right down in my guts, as I never did before, the roots of the music of the old South, of blues, of jazz.

There are some jobs that grown men seldom do. I caused a great deal of merriment by insisting on learning to pound fufu with a pestle and, more dangerous, to turn the ball of fufu in the mortar with one hand, in between the blows of the pestle.

In the course of my professional career, in the course of military duty, I have killed people; once in an extreme situation, to save my own life, I killed a terrorist with a knife. Yet it took me many attempts to learn to cut the throat of a cockerel; and when at last, I could perform that task without retching, I had the same problem dispatching a goat and then butchering it. Of all the skills I learned, those are the ones which give me the least pride. You wouldn't think it but slaughtering farm animals made me ponder my past life as a Marine. And spoiled my appetite for meat.

I wonder whether this insistence on the regular performance of some strenuous productive activity was not Anokye's most important contribution to life in the new Asante. I would return to my simple lodgings fatigued, sweating, dirty. After bathing with a bucket and a jug and putting on a clean shirt, I would feel refreshed and at peace with myself. In the Marines we do plenty of exercise, running, climbing, working out, but none of it produces anything except muscles.

In our society, the "jack of all trades, but master of none" is not someone we admire. Their attitude was different. They were in the process of recovering not only old skills but old attitudes to skill. It was the white man, Anokye told me, who introduced specialization, so that in Ghana days, as in the U.S., a carpenter might refuse to do the work of a mason, and vice-versa. In Asante today, everyone who has a skill, of whatever description, is expected to be a teacher, to share his skills with those around him. There is some specialization, but it coexists with a diffusion of expertise, throughout the society, regardless of age or gender.

There is hardly a village in Asante which does not have a football field. The last hour before sunset is often taken up with an informal game. Saturdays and Sundays there may be as many as four games played through the day: men, women, youngsters of various ages: all play. There are leagues for each with maybe a dozen teams competing and the local team traveling to nearby villages at weekends.

The fields are nothing to write home about, often on a slope. The maintenance, such as it is, is done by the players themselves. The less said about jerseys and boots, the better. Sometimes when a penalty is awarded, the player will call out "Boots," and the team's only pair of boots will make an appearance.

The line markings and goal posts and netting were rudimentary. The balls, made by a factory in Kumase, were often old and much repaired. The referees and linesmen were self-taught and the rules seemed to vary from place to place. Spectators who were not prepared to sit on the ground or stand, brought their own stools.

To start with, I was struck by all these problems; but like the players, I soon learned to ignore them. No one is paid and there are no prospects of glory and riches as a professional, even for the most talented players. They play for pleasure and exercise and delight in demonstrating team work and individual brilliance.

I often had to wait several days in a village either before or after a show. Once I had done my stint of labor I still had time on my hands and might find myself watching a scratch game. In the States my playing days were over and when I was first invited, half in jest, to join in as a substitute, I hesitated. I was anything but football fit but I hadn't quite lost the skills learned back home. At my first attempt I scored a rather dramatic, if somewhat lucky goal. That gained me many instant friends and admirers. The following day I found myself running a coaching session. My reputation ran ahead of me and the local soccer committee often sought me out as soon as they heard of my arrival at a new location. Sometimes I had a chance to play before the show and then my football friends might have difficulty in separating Crash the footballer from Crash the movie's American aggressor.

Anokye must have been keeping tabs on my progress because when we met once by chance or design (his, not mine) two or three months into my travels, he greeted me thus: "Hey, my brother, what do I call you, Crash Ferguson or Abedi Ababio?"

Abedi Pele, I learned, was the name of a legendary Ghanaian football hero from the days when the Black Stars of Ghana had an international reputation. Someone had been spreading a superstitious rumor that I was his reincarnation, Abedi Ababio, Abedi has come again.

Football wasn't my only diversion. Thinking back, I am astonished at how fully occupied I was during the days I spent in what seemed at first to be remote and desperately poor villages.

I was intent on improving my command of the language. A good way to do this, I found, was to ask permission to visit the village school. The kindergarten classes were run by grandmothers who took great pleasure in bossing the gray bearded grandfathers who were required to act as their assistants. Many of these old people could neither read nor write, but each of them had a great store of folk tales and songs and many of them, the men anyway, were expert drummers. So even before the children entered the primary school they could tell a whole range of Ananse stories. As for dancing, I believe that they had all learned to dance while still strapped to their mothers' backs. The old folk spoke to the children in simple language they could understand, and I could too, mostly.

Then it would be my turn to be teacher. I would recite Little Bo Peep and Intsy Wintsy Spider and they would have great fun learning the words off by heart to the extent of mimicking my accent, even before I was able to come up with an Asante translation.

Then I would be invited to give an English lesson to the older children. I guess that I was often the first native English speaker they had come across and they had not a little difficulty understanding me as, indeed, I had understanding them.

Each school had its own farm nearby. There the grandfathers, experienced farmers most of them, would pass on their agricultural and husbandry skills to the older children. Their skills weren't based on science but on long experience and they knew what worked and what didn't. So the school farm was able to supply the school kitchen with corn and plantain and cocoyam; bananas and oranges; and occasionally eggs or even, for a special occasion, chicken.

The kitchen equipment was elementary, pots set on open fires, but the mothers and grandmothers who worked there managed to serve the children a morning snack and a simple midday meal.

These tasks, within the village, kept the young and the old occupied. The able bodied adult men and women worked on the village farms and on communal construction and maintenance jobs and craft work. All this went on without money. It was the job of the chief and elders to see that everyone had work to do and that no one went hungry. How different from the wage economy I had lived in all my life.

Late one afternoon, heading for a new district tour, I got stuck in Edweso and decided to call on Yaa and Bob in the hope that they would offer me a bed for the night.

"Crash," said Bob, "we're just off to the library and we're late. Dump your bag and join us."

The library turned out to be one of the town's many churches.

Up front, to one side, there was a pulpit, occupied by a middle-aged woman. She was testing a microphone ("testing, one, two, three, four") which, like her reading lamp, was powered by a battery. Behind a table, center front, there stood a man, dressed in cloth. I guess there were thirty worshipers, about half near the pulpit and the rest near the man.

"Funny sort of library," I said to Bob as we sat down in the second row, near the pulpit. "Where are the books?"

"Wait," he said.

Maansa, who had come with us, went off to the other group. Little Akua clung to her mother. Bob and Yaa whispered greetings to the congregants near us.

It was some time since I had attended a church service and I was quite looking forward to renewing my acquaintance with the Lord. However, while I was pondering why Bob had taken me to church on patently false pretenses, I discovered that I would have to postpone my meeting with our heavenly Father.

Almost as soon as we had settled down, the woman began. No hymns, no sermon, no chapter and verse; or at any rate, no verse, but chapter: yes. What she read, in English, was a chapter from a book.

The book, I gathered, was a memoir of childhood, set in the Yoruba city Ibadan in the mid twentieth century. The woman read with expression, eliciting laughter and at one point even applause from the audience. After every couple of sentences she paused and the man in cloth, who also had a mike, improvised a translation into Asante.

When the woman had finished the chapter, she said, "We'll take a short break now and then the floor will be open."

"Well, Crash," Yaa said, taking my hand, "what a pleasant surprise. How are you? And where have you been?"

I wanted to ask about the reading but she wouldn't give me a chance. I had to report my itinerary, popular reaction to the movie; and how that reaction was feeding back into my own consciousness and conscience.

As the lady reader climbed the three steps to the pulpit, I said to Yaa, "I wanted to ask you about the book she read from."

"Ask Sister Grace," Yaa advised.

"The floor is open," Sister Grace announced.

Yaa prodded me.

"Go on," she said, but I hesitated, a little shy.

Yaa stood up.

"Sister Grace," she said, "we have a visitor. If you saw my movie a couple of months back, you'll remember Crash, who starred in it. He arrived at our house just as we were leaving so we didn't have a chance to tell him what this is all about. Would you like to do that?"

Grace led into her reply with an effusive welcome. Then she explained that they were trying to address the problem of a dire shortage of books by ensuring that their small stock was used to maximum advantage. It didn't make sense to let books sit on shelves in Kumase while there was a hunger for them in the rest of the country. So the books circulated from village to village and they were read aloud, chapter by chapter, for those who cared to listen. When they had finished their reading of this book they would send it on to Dwaben.

"Before the white man arrived on our shores with his language and his books," Grace said, "our ancestors would sit around the fire at night and tell stories. We are reviving that age-old oral tradition. You see, reading a book, alone, silently, is alien to our custom. It's a Western thing. Here we are getting the best of both worlds. We select finely written works, which are of interest to us and are relevant to our condition; and we share them by reading them aloud. Then, quite often, we discuss what we have read. As you have seen, we also offer an instant translation when the work we are reading is in a language most of us don't understand. The very act of translation hones the storytelling skills of the translator. So Osei, here, has become one of our finest original story-tellers. And we find that our discussions tend to stimulate the story-telling ambitions of the rest of us."

For the twelve months in which I served my sentence, I was on the move constantly. A few days in *Nyame Bekyere* ('The Lord will provide'); a week in *Nkwanta* ('Crossroads'); a weekend in *Brofo ye Duru* ('You can't beat the white man'). Small towns, big villages, small villages.

I could write a book about the unique social experiment that is going on in those parts; and maybe I will. But now I only have time for some broad impressions.

The program of Anokye and his group seems to have been accepted throughout the country. This puzzled me. How did they manage to reach the whole populace with practically no modern means of communication? I can only hazard a guess: the ideas must have been there already, embodied in shared values, perhaps with deep roots in the past. If this hunch is correct Anokye's genius was merely to recognize and articulate these ideas in a way that elicited an enthusiastic response.

I hope I'm not getting out of my depth here. I did just one sociology course at college. That was a long time ago; and my aim then was to get a credit, not to understand the subject. Nothing of what I recall from that course helps me to make sense of what I experienced. So, bear with me.

I identify just two basic principles in their society, and these are interlinked: a collective social responsibility and a rich spiritual life. Democracy, in the meaning we give to that word, does not exist in Asante. Paradoxically, democracy in the sense they give to the word, pervades practically every aspect of their daily life.

Their political units are small. Within those units, there is almost universal participation and much unrestricted discussion, both formal and informal, on any and every issue of concern to them. There is also a regular monitoring of the performance of elected leaders. Those who fail to produce results run the risk of being voted out of office at the next monthly meeting. Apart from a tiny minority of Maxwells, I doubt whether any Asante man or woman

176

feels borne down by a weight of oppression. And even the Maxwells' freedom to organize and propagate their views is unrestricted.

There are limits on freedom there, again using the word as we understand it. I didn't come across a single rich Asante in all the time I was in their country. Production hovers about the subsistence level. If the rains are good, nobody goes hungry. If the rains are poor, most do. There is little surplus available for trade and such trade as there is, is often based on barter. The modern banking system which existed in Ghana, collapsed and has yet to be revived. There is no national currency and no source of investment capital. In a good year they build up stocks of non-perishable crops and invest their spare labor hours in improvements to their capital stock, infrastructure, housing and so on. In this primitive economy, the only way to get rich would be to impose forced labor on the populace. Even if the Asantehcne wanted to do this (and he certainly does not) he lacks the coercive power. So the freedom to accumulate wealth and power is constrained by the harsh realities of economic conditions.

That said, I saw no restrictions on the achievement of what the Asante regard as socially legitimate ambitions. Ambition and competitive drive are valued; however the rewards of success are not material wealth but social approbation.

This is a society so totally different from anything we are used to in the West that, for someone who hasn't experienced it, as I have, it might be difficult to conceive.

Anokye asked me once, "What does a human being need?" and then he answered his own question: "The material things: food, water, clothing, shelter. The immaterial things: love and companionship, spiritual peace, intellectual stimulation, a sense of security. What else?"

"Good health?" I suggested and he nodded.

The new Asante has proved, to my satisfaction at least, that it is possible to live a reasonably good life in conditions of what we would regard as extreme material poverty.

I wonder what my old sociology prof. would have given me for that little essay. Probably no grade at all. I can see the words "arrant Utopian nonsense" scrawled in red across my returned paper.

CHAPTER 15

T HE YEAR OF my sentence passed quickly. By the time it was over, I was fluent in Asante and something of an expert in the geography of the country and the condition of its roads. And spending at least two days every week wielding a hoe or an ax or preparing adobe had done my body no harm.

Anokye had come to end of his period of office and had handed over to his successor. I gladly accepted his offer to accompany me to the coast. But first there was the surprise farewell party. It took place in the same courtyard at the palace where I had seen the dress rehearsal of Julius Caesar and where I had been tried and found guilty. Practically everyone I had got to know well was there, including all twenty Americans. And there too, Anokye introduced me to his wife for the first time.

While I was talking to her, I heard someone say, "Master Crash, *wo ho te sen?*"

"Bra Kwadwo, *awaawaawa,*" I replied.

"*Atuu,*" he laughed.

And we went on to have a conversation in Asante, in which he revealed that Anokye was his son, that is to say, a distant relative..

Bob and Yaa were there, Opoku, Kofi Kanea of course and many more. The Asantehene did me the honor of making a farewell speech.

"Crash, *nante yiye,*" he said at last, Crash, go well.

We traveled on horseback, first to Bekwai and then retracing my journey with Kofi in the reverse direction.

On the first day Anokye was unusually taciturn. I rode up alongside him and looked across, hoping he would want to talk, but he appeared deep in thought. I wondered whether he was unhappy about having given up his office as the Asantehene's *okyeame*. I had asked him about this some weeks before and he had laughed, claiming that he would be happy to be free from the responsibility. He was looking forward, he said, to going back to life as a simple farmer and teacher. Now I wondered whether he had been entirely honest.

Once or twice, he turned to me, opened his mouth and licked his lips and I sensed that there was something he wanted to say. But on each occasion he seemed to think better of it. There were questions which I wanted to ask him, too, but I decided to defer them until he was in a better mood.

On the second day he seemed more relaxed.

"A year ago," I reminded him, "you were giving me a history lesson…"

"Ah yes," he said, "We were interrupted by a call to the theater. OK. We have plenty of time now."

I said I would have like to have made some notes. He replied that it was too late for that now. So, riding side by side, on a broad, empty highway through the forest, he gave me this lecture, which I later recorded from memory. He spoke in Asante, but slowly, asking me from time to time to confirm my understanding.

"I'm going to tell you how we emerged from the era of Things Fall Apart," he said.

"Our intellectual class, those of us who had refused to attempt escape, or those whose attempts to do so had failed, lived in a climate of deep despair. I know: I was among, as we say. Looking back, I can see that those of us at the University were still privileged. There was no central authority to expel us from our bungalows, on which we no longer paid rent. Our library had survived, after a fashion. The university grounds had been generously planned and we had no problem finding land to farm.

"So my wife and I spent part of our day growing cassava and plantain and corn; and looking after chickens and goats and, later, pigs. Our remaining colleagues likewise. And we pooled our time and skills in educating our children, hoping, though with little confidence, for better days.

"In the early years, we were all exhausted by the sheer physical and mental effort needed for survival. But as our bodies hardened, our spirits rose.

"Then one of our number developed an illness which made it impossible for him to farm. He was mentally alert so we delegated some of our teaching load to him and took responsibility for the material support of his family. Initially there were some grumbles, but he was a good teacher and our children loved him, so even the malcontents came round to the view that we had got ourselves a bargain.

"Gradually, professional intellectuals that we all were, we began to analyze our experience and ask whether we couldn't find in it the seeds of a solution to the broader problems of our collapsed society. We were more prosperous than we had been for a long time: the rains had been good for a few years running and we were also becoming more competent farmers. We decided to send out scouts to travel the country and listen to what ordinary people were thinking and saying.

"We found, the years of better crop yields notwithstanding, a mirror of our despair, together with a confused nostalgia for an imagined past, not for the years of Ghana, not for the years of colonialism but for the years of Asante power. At the same time (and this is symptomatic of the confusion) the churches were full. Their ministers had become rich, at least relatively rich, on tithes. With the collapse of the central state they were the principal tax collectors. There were murmurings of discontent but they kept control with promises of blessings and miracles; and threats of eternal damnation. There were still chiefs and elders in most villages but they had little influence; the old structures were a hollow shell.

"Then we began to test popular response to the ideas which were emerging in our caucus. We built up a network of sympathizers all over Asante and we listened to what they had to say. We had our own internal differences but on one principle we were all agreed: this had to be a grass roots movement. We lacked the resources to start a top-down old style political party, let alone rebuild our collapsed state. What is more, those who remembered Ghana days still regarded politicians with deep suspicion.

"We made one exception to this rule. We agreed, some of us reluctantly, that we needed a strong symbol to attract and hold support from those who might find it difficult in the early stages to adopt our ideas. This being Asante, that symbol could only be the Golden Stool; and its custodian, the Asantehene. The last holder of that office, the eighteenth Asantehene, Nana Osei Kwadwo II, and the Queenmother, had both been assassinated during the civil war, together with many of the other royals and their supporting bureaucracy. At the same time the Golden Stool of Osei Tutu and Okomfo Anokye had disappeared. Without these symbols of unity, what was left of Asante as a political entity had disintegrated. We started a search.

"One of our group, Dr. Yaw Mensah, was an eligible (and obvious) candidate. However he was by conviction an incorrigible rationalist and anarchist and, as such, totally opposed to any form of monarchy, whether constitutional or merely symbolic. He rejected our proposal outright. So we set ourselves up, by our own authority, as traditional Asante king-makers. We interviewed every member of the Oyoko clan we could find who was remotely related to the old royal family. The criteria we used were firstly those which would ensure acceptability to the Asante populace. These are appropriate lineage and the traditional qualities of charisma, absence of a criminal record, good health and freedom from disability or physical blemish. The second criterion we used was totally at odds with tradition and we kept it close to our chests. We were looking for someone who would be totally committed to our program. We needed to be sure that the new Asantehene would be our own man and that, once enstooled, he would not attempt to re-assert the traditional rights of his office.

"In spite of our best efforts we failed to find a single suitable candidate. I was then deputed to attempt to persuade Yaw to reconsider his position. I succeeded. His agreement was subject to several conditions, principally his refusal to revive traditions which he regarded as archaic and based on superstition. He agreed to take the stool name of Osei Tutu III as a symbol of a new beginning.

"We had then to decide what to do about the Golden Stool. As a student I had been an enthusiastic and active member of the University Dramatic Society. I suggested to Nana that we have a new Golden Stool made and that we put on a performance which would replicate the descent of the original from heaven into Nana Osei Tutu's lap, but in a way that would subvert the mystical elements. We put a small boy in a tree at Pimpimso, where tradition tells us that the original ceremony took place in 1698, and had him lower the new Golden Stool into Nana's lap. The nylon string was practically invisible in the dusk, but when Nana had received the stool onto his lap, we had a spotlight reveal the small boy hidden in the foliage. The performance was a resounding success and after consecration of the new *Sikadwa* we had to repeat the performance in each of our main towns.

"That is how I acquired the honorable nickname of Okomfo Anokye."

"Excuse me, but what is your real name?" I asked.

"Never mind," he replied, somewhat abruptly, "Anokye will do. That is my real name now."

He continued, "Nana appointed me as his first *Okyeame* and *Gyasehene*, effectively his Chief of Staff and Prime Minister. I served for a year and then gave way to a colleague. Five years have passed and I have completed my second stint. That is a defect in our program: this appointment is so clearly top-down and effected, moreover, by a clique which is responsible to none but our own collective conscience. That is one of our current concerns.

"But let me return to my appointment as Okyeame. I spent the next six months traveling the country, from town to town and village to village. Those who hadn't seen the performance with Nana receiving the new Golden Stool had heard of it, of course. That gave me an opening everywhere. My message was simple. We could depend on no one but ourselves. There would be no material help from Kumase and certainly no foreign aid. We could succeed in transforming our lives, I told them, but only with the direct, active involvement of every citizen, including the elderly, including children and adolescents, including, particularly, women. I warned against the dangers of delegation of powers, against the greedy and power hungry, the Maxwells of this world. I recommended frequent town meetings, involving the whole population. I suggested the qualities to look for in local leaders: selfless dedication to the common good, humility, a readiness to listen, an openness to new ideas. And I set them an ambitious practical agenda: good drinking water and sanitation; adequate food supplies for all, sensible land management, health, care for the sick and aged, education at all levels, sports, entertainment, policing, structures for the resolution of disputes. Then I would get them to elect a temporary chairperson to manage the discussion which followed. And I would sit back and listen. In some places that first meeting continued for several days. In some places the elderly men initially dominated the talk, in some places the young men. We intervened to draw in the women, warning them that they would have only themselves to blame if they failed to participate, encouraging them to raise issues that seemed to be neglected, or even taboo. We did our best to identify people whom we might recruit for tasks in the broader district and regional and national fields. Sometimes we were excited by the contributions, sometimes disappointed and depressed.

"Slowly we built up teams to do the job I had initiated, both from within our core group and with talented recruits. We would send them to each town or village to follow up my visit, assessing progress, always listening, learning. Meanwhile

Nana was working with Kumase, which because of its size and residual population, had somewhat different problems to solve.

"After six months we called a national conference to review progress and exchange ideas. Representatives came from all over the country. There was tremendous enthusiasm. The energy had always been there, it seems, but latent. We had succeeded in sparking it into action. We were thrilled to greet delegations from places which we hadn't yet been able to reach. It seems that we had invented a form of spontaneous political combustion."

He paused.

Then he said, "That's it. End of history lesson. Though not the end of our history. That is still being made. Any questions?"

"Have you ditched the idea of modernization?" I asked him.

"Yes and no," he replied. "Yes, in respect of the unthinking adoption of everything foreign, particularly everything Western: language, religion, technology. No, if you mean a modernization that springs organically from the experience of our own people, expressed in our own language, building on the culture and traditions we have inherited; on our real needs, not on desires cultivated by fantasies of foreign origin. The only modernization we need and can handle successfully is that which grows out of our material poverty and our desire to escape from that. I do not believe in imported technological miracles."

"Like our wristcom?"

"Like your wristcom," he echoed.

"Our view was that we should look critically at what we had inherited from our own past, our past before the coming of the white man; and even more critically at everything we had inherited, good and bad, from the period of our contact with the West: the Atlantic slave trade and its consequences, colonialism and its consequences, capitalism, foreign religion and imported political ideas. Our emphasis was on the word critically. This is a process which, as you know, we call *sankofa*."

"What about the law? You have no constitution. What protection does the ordinary Asante man or woman have from abuse by those in authority?"

"Crash, you must remember that we—I am speaking for Nana Asantehene—have no powers of coercion, or hardly any. We own little more than the clothes we wear. Promulgate a constitution and you must enforce it. We have no police force, beyond the informal unarmed militias at village level, no army to speak of, hardly any funds. Enforcement would require the imposition of taxes. A constitution is just another top-down measure: a national convention peopled largely by western trained lawyers produces a document which suits their class needs. Then they use a YES/NO referendum to give their document a semblance of legitimacy. The people who mark their Xs next to YES have, by and large, neither read nor understood the document. Referenda to approve constitutions are invariably won by large majorities. What real choice do the people have? Have any of the political elite explained to them the implications of voting NO? Have they been encouraged to think what sort of constitution, if any, might meet their needs rather than those of the educated middle classes? Do you understand?

"We have only natural law. Every town or village makes its own rules. The old Law, the Laws of Ghana, provided an opportunity for the judiciary and lawyers to exploit the people. Today our courts work not to punish the offender, but to effect justice, to reconcile the parties, to persuade the offender to compensate the victim and to reform. We have no capital punishment, and only one prison, which is a hospital where we care for the criminally insane, the compulsive murderer or rapist, who may be a threat to society. And those whose minds were ripped apart by the trauma of the bad times, the epidemics, the earthquake, the civil war."

"And human rights?" I asked him. "Isn't your system a charter for abuse? Where are the checks and balances, the opportunity to appeal against an unfair conviction?"

"Crash, every judicial system is a reflection of the class forces at work in society, a reflection of power, class power. Our society is, in any material sense, uniformly poor. We have no governing class to impose its will upon us in the form of laws and magistrates and police. We rely on the good sense of our people and the transparency of the judicial procedures they have devised. The judges, usually but not exclusively older men and women, are elected for limited terms. They report their judgments to the town meeting, where they are discussed and may be overruled, though that rarely happens. Truth is, though, that our judges don't have much work to do. They are part-timers. You would be astonished to learn how little crime we have. Even the criminals of the civil war, those who were unable to flee abroad, have been re-integrated. Most of them, at any rate. And the few incorrigibles, the incurable bullies, have only their fists as weapons.

"All this might sound revolutionary to you, like the "communism" which so scares your own rulers. Don't believe it. Our society is deeply conservative. And yet our lack of formal laws leaves much room for non-conformity. Many of our local leaders have had the wisdom to encourage this, seeing it as a positive challenge to old ideas."

"What happens in a case of murder?" I asked.

"Murder is extremely rare," he replied. "The openness of our society and its emphasis on the good of the community rather than the primacy of the individual, helps us to detect the tensions which might lead a man to kill his fellow. Greed is hardly ever a motive now. We are human of course, and not immune to anger. Fights do break out. Yet our folk seem to have developed skills in controlling violence. We are actively recovering our ancestors' traditional techniques of reconciliation.

"In cases involving death most of our local judicial services have seen fit to follow an ancient rule allowing automatic appeal to Nana Asantehene. Nana is totally opposed to capital punishment. You yourself, if you only knew it, owe your life to him because of this."

I made a little speech. There was no irony in what I said and he seemed to appreciate that.

"Do you see the new Asante as a model for others?" I asked.

"What others? The U.S.A? You must be joking.

"We had no theoretical, ideological agenda. We simply had no choice. No, that is not true. We could have done nothing, allowing our society to be controlled by thugs. That was one choice. The only other way was to begin to rebuild. The pessimists, lawyer Maxwell and his ilk, told us that without the assistance of their former partners in the West, that was impossible. We said that that assistance would not be forthcoming, since we no longer had anything of use to them, to exchange for their pittance. Moreover, we had come to the conclusion that what they used to call 'aid' had been at the root of many of our problems.

"So we decided to start from scratch. We had land, water, sun; and, most precious, our people and what remained of our culture. Those were our basic resources. Our material needs were simple: food, shelter, clothing. It was only when we came to discuss our spiritual needs that the debate became fierce. But that's a story for another time."

CHAPTER 16

ON THE EIGHTH day we hit the outskirts of Cape Coast and headed west.

We soon arrived at Elmina, where every small boy turned out to cheer us and run after us.

We passed by the Castle of Ghosts and headed down to the Atlantic shore. The tide was out and the sand was firm.

Now I had my bearings. I caught up with Anokye.

"We're not heading for Mpoanokrom, are we?" I asked.

I didn't want to pass by without saying hallo to Kofi.

"How did you guess?"

Anokye favored me with a smile.

Then he called out, "Come on, let's give the horses some exercise," and I followed him at a gallop.

They must have had their spies out for they knew we were coming. Kofi was waiting for us, and most of the rest of the town's population too, including the Chief and all his elders, cheering us in as if we were jockeys in a horse-race. It seemed Anokye's fame had spread even to this small Fanti village.

The last time I had seen Kofi was a few days before the invasion at the Kumase Sports Stadium. He now approached me and held out his hand.

"*Madamfo* Crash, *awaawaawa*," he greeted me, Crash my friend, good to see you.

I thought that I detected just a shade of guilty hesitation, as if he felt he had betrayed me (as, of course, he had) and that I might refuse to reciprocate his greeting. I did nothing of the sort. I had liked Kofi from the moment I met him and I still regard him as a friend. It wasn't his fault, nor mine, indeed, that fate had placed us on opposite sides.

"Kofi, *atuu*," I replied and we embraced.

In the late afternoon, the whole village and some guests from further afield, gathered to watch a screening of *Kum Apem, Apem Beba*, and to hear the last narration of my story. As I told it I became aware, more than ever before, that there were gaps in it. I don't mean the gaps that were of my own making, my deliberate concealment of matters of concern to U.S. security, to which only I amongst those present was privy; and which I felt free to withhold because there was no chance that even Anokye would discover them. What was missing was the part of the story which I didn't know. Had Kofi been part of Asante intelligence from the day of my arrival? Was it pure coincidence that I had been landed on the coast less than a mile from his own village? If I had landed elsewhere, would there have been another Kofi waiting for me, rubbing his eyes as if he had just woken from a nap? Had Kofi sent Kwabena to spy on me that morning? Was my arrival expected? How come U.S. intelligence had proved to be so woefully ignorant of the country they were sending me to? Or was their ignorance deliberate? Why had Bud withheld certain information from me? What was the true purpose of William Franklin's visit? Had Bob Service told me all he knew?

There were other questions at the back of my mind, but it took Anokye to bring them to the fore. After the durbar he invited me to join him and we walked down the beach, allowing the incoming tide to wash over our bare feet.

"Are you looking forward to getting back to the States?" he asked.

"Sure am," I replied. "I've missed my wife and kids. "

"Tell me about them," he asked and I did so.

We walked in silence for a while and then he asked, "What about your bosses?"

"What do you mean?" I inquired.

"Well, look at it from their point of view. They sent you on a mission, to find out what had happened to Franklin and his party; and to rescue them from the clutches of the barbaric Asante. You failed."

"I didn't fail," I replied. "You know very well that I did my best. They failed, rather. They failed to brief me properly. They allowed me too little room to exercise my own judgment. Our technology, their technology, proved inadequate. I still don't know how you penetrated it, but the fact that you did so is evidence that my super-miniaturized little box of tricks had holes in it."

"They might not see it like that, Crash."

He was going to go on but I saw him bite his lip, evidently deciding that he'd said enough.

"All I can say is, I wish you the best of luck," he said. "And if you ever want to come back, with your wife and kids, you will be welcome. But without an official agenda, do you understand?"

We laughed over that one. The short tropical twilight descended upon us. We turned back to face a crimson sunset.

"You have served your sentence," Anokye told me. "And with credit. In a way we have together turned a disaster into a triumph. You have seen yourself how the recounting of your story has built up our national solidarity. You have taught us to hate and fear the power of the U.S. and those emotions have brought us closer together.

"There is nothing new in this. One U.S. government after another has manipulated public opinion by fabricating or exaggerating threats to your national security. For a while it was Communism, then Islamic Terrorism, then a revival of the old Yellow Peril. In the past hundred years corporate America, acting through your politicians, has seen to it that you always have a national enemy to divert your attention.

"I hope that our motives were less ignoble. Hatred and fear are negative emotions. We are not immune to them and I would have been happier to build our solidarity on a more honorable foundation. However I had to fight strong pressure. Some of my colleagues would have liked to have had you shot. I proposed your sentence to Nana Asantehene because it was the only way I could see to save your life."

We had reached the outskirts of Mpoanokrom. He halted and turned to face the sea. We stood looking out at the waves. The sky was a deep red. In a few minutes it would be dark.

"My brother," I asked him (and saw him turn to look at my face with an expression I did not understand) "why did you feel it necessary to save my life?"

"Crash," he replied, "my brother Crash. It is a long time since I believed in God. But I do subscribe to one article of faith: a belief in the sanctity of human life. To me, capital punishment is an abomination. Most of my colleagues share my views on this issue. However they regarded your crime as an even greater abomination and were ready, some eager, to make an exception for you, to swallow their scruples to see you executed. To get my way, I had to compromise, devising your sentence and then persuading them that you were more use to us alive than dead.

"That was my first reason. There is another, but that must wait for tomorrow. It's dark: let's go and have a bath and join our friends."

I was woken the next morning by the bizarre call, "Wake up, soldier. Rise and shine!"

It was Anokye.

"Sorry about that," he apologized as I wiped the sleep from my eyes, "but we have just had news that your ship is due in the late afternoon. We have much to do before then. Can you be at the Chief's palace in half an hour?"

The village was a hive of activity: everyone seemed to be

heading for the beach and every head seemed to be carrying a full bag or basket.

There was a table set on the porch of the Chief's house, with a bench on each side. The Chief and Anokye sat on one side; I joined Kofi on the other.

After the customary greetings, the Chief asked, "Will you wet your throat?" and ordered palm wine.

"Crash," Anokye said, "go easy on the drink. This is going to be a stressful day for you."

I looked at him, somewhat puzzled, but said nothing.

"Crash," he continued, "this is difficult. I am going to tell you a story, a true story. I don't know whether you have any inkling of what it might be, but even if you have, it is going to come as a bit of a shock. And when I have finished you are going to be faced with a difficult task. So brace yourself.

"You told us that you came to Africa with two missions. I am not going to talk about the first, the official mission. We have finished with that. Your second mission was to find your natural parents. Did you make any progress?"

I shook my head.

"Negative," I said.

Anokye took a draft of the palm wine. He was sitting directly opposite me. His eyes met mine.

"Sorry," he said. "I shouldn't have asked you that question."

"Why not?"

"Because I already knew the answer. Let me explain."

"Your father, your natural father that is, was called John Owusu-Ansah, John Kwadwo Owusu-Ansah. Your mother was called Abena Saka. Kwadwo's father, your grandfather, worked for the United Nations, now defunct. On his retirement he returned to Ghana, to Kumase in fact. He had invested his savings in U.S. stocks and was able to live comfortably off his foreign income. He sent Kwadwo to a good university in the U.S. Kwadwo wasn't entitled to any financial aid and his father had to pay the full fees. That will give some idea of how wealthy the old man was.

"However…shortly after you were born, several major U.S. corporations collapsed in the wake of the exposure of the dishonesty of their executives. Not long afterwards, the government's general mismanagement of the economy led to a stock market crash, which is how you came by your nickname. Your grandfather, as it turned out, had invested unwisely. He lost his life's savings almost at a stroke. He had to sell the grand house he had built in Kumase and move to more modest accommodation. The old man found it difficult to face up to reality. He convinced himself that the U.S. government, for which he had unlimited admiration, would punish the fraudsters and redeem the luckless investors, including himself. In the meantime, he told your father, with regret, that he would have to interrupt his studies and return to Ghana. Both of them, father and son, thought it would take no more than a year for the old man's affairs to be sorted out. Kwadwo would then return to the States to resume his studies. Your parents decided to leave you in the care of their close and trusted friends, the Fergusons, pending their return. Ma Ferguson, by the way, was a native of Mpoanokrom."

The Chief nodded his head in confirmation.

"Much of this will not be news to you," Anokye continued.

"I didn't know that this was Ma Ferguson's home town," I said. "She always said she came from Cape Coast."

The Chief seemed not too pleased to hear that.

Anokye continued, "The scene shifts to Ghana. And this may be news to you. When they got back, your parents went to live with their parents in Kumase. Your mother bore another son, their last child. They named him after his father, in the American fashion: John Owusu-Ansah junior. They always called him John and insisted on speaking only English to him. But his playmates called him Kwaku and he had no difficulty in picking up Asante."

So, I had a younger brother! I was confused. Where was he? Who was he? I opened my mouth to ask but Anokye stretched across the table and placed his index finger across my lips.

"Patience," he admonished, reading my thoughts. "You'll find out soon enough."

The Chief nodded sagely and Kofi smiled broadly. It seemed that they knew something that I didn't.

"Both Kwadwo and Abena were devout Christians. Their parents on both sides had been Anglicans but they chose one of the newer Pentecostal churches. They took Kwaku with them to church and sent him to Sunday School. Like many children he went through a period of extreme religiosity. When he was an adolescent, their Bishop was caught red-handed in behavior of an extremely unsavory nature which I won't go into here. The Church did its damnedest to arrange a cover-up, but failed. This scandal, and the general malaise in the run-up to the civil war, undermined Kwaku's faith. Much to his parents' despair, he decided first to leave the church and later to declare his agnosticism.

"Let me go back a little. When they returned to Ghana your parents soon realized that your grandfather was never going to recover his fortune. They both got jobs and set about trying to save enough money for one of them to return to the States to collect you. To the best of my knowledge they never did succeed in accumulating the funds they needed. In the course of time your grandfather not only exhausted his remaining capital but also became senile. Perhaps it was his troubles, his frustrated dreams of a peaceful and prosperous and respectable retirement that drove him into a second childhood. So the old folks became a further burden on Kwadwo and Abena's finances. Life was a struggle for them. To their credit they managed, somehow, to give Kwaku the best education on offer in Kumase at that time."

"We don't have much time and Kwaku is not applying for a job so I am not going to recount his curriculum vitae, what you would call his résumé. All I need to say is that as one of our circle he rose to an important position, close to the new Asantehene. His parents, growing old by this time, were proud of him, though they had reservations about the new dispensation. In spite of their poverty their outlook was typical of that of many of our middle class Christians. They paid lip service to our traditional culture but deep down they were incurable admirers of the West, believing that anything of African origin was almost by definition inferior, or, as they would say, pagan. I had long since stopped arguing with them on this issue."

He had said "I," not "Kwaku," but seemed unaware of his slip of the tongue.

Suddenly the blinkers fell from my eyes. How stupid I had been all this time not to read the signs. Now I understood. Anokye was Kwaku. Anokye was my brother, my own kid brother. I couldn't control myself. I began to sob and bowed my head and covered my face with my hands to hide my shame at this uncontrolled display of emotion.

Kwaku—that is what I shall call him from here on—took my hands in his.

"Crash, what is it?" he asked.

"You are Kwaku? You are my brother?" I asked, struggling to take control of myself.

It was as if I had pricked a balloon. Kwaku, too, lost control. We embraced awkwardly across the rough table. I heard Kofi ask the Chief if he had some akpeteshie in the house and soon he was forcing both of us to swallow some of that fire water. The Chief sent for a bowl and a towel and we washed our faces. Looking at each other we almost collapsed again. Then Kwaku pulled himself together.

"I haven't finished," he said. "There is more to tell. I'll try to be brief. In the course of our campaigning in Kumase and in the towns and villages of Asante we ran into opposition from the churches. The pastors felt that we were undermining the grip they had on the people's minds and on their pockets, too. They had grown fat on their exactions and saw us, correctly, as a threat to their relative prosperity. They set aside their disagreements over doctrine and united against us. We decided to mobilize against the pastors. Our aim was to show the people how to recover the churches in which they worshiped and to break down the senseless sectarianism which the missionaries had imposed on us. We challenged the pastors to debate with each other and with us, in public. If I say it myself, they were no match for us.

"We don't have time or I would tell you the whole story. What I do need to tell you is that our parents summoned me and demanded that I stop the campaign, as if I were some sort of tin pot dictator.

"We had a terrible row. The upshot was that they publicly disowned me in their church. That was sad, but no more. Unfortunately our father was so angry that he advised their congregation to take up arms against us. They were arrested. I tried to hush the matter up, dismissing it for the trivial stupidity that it was. Nepotism, if you like. (I practiced it in your favor too.) If they had been prepared to retract their intemperate remarks, the matter would probably have been forgiven and forgotten. But Dad was a proud man and he was also convinced that he had an appointment to meet God and he was determined to tell Him of the battle he had fought for His church on earth. Sometimes I think he saw himself as Abraham, with me in the role of the sacrificial Isaac.

"I tried to talk to them, but they refused to see me. The best I could do was to get an old school friend of mine, who also attended their church, to persuade them to offer to go into voluntary exile. I guess they found some biblical parallel for that too. You can find a passage in the Bible to justify practically anything. Nana Asantehene commuted their sentence to banishment, which is in accordance with time-honored traditional Asante law.

"The last thing they did before they left Kumase was to write me a letter formally disowning me. They couldn't disinherit me—they had nothing to leave. Indeed, throughout all this I was still supporting them, sending them a couple of chickens and a basket of eggs and vegetables from my farm every week. After all they were still my parents and I owed them."

"Did they know the food was coming from you?" I asked.

"I suppose so. I had been sending it for years, since before our quarrel. They never said thank you. I guess they thought it was theirs by right. Honor thy father and thy mother that their days may be long. It doesn't say anything about honoring thy children."

"I had a long-standing friendship with Nana, here" he continued, indicating the Chief, "and particularly with Kofi. In the old Ghana days they had a scheme called National Service and I had spent mine teaching in Mpoanokrom's primary school. Nana was my principal and Kofi one of my best students.

"Without Dad and Mom's knowledge I made arrangements for them to spend their exile here. They could have lived in the village but they preferred to live like hermits in a shack out there along the beach. Kofi saw to it that they had the bare necessities, enough to live on. They lived on the principle, *Onyame bekyere*, the Lord will provide. Kofi, if you'll excuse my blasphemy, played the part of the Lord."

I wanted to interrupt but Kwaku held up his hand.

"Crash, wait please. I have left out one thing. In their last letter to me they expressly forbade me to take any part in their funeral. They said they would make their own arrangements. Those arrangements, I know from Kofi, consisted of writing a letter to their old friends, your adoptive parents in America, telling them that they were near death and asking them to send you, Crash, to come here to see them, presumably (and I don't think I am being unjust to them) to take care of them and, in due course, see them into their graves. You know, we Ghanaians, (though Ghana no longer exists, I am still a Ghanaian) we Ghanaians believe that all Americans are stinking rich."

"How do you know the contents of the letter?" I managed to interject.

Kofi replied: "Dad's eyesight was failing. Mom's too. They got me to write it for them. I handed it to Captain M—you'll meet him this afternoon—and asked him to mail it in the States."

"Ma and Pa Ferguson would have shown it to me," I said. "I'm sure they never received it. Or perhaps they had already passed on by the time it arrived."

Kwaku resumed: "On one of his weekly visits, Kofi arrived to find that both of them were dead, Dad sitting at his desk, Mom lying on a mat on the floor. There was no sign of violence: both of them seemed to have died a natural death. Kofi asked me for instructions. He was prepared to have them buried, but, understandably, only on the instructions of next of kin, that is me, or you, whose place of abode was unknown. By that time the state bureaucracy had collapsed so there was nobody with the authority or interest to order an autopsy or burial. I went through a period of great mental strain. In spite of our differences, I mourned them, choosing to remember a happy childhood and the sacrifices they had made on my behalf. A mental picture of their corpses, decomposing in their shack, haunted my nights. I tried to bring myself to ask Kofi to bury their remains, but, always, there was that last letter of theirs. Fortunately I was no longer serving as Okyeame. I went to ask Nana Asantehene for advice, not in his official capacity, but as an old and cherished friend. He told me that there are two kinds of problems. The first are amenable to solution by active intervention: it is worthwhile tackling those. The nature of the second, bereavement for instance, is such that no intervention on your part is going to solve them. Sometimes they solve themselves, sometimes you just have to live with them. There is no point, he advised, in expending useless energy on problems of the second type.

"I have told you that I am not a believer. But if I were, I would certainly attribute the coincidence of your arrival and, moreover, your arrival right here in Mpoanokrom to divine intervention. If you hadn't been delivered by a U.S. tanker and if your mission had been only to find Mom and Dad, alive or dead, my response to Kofi's astonishing news of your arrival, would have been to come here at once to welcome you and to persuade you, if that proved necessary, to bury Mom and Dad. But soon after, we received a warning from our brothers working on the Half Assini oil platform. They weren't sure what you were up to but advised us to be careful.

I had started my second term of duty as Okyeame and I had to treat you as a potential enemy (as, my long-lost brother, you turned out to be.)"

He was interrupted by a call of "Agôô."

The Chief had evidently given instructions that we should not be disturbed and was annoyed, but when he saw the young man who entered, his expression softened.

"Ah, Sparks," Kwaku welcomed him, "*Bra bekyea me,*" come and greet me.

Sparks did so effusively.

He held a short whispered conversation with Kofi and then took his leave.

Kofi said, "Item one. The tanker has passed Takoradi. It should be here within three or four hours. Item two. The Osofo has arrived. The grave has been dug and the coffins are ready."

Kwaku said, "Crash. Will you go and bury our parents' remains? Kofi will assist you and the Reverend gentleman from Cape Coast will conduct the service in accordance, I hope, with their wishes. Out of respect for those wishes, I shall remain out of sight. Crash, will you do it?"

When the ceremony was over I found the site where I had buried my kit. So I had all the clothes and gear I needed for the trip home and some dollars, too. I presented the inflatable rubber dinghy complete to Kofi, though what use it will be to him I cannot guess.

Kwaku and I still had a couple of hours together. We spent much of the time walking along the beach. The tide was out. We walked barefooted in and out of the water.

"Sea never dry," I said.

He laughed.

"Crash," he said. "There's a question I didn't feel free to ask you as Okyeame. Now I can ask it as a brother."

I turned to look at him.

"Forget about your mission, both your missions. You've had a good opportunity to see what we've been trying to do in Asante. And what you haven't seen, you've heard me lecture about; for which I apologize. What were your impressions? What part of Asante will you take back with you to the States?"

I kicked the water and thought for a moment. He watched me.

"Beggars," I said.

He frowned.

"Beggars?" he asked. "What do you mean?"

"You don't have any. Or at least I never did see one. The sidewalks of our cities are full of beggars. Panhandlers we call them. The police round them up, keep them in cells for a couple of days and then truck them out and dump them in one of the Abandoned Territories. It's futile, of course. They just filter back in. The security fences are too long to police."

He asked me to tell him more about the Abandoned Territories.

"You should know," I said. "On a global scale, this country is an Abandoned Territory. Like Asante, or Ghana, ours have been sucked dry of useful resources. We use them as dumping grounds for the parasites whom we used to support from our taxes before the welfare system collapsed. We still subsidize them to some extent. We wouldn't want them to pass infectious diseases on to us, so we send out medical teams from time to time."

"You say we," he asked. "Who is we?"

"The rich, the prosperous, the owners and exploiters (you would say) of the world's resources; and then those like me whom they need to serve their needs."

"Um," he said. "Forgive me if I sound patronizing, but it sounds like I'm hearing my echo. Did you always see things this way?" and then, "You didn't answer my question. Your impressions of the new Asante?"

"No beggars," I replied. "No billboards. No bribes. Almost no bribes…"

"And?"

"Ramseyer," I said.

He turned to look at me.

"Ramseyer?"

"His ghost. Ramseyer's ghost."

Puzzled still, he shook his head.

"Explain," he said.

"You've laid it. You've laid Ramseyer's ghost."

He smiled.

"I'll remember that," he said.

I took the small kit-bag from my back.

"Here," I said, giving him the book, "You'd better have this. It was on Dad's desk."

He turned it over and read the title, "F. A. Ramseyer and J. Kuhne. Four years in Ashantee. James Nisbet & Co. London, 1875."

"Thanks Crash, but you'd better keep it," Kwaku said. "As a memento. I already have a copy."

"You shouldn't judge Ramseyer too harshly," he told me, as we arrived back at Mpoanokrom. "He was a fugitive from the growing materialism of capitalist Europe, which he despised. So, in spite of my rejection of his religious fanaticism, I suspect that his ghost might have had some sympathy for our social program. We should be grateful to him, moreover, for what he taught our ancestors about building and other trades; and we should value his belief in the dignity of labor."

The tanker appeared on the western horizon around four. It was a sight to see, with three masts each equipped with mighty sails.

"One of the old ones, still running on oil," Kofi explained (as if this would be news to me.) "The sails are to conserve fuel."

Soon after, Mpoanokrom's every single canoe was launched through the waves, every one of them loaded with sacks and baskets. The only exception was Kofi's in which he, Kwaku and I traveled as passengers. It's name, carved in ornate letters on each forward bulwark, was *Sea Never Dry*.

"What does it mean," I asked him, "Sea Never Dry?"

"It means just what it says," he replied with a twinkle in his eye, cocking his head in Kwaku's direction. "If it weren't true, you might have to walk back to America. Of course, you would find your route well sign-posted."

Not for the first time, I felt I was out of my depth.

"What do you mean?" I asked.

"Bones," he replied, "the bleached bones of our enslaved countrymen thrown overboard, dead or alive, mark the shipping lanes from Africa to the Americas."

Kwaku nodded his head.

"Crash," he said. "I am worried about you. Are you quite sure that you won't be blamed and punished when you get back?"

This wasn't the first time he had raised the issue. I dismissed his concern with a short speech extolling the virtues of the American system in general and the Marine Corps in particular.

"They'll probably give me a medal," I told him.

By the time we reached the ship it had furled its sails and dropped anchor and the canoe men were already loading their freight into the nets. As we approached, the gangway was lowered. Captain M was waiting to welcome us on board. He greeted Kofi as if he were an old friend. After introductions he led us to a table under an awning, on which there was a spread of good American food, the best. I had my first Coke in more than a year. While Kwaku and I dug in, Kofi and the Captain did their business, exchanging bills of lading and so on. I gathered that there was a barter deal in progress since once the canoes had been unloaded they were loaded again, with an array of cartons, drums and sacks and bags of cement.

When they joined us Kofi said, "Captain, I have to ask you a favor. We have a passenger for you. Before you reply, let me assure you, firstly, that he is a U.S. citizen, secondly that he is not a fugitive from justice; and thirdly that he has no criminal intent. Having said that, we would like you to exercise discretion regarding his identity."

The captain gave me a searching look which I returned in kind.

"He just wants to go home to his wife and children," Kofi said.

"Kofi, you've always been straight with me," said Captain M. "It's a deal. Let's have a quick drink and then we must be on our way."

CHAPTER 17

THE VOYAGE HOME was uneventful. We stopped at the U.S. colony of São Tomé, or Saint Thomas as we call it now, to take on fuel and supplies and offload, under cover of darkness, the sacks we had taken on at Mpoanokrom. The crew took shore leave in turns and I toyed with the idea of joining them with a view to hitching a ride home on a plane. I decided against. I wanted to use the enforced leisure of the journey across the Atlantic to complete this document, which I have succeeded in doing. I wrote it from the notes I kept throughout my stay in Africa, supplemented by my recollection of events and conversations in the few cases where my notes proved inadequate. My intention has been to reflect my state of mind on a day by day basis, honestly, and without the benefit of hindsight and in so doing to create a record of my experience, while it is still fresh in my mind.

The sea voyage has given me plenty of time for reflection.

I've been thinking about the missionary Fritz Ramseyer.

Dad had evidently been reading Ramseyer's book shortly before he died. Was there some particular reason? I have re-read the book, but an answer to that question eludes me. Perhaps Ramseyer's spirit visited my parents to comfort them with prayer in their last lonely days?

Kwaku shared with me a special family interest in Ramseyer,

which arose, so he told me, like this. In 1836, our ancestor, John Owusu-Ansah, son of Asantehene Osei Tutu Kwame, was sent to England to study. He was then a lad of some twelve years. He returned to the Gold Coast five years later and for the rest of his life lived in two worlds. At the coast he was ordained as a Wesleyan missionary and took charge of the Cape Coast Boys' School. In Kumase, he served as secretary and foreign policy advisor to successive Asantehenes. Ramseyer referred to him as "a man to whom we owe the deepest gratitude, and who seemed to have been expressly sent to Coomassie, to prove a messenger of grace for us during our long trial."

I have given some thought to the question of whether I should change my surname back to that of my biological parents, Owusu-Ansah. I'll have to discuss that with Millicent. Millicent. I've spent much time thinking about her and the state of our marriage. Last but no means least: Fergus and Marilyn. They'll be more than a year older than I when I last saw them. I can't wait.

I have put this story down on paper for them to read when they are older.

Captain M. (not his real initial by the way) provided me with a seaman's I.D. and I had no difficulty passing the dock gates. I prefer not to state the name of our port of arrival. I have deliberately concealed the identity of the captain and his ship. He did me a favor and there is no way I want to get him into trouble for committing some breach of regulations. Apart from that single deliberate omission, this is, to the best of my knowledge and belief, a true recital of my experiences from the date of my arrival in Africa to that on which I left the west coast of that continent in the captain's ship.

My first stop was New York City. I thought to call Millicent but decided I would rather give her a surprise. I hadn't brought any presents back with me so I took a walk to see if I could find something to buy. My cash was running low so I checked my balance at an ATM and finding that it was OK, used my credit card to make the purchases. I mention this because, retracing my actions, I guess that in doing so I was announcing my return to the U.S. If I had had any sense of guilt would I have done that?

I happened to pass along Broadway. In Times Square there were three enormous screens. On the first our President was making a speech. On the second a well known preacher was doing likewise. I paused to watch and listen, but I couldn't make out what either was saying. Then I turned round and saw the third screen. This was showing short episodes of live sex of the most explicit kind, with the addresses of the venues, in Manhattan, where the real thing could be seen, presumably for the payment of a fee. None of the passers-by seemed to be paying attention to any of these images. I wondered what my younger brother Kwaku, "Okomfo Anokye," and my friend Kofi Kom would have made of that.

At Penn Station I paid for my ticket with cash. If I had used my credit card, I suppose there would have been a reception committee waiting for me on arrival.

It was getting dark when the train arrived in Washington D.C. Again I considered calling Millicent and again I decided to give her a surprise. So I took a cab.

I hadn't taken my front door key with me, so I pushed the bell. We have one of those one-way spy holes in the door. I could see from the shadow behind it that someone was taking a look at me.

I called out, "Honey, it's me, Crash."

There was no reply and the door didn't open. I heard the sound of a phone and Millicent's voice.

She said, "He's here," and then, after a pause, "OK."

Then the door opened. I expected Millicent, my wife, mother of my children, to speak my name and fall into my arms.

Instead, she turned her back on me, walked down the hall towards the kitchen and said, "So, you've come at last."

I put down my kit-bag and closed the door behind me.

"Honey," I asked her, "What's going on?"

I was close to tears.

"Honey, what's going on," she mimicked me in a voice

I can only describe as nasty, "'Honey, what's going on,' he asks. Do you have no idea what you have done to me and my children?"

I stood there trying to absorb this. She had said, "my children," not "our children."

The bell rang. She pushed past me and opened the front door. Then she stood aside. Two M.P.'s stepped in, both of them armed. I saw that they hadn't come alone. The street was full of vehicles and uniformed men.

"Here he is," Millicent told the two visitors, as if I were invisible.

"Ekem Ferguson?" one asked.

"Captain Ekem Ferguson, U. S. Marine Corps," I replied.

"You're under arrest," the M.P. said as his fellow turned me to the wall.

My own wall. The wall of the hall in my own house, paid for with my own hard-earned pay.

M.P. number one read me the statutory warning. Number two frisked me. I bore no arms. He took my wallet.

"Papa," I heard Fergus say.

I twisted my head and looked up. He and Marilyn, dressed in their pajamas, were standing at the banister on the top landing. They had grown in my absence. With a shock I realized how much Fergus resembled his Uncle Kwaku, whom he didn't even know existed.

"Hold up your hands," said number two and clicked the handcuffs.

"Fergus, Marilyn, my chickens," I called back; and then to the M.P.'s, "won't you let me say hallo to my kids?"

Millicent interrupted, saying harshly, "Fergus, Marilyn, get back to bed at once."

They didn't move.

"At once," she screamed at them.

They ignored her. Marilyn stretched out her arms to me. After a year's absence, I wondered if she remembered me.

"Papa," she said.

Then there was a male voice which seemed to come from

the direction of our bedroom.

"Fergus, Marilyn," it said.

The voice spoke with authority. A familiar authority. Just two words, "Fergus, Marilyn," and yet I seemed to recognize it.

"There'll be time enough for that," said number one, answering my earlier request.

He picked up my bag and pushed me towards the door.

"Won't you let me give my kids the presents I brought for them?" I begged.

"Let's go, buddy," number two replied and then, holding the door, "Thank you Ma'am and a good night to you."

I have not seen my children since and all my requests to see them have been, not rejected, just ignored. I have asked to see my wife. They tell me that she refuses to visit me and wants nothing to do with me. Moreover, that she has initiated divorce proceedings. It seems that her mind has been poisoned against me, but I cannot fathom who might have done this.

And Bud, my buddy, my best friend, in my darkest hour, where is he?

On arrival at the prison I was stripped, searched and given prison clothes. My possessions were laid out before me and inventoried. I was required to sign the inventory. I was photographed and finger printed.

The following morning I was taken to an interrogation room. There was a long dark window in one wall with shadowy figures moving behind it.

I did not know the interrogator. He refused to identify himself.

I demanded to be allowed to consult a lawyer.

"All in good time," he told me.

The good time has yet to come.

I demanded to be told the reason for my arrest and the nature of my alleged offence.

"All in good time," he told me.

The good time has yet to come.

The interrogator advised me that I would, in due course, be

debriefed on my mission to Africa and that I would be required to sign a statement embodying the content of my debriefing. He presented me with a copy of the private document which I had written on board ship and invited me to assist in my debriefing by amending it and adding to it as I saw fit.

I have re-read it and see no reason to amend it. I have made some additions, relating my experiences since my return to the United States.

I demand to see my children. I demand an interview with my wife. I demand to see a lawyer. I demand that I be either charged or that I be released.

The deposition above was made of my own free will. I declare that it contains the truth, the whole truth and nothing but the truth except for certain details omitted to defend innocent persons (details noted in the text.)

(Signed) Ekem Ferguson, Captain, U.S. Marine Corps.

The cover of the folder carries the following inscription:
    Office of the Commandant of the Marine Corps,
    Headquarters,
    U.S. Marine Corps,
    Washington, DC 20380-1775
    Record of Court-Martial
    Defendant: Captain Ekem Ferguson, U.S. Marine Corps.
    Charge: Treason against the United States of America
    Verdict: Guilty
    Sentence: Execution by Firing Squad.
    Date of Execution of Sentence: September 30, 2052.
    Archived: January 15, 2053.

CHAPTER 18

My name is Fergus Smith. Ekem Ferguson was my father. After his execution my mother re-married. My stepfather's name is Smith. My mother thought it would be in my best interest if she changed my surname to his.

After I graduated from college, I went to visit my mother. I asked her to tell me everything she knew about my father.

"He was a traitor," she said, "a traitor to our country. He got his just deserts."

"How do you know?" I asked. "Did you ever hear his side of the story?"

She did not answer.

"I remember the two of you arguing all the time," I said.

"Fergus," she said, "I don't want to talk about it. I don't want to remember. It's all over. The past."

"Ma, he was my father. I'm entitled to know more," I said.

Again silence.

"Ma," I said, "I'd like to go and see Uncle Bud. Can you tell me where to find him?"

"Colonel Power is in the Arlington National Cemetery," she said. "He's dead."

She refused every request for information. We had a row, some row, believe me. I haven't seen her since.

In a way I'm sorry for her. She's still my mother, after all.

Trying to reconstruct a past I only dimly recall, I guess she was cheating on my father with his best friend Bud. When Dad was arrested Bud must have had second thoughts and walked out on her. While Dad was away Uncle Bud was a frequent visitor; and then he just stopped coming. Mom must have been crushed. We left town soon after and then the Smith era began and my memories of those times started to fade.

After our row, I went to Washington. Hanging around the building where the Marine Corps keeps its archives, I discovered the name of their janitoring firm. Using false papers, I applied for a job. As luck would have it, my very first work site was the Marine Corps Archives. The security check was a joke.

Most of my colleagues were arthritic old black women. (Who else would do work like that?) My supervisor was a black male, like me, a few years older. He was writing a book and using this dead-end job to support himself while he did so. He gave me a good report at the end of my first month. Then, luck again, he received an offer from a publisher and handed in his resignation, recommending me as his successor. Big deal: supervisor of twenty sad old ladies mopping the floors of the Marine Corps Archives every night. If I'd stuck it out, that could have been the first rung on the corporate ladder leading to the studded leather seat behind the desk of DC Janitoring Services' Chief Executive.

It took me just a week to find my father's file. No sweat smuggling it out of the building: the security were snoring at 4 a.m. when we knocked off. A week later the file was back in its box. At the end of the month I tendered my resignation.

I made arrangements to publish the files and at the same time to inform the media, legal and underground, where to find them. It took the Security a month to shut down the website and start looking for me. By that time, the story of my father Captain Ekem "Crash" Ferguson, was widely known.

And I was already on my way to Africa.

I plan to visit my grandparents' grave at Mpoanokrom. Then I'll go to Kumase to see if I can find my Uncle Kwaku, Kwaku Owusu-Ansah also known as Okomfo Anokye.

APPENDIX

Extracts from *Four Years in Ashantee*, Friedrich August Ramseyer
and Johannes Kühne, James Nisbet & Co. London, 1875

As we approached Ashantee proper, we were struck by the
increasing fertility and richness of the well-watered country.
In the vicinity of every important place the roads were good,
and sometimes for miles together, suitable for traffic. Near the
entrance of each village, we noticed yams, sticks, corn, and eggs
heaped up as an offering to the Fetish; and the houses—whether
scattered or in groups—were mostly surrounded by palm and
banana gardens in picturesque variety; sometimes they formed a
street, intersected by lanes and by-ways...(p. 45)

We met with many plantation villages in this fruitful plain, where
corn, rice, pisang, maize, yams, and groundnuts abounded. About
four o'clock we approached a large town named Dwaben, and
prepared ourselves for a noisy reception. We soon reached a
noble avenue of trees, such as I had never before seen in Africa,
and under their glorious shade we entered a fine wide street, with
whitewashed, and two-storied houses. Of course we were speedily
surrounded by the entire population, the youthful portion of which
especially, hailed us with riotous excitement...(p. 52)

We see [the Ramseyers and Kühne] enduring a tedious captivity, full of most cruel privations, in one of the darkest territories of heathen superstition, under a sanguinary despotism, the like of which, even in Africa, exists only in places few and far between. With the abominations and fiendish barbarities of such a government daily before their eyes, their own lives in constant peril, and at the mercy... etc. etc.

May we not believe that God has permitted one of the most powerful kingdoms of Western Africa to be thus terribly humiliated, in order that a free entrance may be opened into that land for the Gospel of Peace? The unbroken power of Ashantee has hitherto—with few and rare exceptions—withstood the influence of the gospel, and would have continued to render the establishment of new missions fruitless, if not impossible. The yoke of despotism is now broken, and the agglomeration of tribes once held together by superstition and fear, is beginning to be dissolved into its constituent elements. The nationalities hitherto enslaved by Ashantee are seeking a closer alliance with England, and wish to be admitted into the protectorate.

Does not all this reveal the hand of God, opening the gates to the messengers of His kingdom? Can we imagine a political situation more favorable to its extension? One of the principal keys of the land, viz., the language spoken throughout Ashantee (Tchi) is already in the possession of the missionaries, who have finished and printed (or are now printing), not only a translation of the Scriptures, but also the most necessary books for schools and churches.

Dr. Theodor Christlieb, in the preface to *Four Years in Ashantee*

Illustration from *Four Years in Ashantee*

GLOSSARY

NAMES OF PLACES

Abono: village on the shore of Lake Bosomtwe

Aburokyiri: Europe, overseas, the country of the white man

Accra: capital of Ghana

Achimota: suburb of Accra; site of an important secondary school

Adanse: site of the creation of the world in Asante belief

Akosombo: site of a major hydro-electric scheme on the Volta River

Anum: Site of mission station established by Fritz Ramseyer in 1869

Anyinam: place of birth of Nana Osei Tutu I, the first Asantehene

Asante: region occupied by people of the same name

Asantemanso: site where the first Asante emerged from a deep
  hole in the ground

Asumegya: (Esumeja) One of the eight founding Asante city-states

Bekwai: One of the eight founding Asante city-states

Bosomtwe: near-circular crater lake in Asante

Brofo Ye Duru: the white man is powerful. Name of a village

Cape Coast: center of the British slave trade

Denkyira: state conquered by Asante in 1700

Dwaben: (Juaben) One of the eight founding Asante city-states

Edweso: (Ejisu) Home town of Nana Yaa Asantewaa

Elmina: center of the Portuguese and Dutch slave trade

Half Assini: town on Ghana's Atlantic coast

Kokofu: One of the eight founding Asante city-states

Kumase: (Kumasi, Coomassie) Asante capital

Kumawu: One of the eight founding Asante city-states
Kuntanase: town in the hills above Lake Bosomtwe
Mampong: One of the eight founding Asante city-states
Manhyia: suburb of Kumase; site of the palace of the Asantehene
  (oman-hyia: the nation meets)
mpoano: coast, beach, shore (literally, the mouth of the ocean)
Mpoanokrom: fictional seaside village
Nkwanta: junction, crossroads. Name of a village
Nok: Nigerian village which gave its name to a culture
  which flourished from 1000 BCE to 300 CE
Nsuta: One of the eight founding Asante city-states
Nyame Bekyere: The Lord will provide. Name of a
  village
Obuasi: site of a major gold mine
Pimpimso: suburb of Kumase where the Golden Stool
  dropped into the lap of the first Asantehene, Nana Osei Tutu
Pra: river which forms the southern border of Asante
Sekondi: port on the Atlantic coast of Ghana, twin city of
  Takoradi
Suame magazine: mechanics' zone in Kumase
Tema: port city serving Accra
Yamoransa: junction where the road from Kumase meets the
  road from Accra to Cape Coast
Zongo: name given to Muslim suburbs of Asante towns

NAMES OF PERSONS

Abedi Pele: famous Ghanaian footballer
Abena: common name of a girl born on Tuesday
Akua: common name of a girl born on Wednesday
Amerikafoo: Americans
Amponsah, Yaa: Title of hit tune of the 1920s. Name of a
  fictional character in the novel
Ankyewa Nyame: mythical woman sent by Onyankopon to
  establish the Asante nation on earth
Anokye, Okomfo: historical priest, adviser to the first As-
  antehene, Nana Osei Tutu. Fictional character in the novel.

Boafo, Kofi: (aka Kofi Kanea, Mansa, Kofi Saman) fictional character in the novel.

Ferguson, Ekem: historical Fanti servant of the British Empire; fictional character in the novel: the narrator, aka Crash

Forson, B: author of a translation of Shakespeare's Julius Caesar into Twi

Karikari, Kofi: Asantehene in the time of the British invasion of Asante in 1873-74

Kom, Kofi: fictional character in the novel

Kühne, Johannes: Historical European trader detained in Kumase with Friedrich Ramseyer

Kwabena: common name of a male born on Tuesday

Kwaku: common name of a male born on Wednesday

Mansa, Maansa: name of an Asante girl

Maxwell: name given to Asante boys in honor of a British colonial governor

Okomfo Anokye: traditional priest instrumental in the founding of the Asante nation

Onyankopon: God

Opoku: fictional character in the novel, producer of the play Julius Caesar

Owusu-Ansah: surname of several important characters in Ghanaian history; also the surname of Crash's fictional parents

Prempeh: name of two Asantehenes

Ramseyer, Friedrich (Fritz): Swiss missionary captured by Asante in 1869 and held in Kumase for four years.

Yaa Asantewaa: heroic leader of Asante resistance to British colonialism

Yaw: common name of a male born on Thursday

MUSIC AND DANCE:
Adowa: traditional Asante dance
Highlife: Popular Ghanaian dance music
Sese: royal Asante dance

TITLES AND FORMS OF ADDRESS

adamfo: friend

Asantehemaa: Asante queen-mother

Asantehene: Asante king

Edwesohene: chief of Edweso

gyasehene: senior minister, chief of staff

krachie: (krakye) clerk, educated person

Maame: respectful form of address to an elder woman

Nana: (plural Nananom) respectful form of address to an elderly person, grandfather

Nananom, agyanom, enanom: grandfathers, fathers, mothers

Obuasihene: chief of Obuasi

okyeame: spokesman (of a chief), linguist

omanhene: chief

opanyin: an elderly person

osofo: Christian priest, pastor

Otumfuo: title reserved for the Asantehene

Owura: sir, mister

Queen-mother: see Asantehemaa

GREETINGS

adwuma ôô: greeting to someone at work

agôô! amêê!: "knock, knock," "come in"

akwaaba: welcome

amêê!: see agôô!

awaawaawa! atuu! Greeting and reply after a long period of absence

bra bekyea me: come and greet me

eye me anigye se me hyia wonyinaa ha enne: I'm pleased to meet you all here today

firi ha: buzz off! Vamoose! (literally, from here)

Kwesi Buroni akwaaba: Sunday-born white man, welcome

maakye: morning greeting

madamfo: my friend

me nuanom: my sisters and brothers

me paa wo kyew: please, I beg your pardon

me papa: my father

nante yiye: go well

Oburoni maakye: white man, I greet you
yaa agya: yes, father (respectful reply to a greeting from an
  older man
Yaa Ohenebaa: respectful reply to a greeting

FOOD AND BEVERAGES:
akpeteshie: locally distilled alcoholic beverage
cocoyam: root crop
fufu: dumpling made of pounded plantain, yam or cassava
kube: coconut
pawpaw: papaya
pisang: banana
tilapia: lake fish, Nile perch

GARMENTS:
batakari: smock from northern Ghana
birisi: funeral cloth
kaba: women's dress style—"cover shoulder"
kente: colorful cloth woven on a hand-loom
ntama: cloth, toga-like article of clothing

CHURCHES AND RELIGIOUS CULTS
A.M.E: African Methodist Episcopal Church
Action and Lighthouse: Pentecostal churches founded in Ghana
Cherubim and Seraphim: church founded in Nigeria in 1925
Tigari: religious cult

WORDS AND PHRASES
aban: stone building, government
abotare ye: patience is a virtue
akyere ase: authored by
amanee: report
Asante Kotoko, kum apem, apem beba: war cry—Asante
  porcupine, kill a thousand, another thousand will come
Asante: people of Ghana, their region, their language
Asantehyiamu: Asante national assembly
Atakpame: technique of building with molded wet mud balls
me ko baabi: I'm going somewhere (to the toilet?)

nwoma: book
odampam: open front of a house
osebo: leopard
Oyoko: clan entitled to the Asante stool
pise-de-terre: rammed earth wall construction
saman: ghost
sankofa: Adinkra symbol, looking back
Sikadwa: Golden Stool, symbol of Asante nationhood
stool: symbol of chieftancy
to wo bo ase: be patient
wo firi he?: where's your home?
wo ho te sen?: how are you?
wo ko he?: where are you going
wo kurom wo he?: where is your home town?
wobenom kube anaa?: would you like to drink coconut milk?
wristcom: fictional micro computer of the 2050s
yadu: we have arrived
yawda: Thursday
ye fre me ...: I am called ...
yenfre me Kwesi Buroni: my name is not Kwesi Buroni (Sunday-born white man)

BY THE SAME AUTHOR

Ama: a Story of the Atlantic Slave Trade

Winner of the 2002 Commonwealth Writers Prize for the
Best First Book

"I am a human being; I am a woman; I am a black woman; I am an African. Once I was free; then I was captured and became a slave; but inside me, I have never been a slave, inside me here and here, I am still a free woman."

In the course of four hundred years some twelve million Africans were forcibly transported across the Atlantic to serve European settlers and their descendants. Only the barest fragments of their stories have survived. Manu Herbstein's ambitious, meticulously researched and moving novel sets out to recreate one of these lives, following Ama, its eponymous heroine, from her home in the Sahel, through Kumase at the height of Asante power, and Elmina, center of the Dutch slave trade, to a sugar plantation in Brazil.

"This is story telling on a grand scale," writes Tony Simões da Silva. "In *Ama*, Herbstein creates a work of literature that celebrates the resilience of human beings while denouncing the inscrutable nature of their cruelty. By focusing on the brutalization of Ama's body, and on the psychological scars of her experiences, Herbstein dramatizes the collective trauma of slavery through the story of a single African woman. *Ama* echoes the views of writers, historians and philosophers of the African diaspora who have argued that the phenomenon of slavery is inextricable from the deepest foundations of contemporary western civilization."

The Boy who Spat in Sargrenti's Eye

Winner of the African Literature Association's 2016 award
for the Creative Book of the Year

Sargrenti is the name by which Major General Sir Garnet Wolseley, KCMG (1833 – 1913) is still known in the West African state of Ghana.

Kofi Gyan, the 15-year old boy who spits in Sargrenti's eye, is the nephew of the chief of Elmina, a town on the Atlantic coast of Ghana. On Christmas Day, 1871, Kofi's godfather gives him a diary as a Christmas present and charges him with the task of keeping a personal record of the momentous events through which they are living. This novel is a transcription of Kofi's diary.

Elmina town has a long-standing relationship with the Castelo de São Jorge da Mina, known today as Elmina Castle, built by the Portuguese in 1482 and captured from them by the Dutch in 1637. In April, 1872, the Dutch hand over the unprofitable castle to the British. The people of Elmina have not been consulted and resist the change. On June 13, 1873 British forces punish them by bombarding the town and destroying it. (It has never been rebuilt. The flat open ground where it once stood serves as a constant reminder of the savage power of Imperial Britain.)

After the destruction of Elmina, Kofi moves to his mother's family home in nearby Cape Coast, seat of the British colonial government, where Sargrenti is preparing to march inland and attack the independent Asante state. There Melton Prior, war artist of the London weekly news magazine, *The Illustrated London News*, offers Kofi a job as his assistant. This gives the lad an opportunity to observe at close quarters not only Prior but also the other war correspondents, Henry Morton Stanley and G. A. Henty.

Kofi witnesses and experiences the trauma of a brutal war, a run-up to the formal colonialism which would be realized ten years later at the 1885 Berlin conference, where European powers drew lines on the map of Africa, dividing the territory up amongst themselves. On February 6, 1874, Sargrenti's troops loot the palace of the Asante king, Kofi Karikari, and then blow up the stone building and set the city of Kumase on fire, razing it to the ground.

Kofi's story culminates in his angry response to the British auction of their loot in Cape Coast Castle. The loot includes the solid gold mask shown on the front cover of the novel. That mask continues to reside in the Wallace Collection in London.

The invasion of Asante met with the enthusiastic approval of the British public, which elevated Wolseley to the status of a national hero. All the war correspondents and several military officers hastened to cash in on public sentiment by publishing books telling the story of their victory. In all of these, without exception, the coastal Fante feature as feckless and cowardly and the Asante as ruthless savages.

The Boy who Spat in Sargrenti's Eye tells the story of these momentous events for the first time from an African point of view. The novel is illustrated with scans of seventy engravings first published in *The Illustrated London News.*

This book won a Burt Award for African Literature which included the donation by the Ghana Book Trust of 3000 copies to school libraries. In 2016, at the annual conference of the African Literature Association held in Atlanta, GA, it received the ALA's Creative Book of the Year Award.

"Manu Herbstein's *The Boy who Spat in Sargrenti's Eye* is a masterwork of historical fiction, with the emphasis on historical. The story is set in the events leading up to the creation of the British Gold Coast Colony and Protectorate in 1874, and its main theme is a boy's—and a nation's—struggle to retain dignity in the midst of their loss of independence. Subtly, then, this is an anti-colonial story…the dastardly deeds witnessed by Kofi in this book are very real indeed. Herbstein's magic lies in the way that he reveals them through such a compelling story of a young man caught in the midst of turmoil and change." Prof. Trevor R. Getz, Ph.D. San Francisco State University

Brave Music of a Distant Drum

This book is about a slave called Ama. She is old and dying but with an amazing tale to tell; she is blind and cannot write her story, so she tells it to her son. It is a tale of violence, heartache, a story of hope and courage, determination and ultimately love. It is a story of Ghana, of its wonderful people, stolen and taken to a foreign land. Ama - scream your story!!! *Glenys Bichan, Cambridge High School Library, New Zealand*

There are some stories that touch you and some that change you. This is what Kwame Zumbi discovers after a visit with his blind mother…Award-winning author Manu Herbstein blends fact with fiction to create a rich story that not only tells a heart-wrenching and powerful tale of friendship, love, and loss, but also chronicles the history of the trans-Atlantic Slave Trade and the scars that it has left behind. It's not an understatement to say that Herbstein's tale is a vital part of history and a key to understanding cross-cultural relations today. *Keilin Huang, papertigers.org*

Manu Herbstein has written an incredible story about the life of Ama, born in Africa but now an aging and blind slave woman in Brazil. She is nearing the end of her life, but is determined she will not go to her grave until her story has not only been told, but written as well. This is a beautifully written, thought-provoking book about age-old questions involving man's inhumanity to man. *Betty Kowall, Waterloo Region Record*

What a beautiful follow up to "Ama". *Talya Honor, Goodreads*

Akosua and Osman

2011 BURT AWARD FOR GHANA

Akosua Annan is a confident and fiercely intelligent student at a posh Cape Coast school. There she comes under the influence of a charismatic feminist teacher.

Osman Said's background is very different. Upon the death of his parents, a police sergeant and an unschooled market trader, immigrants to Accra from the North, he is adopted by a retired school teacher, Hajia Zainab. After a spell as an apprentice in an auto workshop, he returns to school. There, finding the teaching inadequate, he becomes an avid reader and educates himself.

Akosua and Osman are thrown together by chance in the course of a school visit to the slave dungeon at Cape Coast Castle. Their paths cross again as finalists in the national school debating competition where the subject is "The problem of poverty in Ghana is insoluble." They meet for the third time as students at the University of Ghana and as we leave them, it looks as if their relationship might develop into something permanent.

"This fascinating novel tells the story of how these two young people from these disparate backgrounds are brought together as if by an unseen hand, in a process that teaches us about our history, our common humanity despite ethnic differences, the need to pursue our ambitions, the strength of human sexuality and the need for self-discipline, and, above all, the power of love." The Judges, Burt Award for African Literature, 2011.

President Michelle
or Ten Days that Shook the World

The 2012 U.S. presidential election campaign is well under way when Barack Obama succumbs to a sudden heart attack. Vice-President Biden is sworn in as President and the Democratic Party recalls its convention. Jesse Jackson makes a powerful speech proposing that the party adopt Michelle Obama as its candidate. What happens next?

Some quotes:

"The Act to Restore Democracy to the United States of America...would make it an offense for any candidate for public office to accept gifts or loans in support of his or her election campaign; or, indeed, to use personal wealth for such a purpose. Congress would allocate funds to an Independent Electoral Authority and this Authority would in turn fund the electoral campaigns of all candidates qualified to stand for office...At a stroke, this law would level the electoral playing field. For the first time in generations the wealthy would have little or no advantage over the poor in the competition for office. She expected new talents to emerge which would enrich and invigorate American political life. New parties might enter the political arena, breaking the monopoly presently shared by Republicans and Democrats and breathing new life into American democracy...."

"In the first year of my Presidency I shall close down, that is, disarm and evacuate, all our military bases abroad; and hand them over either to the host country, or, if the hosts agree, to the United Nations. All our warships will return to their home ports, tasked with patrolling our own shores, not those of other nations."

She characterized the Middle East, Israel and occupied Palestine, as a "festering wound that has infected the body politic of much of our world." "The so-called two-state solution," she said, was clearly no solution to anything and would no longer receive American support. "In its stead," she said, "I propose to use all the means at my disposal to persuade the parties to negotiate, in a broadly representative national convention, the constitution of a single secular state within the pre-1948 boundaries of Palestine, a constitution that will guarantee full protection for both individual human rights and for the rights of all religious communities."

"What I am tentatively staking out here today," she said, "is a case for leadership, for American leadership. But leadership of a different kind, leadership based not on economic and military power. No. Not that. Not that. I ask, with all humility, that my leadership be judged and that this country's leadership be judged, from this day on, on moral grounds."